AUG 23 2012

P9-CMS-962

LAST LAWYER STANDING

ALSO BY DOUGLAS CORLEONE

Night on Fire

One Man's Paradise

LAST LAWYER STANDING

DOUGLAS CORLEONE

MINOTAUR BOOKS ⚮ NEW YORK

This is a work of fiction. All of the characters, organizations, and events portrayed in this novel are either products of the author's imagination or are used fictitiously.

LAST LAWYER STANDING. Copyright © 2012 by Douglas Corleone. All rights reserved. Printed in the United States of America. For information address St. Martin's Press, 175 Fifth Avenue, New York, N.Y.10010.

Library of Congress Cataloging-in-Publication Data

Corleone, Douglas.
    Last lawyer standing / Douglas Corleone. — 1st ed.
        p. cm.
    ISBN 978-0-312-55228-2 (hardcover)
    ISBN 978-1-250-01487-0 (e-book)
    1. Defense (Criminal procedure)—Fiction.   2. Hawaii—Fiction.   I. Title.
    PS3603.0763L37 2012
    813'.6—dc23

                                                                    2012014697

First Edition: August 2012

10 9 8 7 6 5 4 3 2 1

For Maya
Welcome to the world, baby

ACKNOWLEDGMENTS

Last Lawyer Standing is being released during one of the most exciting periods of my life, largely because of a select group of people. To those who continue to be invaluable to my writing and career, thank you.

Special thanks to my brilliant editors, Kelley Ragland and Matt Martz, and everyone else at St. Martin's Press, including, but not limited to, my publisher Andrew Martin, Hector DeJean, and Elizabeth Lacks.

I am deeply indebted to my literary agent, the extraordinary Robin Rue of Writers House, and her indispensible assistant Beth Miller.

Thanks also to those who, over the past year, have been incredibly generous with their time, advice, and support, including Vincent Antoniello, Stefanie Pintoff, Joel Price, Todd Ritter, David Rosenfelt, and Norb Vonnegut.

For her endless patience, understanding, love, and generosity, *mahalo* to my magnificent wife, Jill. And for brightening each day and night, thanks to my prodigious son, Jack Douglas, and my beautiful newborn daughter, Maya Kailani. Hawaii's my home, but it's you who make these islands my paradise.

Finally, to Dottie Morefield, who kindly joined (and rooted for) me at last year's unforgettable Shamus Awards banquet, I offer my endless gratitude. I may not have left with the award for Best First Novel, but I did leave with a wonderful new friendship, which I hope will last a lifetime.

Chase after the truth like all hell and you'll free yourself, even though you never touch its coattails.

—Clarence Darrow

IULAI

(JULY)

CHAPTER 1

My shadow stretched diagonally across the federal courthouse steps on Ala Moana Boulevard in downtown Honolulu, just an ordinary man in an ordinary suit with a Panama Jack resting on his head. Just another lawyer on his way to court for just another criminal case. Only that's not how it felt. Something palpable lingered in the ether, something akin to the tension I experienced sitting next to a client surrounded by off-white cinder blocks in a cramped, stifling interrogation room in the bowels of a police department's headquarters. I checked my watch to make certain I wasn't due for another few Percocet to relieve the pain in my abdomen where I'd been stabbed with a stiletto not six months ago. But, no, not yet; it wasn't time. The day itself, an ugly young Monday, shrieked in my ear, cautioned me to blow off SoSo's sentencing, to turn around and head the hell home, to turn off the phones, and pretend this morning never existed.

I didn't listen.

Instead I bounded up the steps, briefcase in hand, passed through the glass doors, through the metal detector after dumping my keys and a few coins into a small gray bucket, and checked my cell phone with a bored court officer, who warned me twice to make sure the ringer was turned off.

"I don't wanna listen to that goddamn thing playing 'Funky Cold Medina' for the next three hours, Counselor. Got it?"

"Got it." I took the ticket he offered as a receipt then made for the elevator bank at the end of the hall.

When I stepped through the ten-foot-tall, mahogany double doors into Justice Harlan Platz's empty courtroom, my partner, Jake Harper, already seated at the defense table, turned in his chair and greeted me with a slow nod.

"What the hell are you doing here?" I asked him, tossing my briefcase onto the table, slightly shuddering at the exaggerated echo of the thud.

"Wouldn't miss SoSo's sentencing for anything, son."

"It's routine. Both sides are resting on the papers. Platz is going to give him twenty years and we're done."

"I've yet to see a routine appearance in front of Harlan Platz," Jake said. "Never mind a routine *anything* involving SoSo."

Forty-five minutes later, four priggish US Marshals led our client Solosolo Sinaloa through a side door into the courtroom. SoSo, shackled at the wrists and ankles, towered over each of them, his muscular bulk preventing any of the four from accompanying him side-by-side up the aisle. The single-piece, orange jumpsuit befit the Samoan so well, I couldn't imagine he ever wore anything else. Then again, I'd never seen him wear anything else. And unless in twenty years SoSo returned to

Honolulu to shake my hand or slice my throat, chances were I never would.

"Howya doin'," SoSo greeted me, as two of the Marshals stepped away from the table. The other two took positions behind the prisoner.

"Comme ci, comme ça," I said, but SoSo was apparently in no mood for levity. On the upside, my French earned a light chuckle from Jake.

Jake and I represented SoSo pursuant to the Criminal Justice Act, which was to say that the federal government rewarded our firm a paltry seventy-five bucks per hour to play advocate to the most menacing, callous monsters federal law enforcement could capture and charge. Although I'd adamantly opposed joining the CJA panel, Jake insisted on it. With a mere two dozen murders on the island each year, it's rare to hit on a state case with any teeth. But the feds never fail to scrounge up a few supervillains per annum, providing the dose of excitement Jake seems to need to thrive.

Of course, I lacked standing to argue. I'm the one who got the old man addicted in the first place.

Or was it the other way around?

Another twenty minutes passed before the Honorable Harlan Platz rose to the bench. Platz looked as though he chose his skin off a rack this morning, then dotted it with liver spots before stepping into the long, flowing black robe that made him look like Death itself. Approximately sixteen white hairs loitered on a scalp that would've made Mikhail Gorbachev cringe with disgust. When the founding fathers drafted Article Three of the US Constitution, providing that federal judges serve for life, they couldn't possibly have foreseen the likes of Harlan Platz. Then again, maybe Platz knew one of the founding fathers personally.

"I have reviewed the Government's sentencing memorandum," Platz rasped from his perch, "as well as the Defendant's. I must say, Mr. Corvelli, you receive an A for creativity. I had to reread the Federal Sentencing Guidelines twice because I did not quite believe some of the provisions you cited even existed. Yet, there they were in black and white. Although, I think you will concede, Counselor, that it is somewhat of a stretch to contend that Mr. Sinaloa accepted responsibility for his crime by nodding his head after the jury foreman read off the verdict of guilty."

I had little to work with. We were appointed SoSo's counsel only after trial, for the sole purpose of preparing a sentencing memorandum on his behalf. About a year ago, SoSo beat a man to death outside a strip club in Honolulu's red-light district, following a "Miller Lite: Tastes Great/Less Filling" debate. Or something like that. The victim, Marc Dalton, was a US immigration officer, which landed the case in federal court. At a post-verdict visit at the Federal Detention Center, SoSo handed a sample of what he'd given Dalton to his trial attorney, Clyde Harris. Harris begged off the case and the CJA panel appointed yours truly.

"Mr. Boyd," Platz said to the assistant US attorney, "do you have anything you wish to add to the Government's sentencing memorandum?"

AUSA William F. Boyd was a typical government lawyer, complete with the personality of a houseplant and all the style of a toaster.

"I have nothing further, Your Honor," Boyd said in a mechanical voice. "The Government's memorandum speaks for itself."

"Mr. Corvelli," Platz said, "have you anything else to say?"

"No, Your Honor," I replied.

Then Justice Platz began hacking, a hideous, loose cough that echoed through the gallery like a ricocheting bullet from a .44. Platz's sagging facial skin flapped violently, his liver spots dancing in unison.

Platz's clerk, a round kid just out of law school, came to the judge's rescue with a clean hanky and a gentle, oddly affectionate pat on the back.

"I am sorry," Platz said once he regained his composure. "Let us move on. Mr. Sinaloa, have you anything to say before I sentence you?"

The correct answer, of course, was *No.* Or at most, *No, Judge*, maybe *No, Your Honor.* I'd gone over the straightforward federal sentencing procedure with SoSo at least a half dozen times. Since it was no longer mandatory for judges to strictly follow the rigid provisions of the Federal Sentencing Guidelines, and since Harlan Platz was known to be a fairly liberal judge, both sides anticipated a prison term of twenty years in a maximum-security facility. Not bad for killing a federal agent with your bare hands outside a strip club at four in the morning. Especially considering SoSo was only twenty-six years old.

This hearing was a mere formality. Justice Platz had already read our memorandum; nothing added today could aid us in any imaginable way. Anything said could only do us harm, could only lengthen SoSo's prison sentence. Thus, I had instructed SoSo—had done everything but hold a gun to his head—to simply reply in the negative when asked whether he had anything to say. "No," I had told him. "Just say no. No. No. No. No. No."

"Yes," SoSo said to Justice Platz.

Shit.

"Your Honor," I interrupted, "SoSo—I mean, Mr. Sinaloa—has nothing further to add at this time."

Platz coughed into the elbow of his robe and looked at my client for the first time. "Is that right, Mr. Sinaloa? Or do you have something you would care to say to this Court before I sentence you?"

"Yes," SoSo said again.

"See, Mr. Corvelli?" Platz said with what might have passed for a smile in a casket. "Another county heard from."

"Your Honor—," I tried again.

"Proceed, Mr. Sinaloa. It is your right. What say you?"

SoSo's face remained perfectly stoic as he addressed Justice Platz. "I say you the oldest, ugliest motherfucker I ever seen in my life."

A nauseating silence hung over the courtroom like tear gas. The houseplant standing at the Government table glanced over at me, the slightest attempt at a smirk playing on his lips. But quiet the courtroom remained for at least the next three minutes. Then the Honorable Harlan Platz slapped his gavel with all the savagery a two-hundred-year-old man could muster. If looks could kill, the Marshals would've been wheeling SoSo out of the courtroom on a stretcher, a white sheet draped over his face.

"Very well," Platz finally said with a calmness that betrayed his face. "Mr. Sinaloa, the Court hereby sentences you to imprisonment at a federal penitentiary of maximum security for a period of thirty-five years."

All four Marshals instantly convened behind my client to recuff him and take him away.

"But, Judge!" SoSo pleaded, the stoicism suddenly melting from his body like crushed ice on hot sand. "Judge, I can't *do* that much time."

Platz waved a skeletal hand in the air, and the Marshals immediately halted their movements.

"Oh, I see," Platz said. "You cannot do that much time; is that so, Mr. Sinaloa?"

"No, sir, Judge," SoSo replied, relief already washing over his mammoth frame. "I can't do no thirty-five years. I can't do that much time."

"Very well, then, Mr. Sinaloa." The corners of Platz's mouth turned up as though on strings as he glared at my client and stated flatly, "In that case, do as much as you can."

CHAPTER 2

"That was some statement your client made, Corvelli," Boyd called out as Jake and I plodded toward the towering double doors. "You prep Sinaloa yourself?"

"It speaks," I said to Jake as I turned to face the houseplant.

Boyd was dressed as always in an uninspired navy suit that hung scrupulously on his perfectly average frame, a crisp white oxford and muted red tie peeking out over two ever-closed, vertical brass buttons.

"Ah, more botanical humor," it said, marching toward us. "Played really well before Justice Ingraham last week."

I was fast running out of patience. "Did you initiate this conversation for a reason or are you simply working on your social skills, Boyd? Because my partner and I both have appointments this morning."

As I pushed through the heavy wooden doors, Boyd said, "Just wanted to know if we can expect you here at the court-house tomorrow morning."

"Not likely," I muttered, ushering Jake into the lavish hall. In state courts, law is practiced on small, weathered Little League fields; federal courthouses, on the other hand, are Major League ballparks all the way.

Boyd caught the door before it closed. "You're not joining us for the arraignments tomorrow?"

Jake sprang to life. "What arraignments?" Jake would fancy nothing more than another nickel-and-dime CJA appointment.

"You haven't heard?" Boyd said. "There was a DEA raid on a meth superlab up North Shore this morning. I'm sure you'll see it on the news tonight at whatever dive bar you're frequenting these days."

I snatched Jake's elbow and led him toward the marble staircase so that we wouldn't get caught in an elevator with Boyd.

"You hear about this?" Jake said, breathing heavily as we hustled down the stairs.

"You all right?" I asked as we hit the second landing.

"Fine," he said, though he paused for a breath. "So how about it, son? You hear anything about this raid?"

I shook my head. "No surprise. It's an election year. Someone wants to look tough in the so-called war on drugs."

When we reached the first-floor lobby, I handed the same bored court officer my ticket, and he took his time retrieving my phone. As he slapped it on the table between us, he asked if I was fucking deaf.

I told him I wasn't.

"Well, then, Counselor, you'd better clean the shit out of your ears, because I told you twice to make sure the fucking thing was turned off, and evidently you didn't hear."

I stared at the cell, which alluded to eight missed calls, eight voice messages, at least one of them marked urgent.

Before I could respond to the federal court's answer to the coat-check girl at Club Tsunami, my cell phone started going off again. A simple ring; no "Funky Cold Medina."

I opened the phone and put it to my ear. "Speak."

"Take it outside, Counselor," the court officer warned.

Jake and I started walking toward the exit as a frightened voice spoke in my ear.

"T'ank God you finally answered, Mistah C."

"Turi," I said. Turi Ahina was a lawyer's best friend: a career criminal. A hell of a nice guy who always carried a gun, and who had once used that gun to save my life. "What's the trouble?"

"I got myself pinched again, Mistah C."

"That's no trouble," I told him as Jake and I stepped outside. I placed my Panama Jack back atop my head to shield my eyes from the midday Hawaiian sun. "I'll come straight over to County and arrange bail."

"I ain't at County, Mistah C," Turi said glumly.

"Then where the hell are you?"

"I'm at the Federal Detention Center. Wasn't the HPD that arrested me this time."

I stopped cold on the cement steps, in the same spot I stood this morning, though this time my shadow simply surrounded me like a pool of blood.

"Who was it?" I asked Turi, though I was pretty sure I already knew.

Turi confirmed my suspicions by uttering the three ugliest letters in the English alphabet, bar none: "DEA."

CHAPTER 3

After stopping at the Federal Detention Center to meet with Turi Ahina that evening, I headed home to my villa in Ko Olina on the leeward side of the island. Boxes littered the hardwood floors, the walls were stripped bare, and most of my furniture had already been donated to Goodwill. I set a plate of yellowfin tuna on the kitchen floor for Grey Skies, then nuked a leftover slice of pizza from Boston's North End for myself. I ate quickly from a paper plate over the counter, washed it down with a cold bottle of Kona Longboard, then turned out the lights.

I wanted to move. Even though Erin Simms had never once set foot in my villa, she'd opened her veins in a lagoon just a short walk from my door. I could no longer frequent my favorite bars or restaurants in the resort community because they each boasted views of that azure lagoon. Erin's blood no longer diluted the salt water, of course; her naked body no longer floated along the surface. But for me, it seemed, she would always be there.

And I wanted to be somewhere else.

The problem was I didn't know where. Three years ago I'd fled New York following the death of Brandon Glenn, an innocent client who had been raped and murdered at Rikers Island after I blew his defense. Here I was in a tropical paradise and—albeit for entirely different reasons—ready to flee again.

I had disappointed my New York mentor, Milt Cashman, and now I was about to let down my Honolulu law partner, Jake Harper. But just as it was three years ago, it felt as though I didn't have a choice.

I lay down on my bare mattress in the middle of the living room and fondled the softcover book at my side. Ostensibly, it was a work of nonfiction: true crime. The author was a lover I picked up here in Ko Olina more than a year ago. Sherry Beagan. Ironically, at one point I couldn't even remember her name. It's now etched into my memory, as vivid as the blue-white corpse of Erin Simms.

I held the book above my eyes and squinted through the darkness at the title: *Paradise on Fire: The True Story of an Innocent Young Bride and the Lawyer Who Saved Her Life*. A bullshit subtitle if ever there was one. And not only because Erin Simms suicided before any verdict was ever read.

I sat up on the mattress and flung the paperback across the room. The book smacked into the sliding-glass door like a blind pigeon, the racket frightening Skies, sending him scampering out of the kitchen before finishing his meal, his claws scratching the hardwood as he skidded into a turn. I tried to call him back with a soothing voice, to no avail.

Time for a move. *But to where?* Another island? Another state? Another country?

The silence was suddenly interrupted by the obnoxious peal of my cell phone, and I felt a sudden rush of empathy for the court officer I'd nearly cursed out earlier. I stood and searched the cluttered kitchen counter for my cell.

The caller ID read RESTRICTED.

"Speak," I said into the phone.

"Is this Mr. Corvelli?"

"Yeah."

"Mr. Corvelli, my name is Jason Yi and I'm calling on behalf of the governor."

The clock on the microwave read 11:02 p.m.

"Are you kidding me?" I said. "You're soliciting votes at this time of night four months before the election? Good luck with that."

As I searched for the PWR button, the voice on the other end protested, "No, sir, you misunderstand. I'm Governor Omphrey's chief aide. I'm not calling to secure your vote, Mr. Corvelli. I'm calling to secure your services."

"I'm a criminal defense attorney. Not an election lawyer."

"The governor is well aware of the type of law you practice, Mr. Corvelli. And of how well you practice it."

I smirked. Wade Omphrey was up for reelection this year, and according to the polls and the pundits, he had an incredibly slim chance of losing the governor's mansion. But that could all change with a single headline.

"The governor has been charged with a crime?"

"Not charged, Mr. Corvelli. At least not yet. And probably he never will be charged. That's what we want to make certain of, and that is why we're getting you involved so early in the investigation."

"What type of investigation are we talking about?"

Jason Yi hesitated, swallowed audibly. "Murder, Mr. Corvelli. Your specialty."

CHAPTER 4

As a defense attorney it wasn't often that I got the opportunity to visit a fresh crime scene, but this scene was as fresh as a lobster plucked straight from the tank at John Dominis. Not that I felt lucky to be here. I was one of the few people in this voyeuristic nation who actually looked away when they glimpsed yellow police tape. I wanted nothing to do with blood and gore, wasn't the slightest bit intrigued by the macabre. So when I entered the elite residential complex on Diamond Head Road, I did so with dread, with trepidation, with a feeling like sharp metal lodged in the pit of my stomach.

"Fourth floor," Jason Yi said as he opened the door to the stairwell. "All the way to the top."

The police had shut down the lone elevator. We passed a number of uniforms in the sterile white stairwell on the way up, each of them eyeing us without attempting to mask their contempt for our trespass onto their playing field.

We stopped at the top of the steps, and I presented my attorney ID to a young officer guarding the door.

"Mr. Corvelli's with the governor," Yi told the cop.

The cop handed me a pair of latex gloves.

"I'm allergic to latex," I said.

"Tough shit, Corvelli." Staring at me from over the young cop's shoulder was Detective John Tatupu, Honolulu Homicide. Tatupu was a good cop who had found himself on the losing end of two major murder trials since I'd arrived in the islands. "Put the gloves on and come with me, Counselor. But don't touch a goddamn thing."

Yi nodded, and I slipped on the gloves, itching already, and stepped past the guard, following Tatupu into the center of the flat.

The apartment was a vision, the entire living area open to the air, with a view of the Pacific few five-star hotels on the island could rival.

"I don't know what Omphrey's lapdog has already told you," Tatupu said, "but you're here as a courtesy to the governor's office only. On the condition that nothing you see here finds its way into print. At least not until the FBI has concluded their investigation."

"The FBI?"

"Didn't you see the suits on your way in?"

"I thought maybe your boys were playing dress-up."

Tatupu, a native Hawaiian, cast a dark glance in my direction. "Better get the laughing out of your system now, Counselor. Because after you see what's behind Door Number One, it's going to be all you can do just to sleep."

And the son of a bitch was right.

The corpse was already in the grip of rigor mortis, frozen, apparently, in the middle of a violent convulsion, her backbone curved like the St. Louis Arch. Her body was dressed in a sheer nightie. From the neck down, she resembled the young girl from *The Exorcist* when she spider-walked down the stairs.

I swallowed hard and set my jaw. "What the hell happened to her?"

"I'm not here to give you a tour and hold a Q and A, Corvelli. Look but don't touch, and you're welcome to draw your own conclusions. But in a few minutes you'll have to clear out so Dr. Tong can do his thing."

"Tong?"

"Yeah. You didn't hear? Derek Noonan handed in his resignation following the Simms trial. Last week was his final week as chief medical examiner. Turned the reins over to Charlie Tong."

I took a step toward the corpse. Downstairs, Jason Yi had retained me for $10,000 in cash, which now felt like a cumbersome bulge in my left pants pocket. Yi's chief concern was that Governor Omphrey be protected by the attorney-client privilege. Of course, that was the case the moment I answered the phone.

Jason Yi had filled me in on a few facts. The deceased, Oksana Sutin, twenty-six, was a Russian national and the governor's latest mistress. The affair had been going on for the past six months. That was undoubtedly why the feds were involved, though who leaked the affair to the feds remained to be heard. Yi assured me that Omphrey had an alibi. In fact, the governor was still in Washington, DC, for meetings with White House officials, and he'd been there for the past two weeks.

"Then what do you need me for?" I'd asked.

Yi didn't hesitate. "The press. The governor is up for reelection. If news of the affair breaks, there's going to be tremendous pressure from the party for the governor to step aside."

"I can't control what gets leaked to the press."

"No, but you can spin it. You can also threaten to go after anyone who commits libel and slander by implicating the governor in this crime. And you can deal with the police and prosecutors if and when they have questions for the governor."

Now I knelt at the side of Oksana Sutin's body. No visible bruises, no visible wounds. I glanced around the room at the high-end dark-wood furniture arranged in the ancient Chinese method of feng shui. No sign of a struggle, nothing conspicuously out of place.

I stood and stepped over to the dresser, caught a glimpse in the oval mirror of the midnight shadow on my face. I stopped myself from picking up a framed photo of the deceased, a picture of the ravishing brunette alone at sunset on Lanikai Beach, the Mokulua Islands idling in the background. She looked nothing like the grotesque form strewn out behind me. In the photo, her blue eyes lit the sky, her cheekbones looked as though they'd been chiseled by a sculptor, her lissome body filled a plain white two-piece. Oksana Sutin could have passed as a *Sports Illustrated* swimsuit model; in fact, this shot could easily have made the cover.

"You about done here, Counselor?" Tatupu asked from the doorway. "Dr. Tong just arrived, along with an ME from the Bureau."

I backed away from the dresser and nodded.

As I passed Tatupu in the doorframe I said quietly, "Want

to save me a three-second Google search and tell me which poison could have done something as hideous as this?"

"Off the top of my head?" Tatupu said with a shrug of his broad shoulders. "I'd say strychnine."

CHAPTER 5

I arrived at the Federal Detention Center early the next morning. The FDC stands adjacent to Honolulu International Airport, and after I parked and popped a few Percocet, I sat in my
Jeep listening to Eddie Vedder and watching the planes take off
from the Hawaiian Airlines terminal. I could do it, I thought. I
had enough money to pack it all in and start over somewhere
else. In a small town maybe. Just buy a two-family house out in
the sticks and set up shop downstairs, drafting wills, reviewing
contracts. Maybe run for mayor someday.

I stepped out of my Jeep and slammed shut the door. First I
had a job to do.

Turi Ahina first waddled into my office about three years
ago, while I was defending a young New Jersey man named
Joey Gianforte, who was accused of stalking and killing his ex-
girlfriend Shannon Douglas on Waikiki Beach. Turi had been
caught up in a simple buy-and-bust operation set up by the Honolulu PD in which he'd sold an undercover officer a $40 bag of

crystal methamphetamine, otherwise known as ice. Thanks to some creative lawyering on my part, all charges against Turi Ahina were ultimately dismissed. But that was just the beginning of our relationship. As a gesture of appreciation, Turi sent me a steady stream of criminal clients—in other words, his associates—which aided me in building the successful law firm Harper & Corvelli eventually became. Later, during the Gianforte murder trial, Turi Ahina shot a man dead in order to save my life. Since then I had successfully represented Turi in at least a half dozen other matters, but as far as I was concerned, my debt to Turi wasn't paid. I still owed him. No matter what it took, I promised myself as I entered the Federal Detention Center, I would extricate Turi from the DEA's dragnet in this case.

Forty-five minutes after signing in, I spotted Turi carrying his wide load across the packed cafeteria toward the tiny Plexiglas cube in which I had been scanning a copy of this morning's *Honolulu Star-Advertiser* for news about Oksana Sutin's death. Nothing yet. Fortunately, the local media sometimes operated on aloha time.

As Turi Ahina squeezed through the door to the Plexiglas cube, I stood and braced myself for what was coming next: the patented Turi Ahina bear hug. Only Turi didn't move to hug me, didn't even attempt to shake my hand. He simply sat down.

The wide smile that was all but painted on Turi's face was absent, possibly confiscated during the raid. For the first time since I'd met him, Turi Ahina appeared scared.

I sat across from him as the Plexiglas door closed, sealing us in. I angled my metal chair slightly so that I wouldn't be distracted by the goings-on in the cafeteria: the wives and girlfriends, sisters and mothers, sitting, talking, weeping, with their loved ones; young children—sons, daughters, younger siblings—running around the tables and playing on plastic chairs, undaunted by their surroundings, acting as though this were simply a theme park, a carnival, some sad, chaotic county fair.

"All right," I said. "Let's begin where we left off yesterday."

Yesterday Turi described for me the early-morning raid by the US Drug Enforcement Administration. Turi and two others were working at a clandestine meth laboratory in Waialua at exactly 6:00 a.m. when agents busted through the door. The lab was a simple one-bedroom home set off a distance from its neighbors, not only to protect its privacy but because the chemicals used to manufacture methamphetamine are toxic, flammable, and explosive. Explosions and fires at meth labs are common and deadly. Thus, at least two workers charged with damage control and cleanup remained on-site at all times.

"We called the lab the Tiki Room," Turi said in pidgin English. His t's sounded like d's, his r's often disappeared completely. "Biggest lab on the island, maybe in all of Hawaii because of the flyovers over the Big Island." Turi was referring to the recent crackdown on marijuana fields on the Big Island of Hawaii.

"Aside from the product itself," I said, "what were the agents able to seize?"

"Everyt'ing," Turi said, eliminating the h as always. "We didn't have time to dispose of nothing, Mistah C."

"Specifically?"

Turi took me through a laundry list of chemicals, which included ephedrine and pseudoephedrine—ingredients extracted from cold tablets and diet pills. Kerosene, lye, anhydrous ammonia, lithium from batteries, drain cleaner, red phosphorous from the heads of matches and flares, and iodine.

I leaned forward and told Turi to cover his mouth. We were visible to other inmates, and although lip-reading wasn't a common talent among the criminal crowd, you could never be too careful. We were about to enter extremely dangerous territory.

"I need you to tell me about the organization, Turi."

My client's thick lips folded in on themselves and his eyes seemed to close of their own accord as he drew in a colossal breath.

"There's no getting around it this time," I told him. "This isn't like getting caught with a gram of ice or an unregistered handgun. If getting popped for simple possession were the common cold, this is a heart attack, a stroke, and a positive HIV test combined."

My analogy didn't seem to ease Turi any.

"Turi, I've been in this game long enough to know and understand the rules. 'Keep your mouth shut and take your medicine like a man.' But not this time. I can't play Beat the Speedy Trial Clock or ask the prosecutor on a date to get you out of this one. And we're not talking six months in Halawa if you plead guilty. We're talking fifteen, twenty years *minimum* at a maximum-security pen on the mainland."

"What do they got me on?"

"If they can prove everything set forth in the complaint— and, believe me, Turi, the feds don't move on a suspect until they're absolutely sure they can get a conviction—then they have you on racketeering and everything that comes with it."

"And there's no chance at trial?"

"Turi, the feds in this case are going to parade photos, wire-taps, chemicals, corpses, and testimony from your cohorts in front of the jury. You'd have a better chance of escaping the FDC than walking out of federal court with an acquittal. No pun intended, big guy, but this is much larger than you."

"Awright," he said grimly. "What do we gotta do?"

I glanced past the Plexiglas again, covered my lips when I spoke. "There's only one way to handle this, Turi. And I think you already know exactly what I'm about to tell you."

Turi wouldn't look at me.

"You're going to have to flip."

Turi started sobbing and shaking his head before I even finished the sentence, but I continued nonetheless.

"You're going to have to offer the US Attorney's Office something they don't already have. You're going to have to sing about everything and every*one* you know, and you can't hold anything back."

By the time I finished speaking, Turi's head was on the table, his enormous shoulders shaking up and down like mountains in the midst of an earthquake.

"No way, Mistah C," he mumbled into his fleshy forearms. "No can."

"You can, Turi. You saved my life a few years ago. Allow me now to save yours."

A long while passed before Turi finally looked up again, his cheeks bright red mounds, the whites of his eyes encased in thin, red spiderwebs. "I need some time to think."

I shook my head. "I wish I could grant you that time, Turi, but it's not mine to grant. The two others who were arrested with you are going to be having this same conversation with their own lawyers soon, if not already. Then it's a footrace to the US Attorney's Office, and the first one in the door wins. The two who are left behind can get nice and comfy in their cells."

Turi turned his head and eyed the guards, the inmates, on the other side of the Plexiglas. Then he stared at me. "You're looking at a dead man," he said.

Maybe, I thought sadly. But it wouldn't be the first time.

And it sure as hell wouldn't be the last.

CHAPTER 6

When I opened the door to our thirty-third-floor office on South King Street, our receptionist, Hoshi, immediately leapt from her chair and scurried around her desk.

"I wanted to call you, Kevin," she said, her words hurried and hushed, "but Jake told me not to. He said you'd take off for Tokyo and leave him holding the bag."

Before Hoshi could further fill me in, the door to our conference room opened and Jake stood in the doorframe.

"Good, son, you're here. Let's duck inside the conference room. There's someone you need to meet."

I crossed the reception area, tossing my Panama Jack on Hoshi's desk along the way. As I stepped through the conference room door, I already regretted coming straight to the office following Turi's uneventful arraignment in federal court. I'd been shanghaied again.

Jake coughed into his fist, then said, "Kevin, I believe you already know Mr. Jason Yi."

Yi stood and nodded his head.

"And this gentleman," Jake said, motioning to the older Caucasian sitting next to Yi, "is, of course, Governor Wade Omphrey."

"Governor," I said.

Neither of us made a move toward the other. The heavyset governor remained stoic and seated, and I stationed myself just inside the door. Client or no client, I had no intention of shaking hands with a politician. Particularly this one.

At first glance Omphrey seemed like the typical politician, right down to the mistress (with the exception, of course, of the possible murder charge). But governing the Hawaiian Islands wasn't anything like governing New York City. When unpleasant actions were taken by the government here, they were often irreparable; decisions, for instance, to pave over the state couldn't be reexamined following the next election cycle.

Jake pulled a chair out for me and asked me to have a seat.

"I apologize," I said to Yi and Omphrey, declining Jake's offer of a seat, "but my meetings are by appointment only. If you check with our receptionist, Hoshi, I'm sure she can schedule a brief conference for sometime later this afternoon."

The governor smirked. A criminal client with money and clout will bully a defense attorney right out of the business if he allows it. I'd seen my mentor Milt Cashman handle these situations in New York, with clients such as mob boss Vito Tagliarini, with the rap stars Rabid Dawg and Shave Ice. Constant calls to the lawyer's cell phone at all hours of the day and night, "emergency meetings" set up at the time and place of the client's convenience. Just recently Milt called me to bitch about one of his newest clients, the gangsta sensation M.C. WMD.

"You won't believe it, Kevin," Milt said. "One night this fucker M.C. WMD shows up unannounced at my home. My *home*, Kevin. Where my fifth wife sleeps and my mistress comes to play with my balls."

Jake shrugged in the general direction of the governor. "Son, maybe—"

But before Jake finished speaking, I was halfway down the hall to my private office.

When I stepped inside, I closed the door. My heart raced and lead settled in the pit of my stomach. It took me a moment to realize that the painkillers were calling. I popped open my pill bottle, tossed back three Percocet, and washed them down with a warm bottle of FIJI water.

I sat behind my desk and replayed the image of Hawaii's governor. Wrong politician, wrong party, wrong attorney to represent his interests in a criminal case. *What the hell was I thinking last night?* I'd acted solely on instinct, saw myself in the papers standing next to the governor, a possible candidate for vice president or at least for a cabinet position, maybe the US Supreme Court, and I'd jumped like a predator toward its prey. But now, memories of microphones and heartrending headlines rose to the surface like bubbles in boiling water. How could I even *consider* accepting a press case of this magnitude after all I'd already lived through?

Hoshi's voice over the intercom broke through the silence. "Kevin, you have a call on line two. It's Milt Cashman."

"Speak of the devil," I said when I picked up the phone.

"And the devil appears," he said, "with a little help from AT and T."

In the three years following my move to Honolulu, most

telephone conversations between former mentor and protégé were initiated by me. But this was the second time Milt had called me in less than a month. Something was up. Milt wasn't one to call to shoot the shit. He wanted something.

"I need a favor," he said.

My gut flipped. Right now I had enough on my plate without having to research issues on appeal for the great Milt Cashman. Still, after all he'd done for me, how could I say no?

"What is it, Milt?"

"You remember a kid named Scott Damiano?"

"He wasn't a kid, he was around my age, Milt."

"Whatever. Anyway, when the kid got out of prison after his three-to-five stretch upstate, he came to me and said he wanted to get out of the game. But he didn't know what in the hell else to do. He got his GED up there, but in this economy, an ex-con with a GED, he might as well slam his dick in the drawer and collect disability. So, pussycat that I am, I cut the kid a break and gave him a job. First he was just running papers back and forth to the Bronx, but then I had him meet with a few witnesses, and I'll tell you, the fucking kid's persuasive. Best unlicensed investigator I've ever come across."

"So what's the problem?"

"Problem is his fucking father and brother, they wouldn't let him alone. They continued keeping books and selling dope for the Tagliarini family, and last week the shit hit the fan. Nico Tagliarini—you remember him?"

"Nico 'Head Case' Tagliarini? How could I forget?"

"Yeah, well, Nico Tagliarini and most of his crew, including Scott Damiano's big brother and dear old dad, were picked up by the feds last week. Word is, one or both of the Damianos are going to flip. There's a contract out on them, only the feds hid them better than Hitler's gold. So I don't have to tell you who they're going to come after next."

"Scott," I said.

"Exactamundo. So last night I put Scott Damiano on a plane to Honolulu. He's got no passport, so that's the best I can do."

The Percocet nearly came up in my throat. "You're asking me *to take him in*? You want me *to take an ex-con with a contract out on his head into my home*?"

"No, no. And quit being so fucking dramatic. All I want is for you to pick him up at the airport. I rented him a one-bedroom apartment in Waikiki where he can live on his own."

I exhaled, enjoyed the warm sensation of relief. "I can do that."

"Good."

With that settled, I moved on to my own problems, explaining to Milt how Hawaii's governor was waiting impatiently in my conference room. I told him how I became involved in the case, I described how I felt about him as a person, as a politician, as a high-profile client.

Milt stopped me midsentence. "What is this shit all the time with you and your *feelings*? This is a fucking business, Kevin. You don't pick and choose your clients based on personality. You take the ones with money in their pockets and you tell the rest to fuck off. It's that simple. You think I *like* Mr. Fucking M.C. WMD? No, but he's got millions to spend on legal defense, and I want to buy my mistress a new condo in Belize. So there you have it. Feelings," he said with a theatrical sigh. "Is that the kind of shit I taught you here in New York? Because if it is, you should come back and shoot me."

"No," I conceded.

"Good. Now listen, Kevin. One more favor I have to ask. When he gets there—my secretary, Candi, will give you the airport pickup information—I need you to give Scott Damiano a job as an investigator with your firm."

Before I could say another word I was on hold, waiting for Candi.

"Hi, Kevin . . . ," she said.

I swallowed hard and took down Scott Damiano's flight information.

When I finally hung up the phone I thought, *When all this is over, I just might go back to New York and shoot Milt Cashman anyway.*

CHAPTER 7

"They don't think I did it," Omphrey said, "they think I *hired* someone to do it."

Jake had asked the governor whether the feds were going to find his fingerprints all over Oksana Sutin's apartment.

"We understand that," I said. "But in order to establish motive, they are going to have to produce evidence of the affair. And that evidence can't be hearsay; in other words, it can't be based in rumor and conjecture."

"I *know* what hearsay is, Counselor. I was a lawyer and a judge for twelve years."

A traffic court judge, I wanted to remind him, but I held my tongue. He knew that I knew that he was being evasive, avoiding the inevitable, but he wanted me to know that he had no reservations about wasting my time, just as I had wasted his this morning.

We were seated in the conference room, Jake to the left of me, the governor and Jason Yi across from us. It was just after

lunch and the three cans of Red Bull I'd drunk were beginning to kick in.

"Yes or no, Governor?" I said. "Were you ever in Oksana
Sutin's Diamond Head home?"

"Yes," he said with a slow bob of the head.

"How many times?"

"I don't know."

"How frequently then?"

"I don't know."

"Es-ti-*mate*." Part of me wanted the governor to stand up
and call this meeting to an end, to spit in my face and walk out
the door never to return.

But he didn't. He kept his cool just as he did in debates. "A
few times. Maybe once a month over the past few months."

Assuming his pudgy fingers had left at least one full usable
print, the issue of whether the governor had had an extra-
marital affair with the victim would be resolved by reasonable
inference. This simple truth now saved me and my staff the
time, energy, and pure hassle of investigating whether evidence existed that Wade Omphrey knew Oksana Sutin. It was
that simple. The bad news, of course, was that this fact most
likely established motive.

"So you were having an affair with Ms. Sutin," I said. "Did
Mrs. Omphrey know about the affair?"

The governor's wife, Pamela, was an outspoken and well-
known, well-loved first lady, a fierce advocate for the environment and for the native Hawaiian people—a vast departure
from the governor himself, who was often accused of not giving a shit for either. Wade and Pamela Omphrey weren't
quite the Arnold Schwarzenegger and Maria Shriver of the

Hawaiian Islands, but from what I knew of the pair, they were pretty damn close.

"No," Omphrey said, "she did not. At least not to my knowledge."

"Let's talk about Oksana herself," I said. "Did she ever express any fears to you? Was she concerned that someone was going to try to harm her?"

"No, never," the governor said without hesitation. "I know of no enemies, no one who might . . . have done *this*."

It was the first bit of raw emotion I'd seen from the governor, but I didn't trust it; I never did. More often than not tears and trembling voices at the mention of the victim's name were the result of the clients' own fears, a recognition that this was serious, not some game, a realization that their trial could bring about an abrupt end to their own lives as they knew them.

I followed by asking the governor about Oksana Sutin's life outside their relationship, and he could tell me little. Or at least he *did* tell me little. He didn't know much of her history, how she'd earned money, who owned or paid for her expensive Diamond Head apartment, how long she'd been in the islands. Didn't know whether she had family here or anywhere else for that matter, only that she was a Russian national.

"How did you meet her?" I said.

"At some function," Omphrey said, looking to Jason Yi for help.

"A fundraiser at the Blaisdell Center," Yi said. "There was a production of *Phantom* in the concert hall. They met during the intermission between acts one and two."

"Who was she in attendance with?" I asked. "Who made the introductions?"

Yi shook his head. "That I do not recall."

As he spoke, Yi's BlackBerry began rumbling on the conference table. He picked it up, made a few moves with his thumb, then looked glumly at the governor.

"It's Dias from the *Herald*," Yi said to his boss. "Somehow the media has already made the connection."

Both men looked soberly up at me.

"They're looking for comment," Yi said.

CHAPTER 8

I sent a car to pick up Scott Damiano at Honolulu International, then drafted a written statement on behalf of the governor's office for release to the media in connection with the ongoing investigation into Oksana Sutin's death. I cautioned the press not to jump to conclusions and reminded the public that Wade Omphrey, like any sitting governor, had made powerful political enemies while fighting for the citizens of the state of Hawaii. I promised further comments would follow the FBI press conference scheduled for tomorrow afternoon.

Then I placed a call to the houseplant, aka Assistant US Attorney William F. Boyd. "My client Turi Ahina and I would like to come in for a chat."

"Smart decision, Counselor."

"Thanks for the compliment. Name the when and we'll be there."

"How about right now?"

I glanced at my watch. "A little late in the day, isn't it?"

"You can stand to miss one happy hour, Counselor."

"Let's not make this about me and you."

"If this were about me and you, Counselor, I'd tell you to go to hell and I'd begin prepping for trial so that I could nail your ass to the wall. But I'm willing to speak to your boy. As you may know, one of his codefendants drew Clyde Harris, and I expect a call from Clyde in the morning, in which case I won't need you *or* your client anymore. So it's now or never, Counselor. What's your call?"

"I'll see you in forty-five minutes," I said quietly.

"Smart decision." Then the line went dead.

A little over an hour later Turi and I were seated alone in a small room with no windows at the Federal Detention Center, and I was sweating, itching from the Percocet, yet trying to maintain my calm. Turi didn't appear to be much better off, his legs shaking beneath the table, his hands taking turns wiping the perspiration from his brow.

"This document is called a Queen for a Day agreement," I said, pulling a form out of my briefcase.

"I don't think I like the sound of that, Mistah C."

I set the form in front of Turi on the table. "Don't worry, Turi. It doesn't mean you have to dress in drag. This document is meant to protect you, and I won't allow you to say a word before I have a fully executed copy in my briefcase."

"How does it protect me?"

"This agreement provides that no statements you or I make this evening can be used as evidence against you in any criminal proceedings. *But* the government may use your statements against you for the purpose of cross-examination or impeachment should you testify at any proceeding contrary to this proffer. In other words, don't lie because lies *can* come back to haunt you."

"No lies," Turi said as though instructing himself.

"No lies. Remember, in addition to the charges already filed against you, you can be prosecuted for perjury, giving a false statement, or obstruction of justice if you knowingly provide false information."

"What's the government promising me in return, eh?"

"Nothing," I said flatly. "In return for your willingness to talk, if you provide the government with useful information during this debriefing, you *may* receive some form of leniency such as a plea to a lesser charge or ideally, immunity from prosecution. But they've made no promises so far. You have to make it worth their while to make you a promise. The better the information, the better the deal they'll cut."

Turi filled his large lungs with the stale air of the sealed room. "What do they want to know?"

"Everything." I stood and removed my suit jacket, hung it neatly over the back of my chair. "One more thing. The government lawyer will be gauging how well you handle yourself to determine what kind of witness you'll make. Be certain of what you say, maintain eye contact, and speak loudly and clearly. Understand?"

Turi nodded to me just as the metal door creaked open and AUSA William F. Boyd stepped in, followed by a man and a woman. Turi and I shifted our chairs so that we were seated side-by-side, ready to address our adversaries. Boyd took a seat on the opposite side of the table, flanked on either side by the man and the woman. The woman looked strikingly familiar.

"Mr. Corvelli," Boyd said, "thank you for coming." Boyd

completely ignored Turi in an effort to show my client how insignificant he was. "Seated to my left is Special Agent Michael Jansen of the Drug Enforcement Administration. And seated to my right is Assistant US Attorney Audra Levy."

Audra. I peeked at her slender left hand; no ring. She somewhat resembled a brunette I graduated high school with, but her last name had been Karras. *Audra Karras.* A tight-ass who had once turned me in for smoking a joint in the faculty parking lot.

Boyd presented a fresh copy of the proffer agreement and reiterated what I'd already said to Turi, then he pushed a silver Montblanc across the table to me and I handed it to Turi, indicating where to sign. After adding my John Hancock, I passed the document back to Boyd and stuffed the Montblanc into the inside pocket of my suit jacket.

"All right," Boyd said. "Let's get started. Mr. Ahina, why don't you begin by telling us everything you know about Orlando Masonet."

CHAPTER 9

"Counselor," Boyd said an hour later, "your client is wasting my time."

"I'm telling you everything I know," Turi protested.

I motioned to Turi to keep silent. "Let's you and I have a word outside in private," I said to Boyd.

Jansen and Levy both nodded in agreement, and the four of us stood up and stepped into the hall, leaving Turi alone in the tight room. Jansen and Levy made for the vending machines at the end of the hallway, while Boyd crossed his arms and waited to hear what I had to say.

"Help me help my client help you," I said. "We both know that the DEA doesn't make a move until they're certain they can nail the entire organization, top to bottom. So what is it you want confirmed?"

"It doesn't work that way, Counselor. Maybe some dim-bulb state prosecutor might fall for your shit and play ball with you, but not me."

I glanced over my shoulder down the hall; Jansen and Levy were nowhere in sight. "Every single question you asked my client was about Orlando Masonet. My client told you that he never spoke to him, never saw him. My client doesn't even know what he looks like."

"That's too bad for all of us."

I felt my cheeks glowing red under the fluorescent lights. "What evidence do you have that this guy even exists?"

"Oh, he exists—maybe not on paper—but that's none of your concern, Counselor. But I *will* give you an idea as to why we're moving on this now." Boyd leaned in and lowered his voice. "We have word that Orlando Masonet is on this island right now, which according to everything else we know, is as rare as Halley's Comet. So, if you want your client to have any chance at all at walking in this case, you're going to have to get him to cooperate. And fast."

"He's *been* coopera—"

"Not that way," Jansen said from behind me.

I spun, my heart pounding. Since the stabbing, I hated being snuck up on.

Jansen said, "We need your boy on the street. We need a CI."

I swallowed hard; there was no way I was allowing Turi Ahina to act as a confidential informant. Not with what I already knew about Orlando Masonet and his organization.

"My client is no good to you in a coffin," I said.

"And he's no good to us behind bars," Jansen volleyed. "But that's where he's going to be spending the next thirty years of his life if he doesn't play ball. And that's if he's lucky. Because you, Mr. Corvelli, know as well as anybody that if someone wants to get to your client on the inside, it's as easy as pie."

The image of Brandon Glenn's gravestone flashed through my mind. "Even if you put my client back on the street—even if he isn't immediately killed—what makes you think he can get anywhere near Orlando Masonet?"

Jansen shot a glance at Boyd, then said, "Orlando Masonet is trapped on this island. We're watching everything, every airfield, every harbor, every military base. Oahu is on lockdown, Counselor. Masonet won't make a move until he knows it's safe."

"If you can't identify Masonet," I said, "what good does a lockdown do? And if Masonet knows you can't identify him, why the hell does he have anything to fear stepping into an airport terminal?"

Boyd pursed his lips, no doubt weighing the odds of disclosing sensitive information to a defense attorney he wouldn't trust pet-sitting his goldfish. Reluctantly he said, "We can't identify Masonet by his face or even by any external markings such as tattoos or scars. But we do have information from a credible source that Masonet has a fraction of a large-caliber bullet lodged in his skull, an inch or so above the left ear. Too deep and too near the brain to risk surgery to remove it. It never presented much of a problem for him before, but now that the TSA can ostensibly subject every individual who boards a plane in this country to a full-body scan, it's a whole new ballgame. Masonet knows we have this information; we know that because he slaughtered the doctor who provided it to us. So Masonet won't risk leaving this island now that we know he's here."

"That's where your client comes in," Jansen added.

"And how's that?" I said.

"Your client is going to offer Masonet an out."

I stared at Jansen, smirked at Boyd. "Are you both out of your fucking minds? Turi sells forty-dollar bags of meth just to keep himself stuffed with kalua pig and poi. Masonet won't believe for a second that Turi has the resources to transport him safely from Honolulu to the North Shore, let alone off the island entirely."

"Of course not," Jansen said. "And that's where *you* come in, Counselor."

"Me?" I said incredulously. "You *are* out of your fucking mind."

As I started back toward the room holding Turi, Boyd grabbed my arm with such force that I nearly turned and cracked him across the face.

"You'll want to hear Special Agent Jansen out," he said firmly.

"I'm a lawyer," I said quietly. "What incentive in hell could you possibly offer me to get me involved in this shit storm?"

"This is the only way your client walks," Jansen said.

"Don't believe everything you read in the racks at the airport," I said, seething. "What makes you think I'd put my neck out for a client?"

"Not just any client," Boyd said.

"What the hell does that mean?"

"It means," Jansen said, "that we know that Alika Kapua didn't fire two bullets into his own chest the night he attempted to kill you in Kailua three years ago."

CHAPTER 10

The plan was simple. Simple and as dangerous as a foolproof suicide attempt. The feds would move money to make it appear as though I surreptitiously bailed Turi out, a move that could get me suspended or disbarred in and of itself. Once Turi was back on the street, he'd get word to his associates that he needed to rendezvous with the kingpin Orlando Masonet himself, that he had under his thumb a criminal lawyer named Kevin Corvelli, who was highly indebted to him and who could get Masonet safely off the island with a single wave of his magic wand. If everything went according to plan, a meeting would be arranged between Orlando Masonet and me. Once the feds had enough to identify Masonet, the rest was up to them. The only guarantee I was given was that the arrest wouldn't come back to me.

I pulled my Jeep off H1 West into Ko Olina and passed through the gate, thinking about what Turi had told us about this Orlando Masonet. Or "Keyser Söze's evil twin," as some

were known to call him. The details of Masonet's past were
unknown, but he was said to have come to power in the early
nineties when the family-run Mexican cartels seized control
of the Hawaiian drug trade.

Some insisted that Orlando Masonet was Colombian, others said that he was the bastard son of Panama's former military dictator Manuel Noriega. Still others claimed he was an
orphan raised by jackals on Mexico's Yucatán Peninsula. Whatever his background, all agreed that Orlando Masonet was a
man-killer. He took control of the cartels and consolidated
power through brute force and intimidation, leaving a wake
of bodies only the hardest of Mexicans had ever seen. He
oversaw every aspect of the business personally until the late
nineties. Just as his ruthlessness became legend, Orlando Masonet disappeared. But only in the flesh. His organization continued on as fluidly as ever with all members behaving to this
day as though Orlando Masonet were steps away, watching their
every move, hearing their every word. And sure enough, even
now, when someone crossed Masonet, his body turned up on
the rocks off Ka'ena Point, if it ever turned up at all.

Of course, few successful criminals achieve power without
the help of the cops. It was said that Orlando Masonet was no
exception. In return for protection, Masonet aided Hawaiian
law enforcement in their efforts to take down Asian gangs.
When upper-echelon Asian gang members couldn't be caught,
they were killed. Masonet didn't care how he eliminated his
competition—through force or through the courts—so long as
they said their last aloha in the Hawaiian Islands.

As I pulled into my driveway, I was hit with a wave of nau-
sea. Time for my pills. But they could wait until I got inside.

I needed to feed Skies, and I needed a nice tall glass of Glenlivet.

The moment I stepped into my living room I noticed a small red-orange dot glowing in the far corner.

My first thought was, *Who in hell would have the balls to smoke in my home?*

My second thought was far more practical. I reached for my cell phone as I flicked on the lights.

"Relax, Kev. It's a joint, not a cigarette."

Scott Damiano sat cross-legged on a folding chair blowing smoke out his nose.

"We're on a first-name basis now?" I said, trying to catch my breath without demonstrating that I'd lost it.

"I figured if we're going to be working together and all . . ."

"Yeah, well, if this is the interview, you'd better start jazzing up the résumé and searching on Craigslist." I tossed my keys onto the kitchen counter and moved toward the liquor cabinet. "How the hell did you get in here anyway?"

"Your garage door was unlocked."

"No, Scott, it wasn't."

"Well then, it wasn't locked enough."

I twisted the cap on the Glenlivet and took a swig straight from the bottle. "You've been in Hawaii, what, eight hours? How the hell do you have a joint already?"

"One of your neighbors."

"Really? Which one?"

"I promised I wouldn't tell."

"Fine," I grumbled. "But pass it over; I'm having one hell of a day."

CHAPTER 11

A few minutes after I arrived at the office the next morning, Jake stepped through my door, waving a pink message slip.

"FBI called, son. A Special Agent Neil Slauson. Says he'd like you to bring the governor in for a sit-down."

I tossed back the pills I had in my hand and washed them down with Red Bull. "It was just a matter of time, I guess. I'll have Hoshi set something up for this afternoon."

"I realize it's none of my business, son"—Jake motioned with his sagging chin to the prescription bottle on my desk—"but are you still experiencing pain from that stab wound to your gut."

I stared at the bottle. "I'm experiencing pain from the entire event."

He gave a slow nod. "Fair enough, I reckon."

We were saved from any further discussion by Hoshi's voice over the intercom: "Flan's here."

"Good," I told her. "Ask him to wait in the conference room. Jake and I will be right down."

Once we settled into the conference room, I explained to Jake and Ryan Flanagan, our full-time investigator, the plan that Jansen and Boyd expected me to carry out.

"This is as dangerous as it gets," I told them, "but for reasons you both know, it's something I've got to do. But I don't expect either of you to put your lives on the line for my debts."

Jake whistled. "We're not only talking bodily harm here, son. We're talking serious ethical violations with no safeguards in place. When all this is over, the state bar can come after your license, and I guarantee that Jansen and Boyd will be in no position to help your cause, even if they wanted to."

I nodded. "That's why I'm proposing a temporary split. We dissolve the firm of Harper and Corvelli on paper, and each of us flies solo until the heat clears."

Jake stroked his chin. "May be for the best. If you get your license yanked, at least we can continue under the Law Offices of Jake Harper until the dust settles. We can recruit a young associate and you can play Cyrano de Bergerac for as long as you need to."

"Then it's decided," I said. "The feds will move one million dollars into a Swiss account, which I'll then use to make Turi's bail. I'll use a fake identity, but the paper trail will lead back to me if and when Orlando Masonet goes looking."

Flan shook his head. "What if Masonet has Turi smoked the minute he steps out of the FDC?"

"He won't," I said. "Masonet is going to want to know what Turi told the feds, so if he does anything, he'll abduct Turi, maybe torture him to find out if he sang."

"Well, then," Flan said with a smirk, "sounds like you've got everything under control. Remind me not to save your life because I sure as hell wouldn't want to be in Turi's shoes right now."

"Turi will be protected," I said. "I've already hired a private security firm to watch him from the minute he steps out of the FDC. And while he's on the street, he's going to have his own personal bodyguard."

"Won't that appear a little suspicious?" Jake said.

"Not if the bodyguard is one of my own guys. That plays right into Turi's story to Masonet about how I'm indebted to him and will do anything to protect him."

"One of your own guys?" Flan said, gulping visibly.

"Not you," I assured him. "You work for Jake, and Jake and I are going to be handling the governor's matter collectively. You'll be assigned to that investigation for the time being."

"Then who's playing Secret Service?"

"Scott Damiano." I filled Jake and Flan in on Scott's story.

After a few moments of silence, Jake sighed heavily. "What the hell did I get myself into when I rented you that office, son?"

I shrugged. "No one lives forever, Jake."

"Not around you they don't."

I pushed my chair out, stole a look at the mountain range in the distance, the clouds so thick around its peaks, it looked as though the mountains themselves were on fire.

"All right," I said. "Enough fun for this morning. It's time to get to work. I've got to call this FBI agent Slauson and escort the governor in for questioning."

As I made for the door, Jake half-chuckled, half-coughed. "Good thing you moved out here to paradise to avoid any real responsibility."

Good thing, indeed, Jake.

CHAPTER 12

Special Agent Neil Slauson of the Federal Bureau of Investigation met with us in his office on Ala Moana Boulevard late that afternoon, accompanied by a younger female agent named Wendy Chan. Once introductions were made, Chan remained silent as Slauson, with his slicked-back gray hair, launched into a needless preamble as to why the FBI was involved in the Oksana Sutin homicide investigation.

"We're concerned about certain individuals within the Honolulu Police Department," Slauson said matter-of-factly. "And this particular investigation involves a number of sensitive issues, not the least of which is the governor's apparent relationship with the deceased."

I sat forward in my chair, hoping to cut short another long-winded diatribe on the FBI's national efforts to combat public corruption on all levels. "Governor Omphrey understands why you've requested this meeting, and he wishes to assist your investigation in any way that he can. Unfortunately, the governor's knowledge of the victim is exceedingly limited, and his knowledge of the circumstances surrounding her death is practically nil. So with that in mind, we'd ask that you commence your questioning so that the governor can continue his day's itinerary with as brief an interruption as possible."

Slauson bobbed his head slowly. "Understood, Mr. Corvelli." He made a show of shuffling some papers around on his neatly arranged desk, then planted his elbows and folded his hands together just below his chin. "Governor, are you familiar with the name Lok Sun?"

Omphrey's cheeks puffed up and a smug smile played on his lips. "I'm sorry," he said, glancing at Chan, "is that a restaurant of some sort?"

I bit down hard on my lower lip and let Slauson field the question.

"No, sir," Slauson said without humor. "Lok Sun is a name."

"Either way," Omphrey said, "I'm afraid I'm not familiar with it."

"How about your wife, Pamela? Might she know the name?"

"You'd have to ask her."

A brief silence followed. Not for the first time I wondered what the hell I was doing sitting next to Wade Omphrey. Surely the state of Hawaii would be better off without him at the helm, his guilt or innocence aside.

Slauson said, "I was made to believe by your attorney that you would prefer to keep your wife out of this investigation, if at all possible." He paused a moment. "Considering the circumstances."

Omphrey glanced at me, then said, "Of course, of course." His jowls trembled as he shook his head. "No, I'm certain Pamela has no knowledge of . . ."

"Lok Sun," Slauson said again. "He may also use the name Park Wu."

"I'm sorry," Omphrey said. "Again, no knowledge."

"Maybe if you put these names into some context," I suggested.

"At this point, I suppose there is no compelling reason not to," Slauson said. "The evidence gathered thus far suggests that Ms. Sutin was murdered using the colorless, crystalline alkaloid called strychnine. It is a very well-known poison but it is very seldom seen in homicide cases."

"If I'm not mistaken," I said, "strychnine is commonly used to cut cocaine and heroin. Is it possible Ms. Sutin's death was accidental?"

Slauson shook his head. "There was no evidence of any street drugs found at the victim's residence, and by all accounts Ms. Sutin was not a recreational drug user."

"No," the governor said. "Oksana was a social drinker but she didn't dabble in drugs."

The way Omphrey said it, it sounded as though he'd tried to get her to partake on an occasion or two.

"Toxicology tests are pending," Slauson said, "but we think the poison was slipped into one of Ms. Sutin's food or beverage items in the home. Maybe a strong black tea she was known to drink."

"And this Lok Sun you mentioned," I said, "you believe he was the delivery mechanism."

"Lok Sun," Slauson said, "is a world-renowned hitman high

on Interpol's wanted list, though I know of no country with enough evidence to convict him. He's known to most in the underworld as the Pharmacist, and poisons such as strychnine are part of his MO. Lok Sun is typically out of a country before a body is ever found. But this time, we got lucky."

"Lucky?"

"As part of an unrelated investigation, the Drug Enforcement Administration has been watching all airports, all harbors, and all military installations since Sunday evening. Late Monday night, shortly before Ms. Sutin's body was discovered, a Chinese national named Park Wu missed his flight back to Beijing. We have reason to believe that Park Wu is actually Lok Sun. We think he caught wind of the lockdown on Oahu and purposefully missed his flight. Logic would dictate that he is presently lying low in Chinatown."

I immediately understood Slauson's reasoning behind bringing us in, knowing damn well the governor—savvy enough and lawyered up—would not be forthcoming with any useful information. The sole purpose for the meeting was to feed us this information, hoping the information would make its way over the tapped phone lines and ever-watched Internet service providers of Hawaii. Slauson's aim was to flush out Lok Sun, and he made no effort to mask his objective.

"We *will* find him," Slauson said flatly an hour later when the meeting finally ended. "And we *will* find out which party is responsible for hiring him."

CHAPTER 13

On the sidewalk outside the Federal Detention Center, I inadvertently stepped on a long brown slug, squashing it beneath the hard sole of my shoe. I felt it wriggle and die beneath my foot. I looked down at the length of ooze and wondered briefly how old the slug was, how long slugs were expected to live. The hand of grief reached out and grabbed me by the throat, and for a moment I thought I might vomit on the sidewalk in the blush of the setting sun.

Turi's wide smile spared me any further despair. He peered up and down the boulevard before finally staring straight at me. Being released from federal prison is typically an invigorating experience, but not when far darker forces are likely waiting for you on the outside.

"Thanks for going along with all this, Mistah C," Turi said immediately after greeting me. "Ya know, you're going to heaven for this, brah."

I started down the street without saying anything.

Turi followed me in the direction of the garage where I'd parked my Jeep. We took the elevator up to the third floor, then walked briskly toward my white Wrangler. Turi waited until we were both inside, then said, "I need one favor, yeah? I need you to come with me tonight around midnight to meet up with Tam in Chinatown, eh?"

"Tam?" I said, turning the ignition with no small amount of trepidation. "Who's Tam?"

"He's one Vietnamese guy I know. If anybody can get one message to Masonet, it's Tam, brah."

I backed slowly out of the tight space, then threw the transmission into drive and rolled forward. "Why me? Why tonight?"

"Because, brah, I might not make it till dawn. And I need you with me or else no one's gonna buy my story that I got one haole lawyer gonna help me out by helping the big boss. I go to Tam's bar with that shit, and I'm not coming out, eh?"

I pulled the Jeep onto Ala Moana Boulevard. "All right. But for now we're headed up to my home in Ko Olina. We can hang low there until it's time to take off for Chinatown."

"We need to make one stop first, brah."

"One stop where?"

"Kailua, yeah? We gotta stop by my house."

"What for?"

"I need something."

"Anything you need—clothes, toiletries, snacks—we can buy at the ABC Store near my villa. I'll pay or you can borrow some of my things."

Turi twisted his thick neck to look at me, then shook his head. "No offense, Mistah C, but you don't got what I need."

"What's that then, Turi?" I asked, checking my rearview to make sure we weren't being followed.

"If we're going to Chinatown, we're going strapped. So I gotta get my gun."

By the time we drove to Kailua and picked up Turi's .44 Glock, it was already dark, so we grabbed some steak sandwiches at Buzz's in Lanikai and waited. Then we waited some more. Few words were said; even fewer were necessary. We both knew we had our backs against the wall. One wrong move and the two of us were fish food.

At a quarter past eleven we finally began the anxious drive from Lanikai to Chinatown.

Once Honolulu's red light district, Chinatown had undergone a recent face-lift. The area was now more known for its cutting-edge art and world-class cuisine than for its violent drug gangs and dilapidated buildings. But Turi and I weren't heading into Chinatown to admire its oil paintings and sculptures or to dine at one of its four-star Asian eateries. We were making for Nuuanu Street and one of its relics—a dive bar that few knew about and even fewer entered, a place where you could go in the front whole and come out the back in pieces.

We parked in the business district and walked. I knew we'd hit Chinatown once the street names were accompanied by Chinese symbols. The moon offered the only light, and from the corner of my eye I caught more than a few of the district's nocturnal denizens lurking in the shadows. Not too many of the men looked Chinese, but plenty looked plenty tough. Face-lift or not, Chinatown wasn't a place where you wanted to walk the streets after dark.

"There it is," Turi said, motioning toward a nook between two abandoned storefronts.

The joint had no sign, the door was hidden in shadows, and I thought, not for the first time, *There's nothing more indecent than a dive bar that doesn't want to be discovered.*

"All right," I said. "What's the play?"

"We go inside, brah. And we try not to get killed."

Sounded like a plan. I'd passed through Chinatown plenty of times before but only once spent any length of time here—for the Chinese New Year back when I was dating Nikki Kapua. We'd stood on crowded sidewalks and watched colorful dancing lions snake through the streets while sipping *baijiu*, welcoming—now ironically—the Year of the Rat.

We crossed the street and ducked into the nook, then Turi rapped on the door.

Nothing like a bar where you've got to knock.

When the door finally opened, an Asian man the width of Turi with twice the height prevented us from seeing inside.

"Ahina?" the giant said, glowering at Turi. "The fuck you doin' here?"

"I need to see Tam, brah. I got one message for him, yeah?"

"Nah." The giant shook his head. "No can." He looked at me. "And who's the fucking haole, eh?"

"That's Mistah C. He's my lawyer, yeah?"

"Whatevahs. You bettah get from here before you and this muff get your heads blown off." The giant started closing the door.

Turi stopped it with one mammoth sandaled foot. Then he pulled his piece. Held the business end flat against the giant's temple.

"Oh, fuck," I muttered. This plan had just gone from bad idea to suicide in under sixty seconds.

"Easy, brah!" the giant said. "No *huhu*, brah. No get upset."

Turi didn't flinch. "Feel that chicken skin, eh?" he said calmly. "Them goose bumps telling you to open that door and no make ass. One funny kine move and I make you parallel fo' real, eh?"

"Easy, brah," the giant said quietly. "No need."

Behind the giant I detected movement.

"Quickly, Turi," I whispered.

Turi got the message. "You got three seconds, moke, then I cut you down peanut-size."

"Oh, wow, like that, eh?" the giant said, raising his voice. "'Kay, fine then!"

The giant moved out of the doorframe and Turi aimed his pistol at the bartender, who was rising from behind the bar with a shotgun.

"No act!" Turi shouted.

The bartender lowered his weapon and Turi led the way inside, gun still raised.

A half dozen people were in the bar, counting the giant and bartender. Two men—one Asian, one Caucasian—sat at the bar, their eyes trained on Turi's weapon. In the rear of the cramped space, a scarred man sat on an old maroon velvet couch, a young woman straddling his lap. Her back was completely bare, displaying a torso-length tattoo of a rare bird escaping its cage.

The scarred man dumped the girl off his lap and rose.

"What the fuck you think you're doing?" he said to Turi in near-perfect English.

From the side of his mouth Turi said to me, "This here is Tam. He no like Americans. They kill his whole *'ohana* back in 'Nam."

"You might have mentioned that sooner," I said through clenched teeth.

Turi shrugged. "You no ask."

I stole a glance at the Caucasian idling at the bar; he suddenly appeared very European. I swallowed hard and vowed to keep my lips shut. Until we left this shithole—*if* we left this shithole—I was 100 percent Canadian. *Je suis de Québec, amigo.*

"I no want no beef, Tam," Turi said evenly. "I just come to bring you one message."

"And what's that message, Ahina?" Tam sounded as though he'd just swallowed a mouthful of gravel. "That you have one death wish or something?"

"No get wise, Tam." Turi glanced over at the bartender, shouted at him to keep his fucking hands raised, then he looked back at the giant and ordered him to stand in the far corner where we could keep our eyes on him. Then he turned back to Tam. "Your wahine speak English, yeah?"

The young Asian girl with the uncaged-bird tattoo nodded. "I speak English."

"Good," Turi said. "You come here, eh?"

"What are you doing?" I whispered to Turi. "Why not go back there and tell Tam himself?"

"In case you no notice," Turi whispered back, "I'm a big

guy and I no move too fast. I get close to Tam, and he'll stick me like a pig."

The girl—she couldn't have been more than eighteen—swayed forward slowly. When she was just a little more than an arm's length away, Turi ordered her to stop.

In a hushed voice Turi said to her, "You tell Tam I have one way for big boss man to get off the island. My lawyer here, he owe me one favor, and he have one jet ready to take off for anywhere big boss man wanna go. No need file flight plan." He motioned with his head to Tam. "Now go."

My fingers tingled, and the stagnant air of the bar was causing me to sweat through my shirt and suit jacket.

Tam listened to the message then pushed the girl away hard enough to drop her to the floor.

"Big boss is gonna ask how the fuck you got out of the FDC," Tam said.

As the girl uneasily got to her feet, Turi motioned her over again. But I didn't want her involved, and I didn't think I'd make it through another round of telephone.

"*I* bailed him out," I said aloud.

"And why would you do that for a half-ton bag of shit like Turi Ahina?"

"Hit the archives of the *Advertiser*," I said, my voice surprisingly steady. "Go back three years and you'll find out why."

Tam smiled, the long, jagged scar stretching across his face. "Alika Kapua."

Small island, I thought. *Too damn small.*

I ignored the name and said, "Bottom line is, I have the means and the motive. Turi remains untouched, and I send your boss anywhere on the planet that doesn't share reciprocity with the United States."

Tam scratched at his scar, which ran like the Kaukonahua River from his brow all the way down to his chin. "I will deliver the message. How does he get in touch with you?"

"No need. I'll get in touch with him through you in forty-eight hours. That should give him enough time to check me out and confirm everything I just told you."

I turned around and went for the door while Turi backed out slowly.

"Lawyer!" Tam called just as my fingers grazed the door handle. "What's your name?"

I turned back to him. "Kevin Corvelli."

"Corvelli. You are an American?"

"Worse. I'm a New Yorker."

CHAPTER 14

When I opened the door to our offices late the next morning, I found AUSA Audra Levy sitting in our reception area reading the latest issue of *Time*. I ignored Hoshi's good morning and turned to the assistant US attorney. "What the hell are you doing here?"

"Excuse me?" she said, looking up from the magazine.

"You heard me. Are you *trying* to get me and my client killed by coming here to check up on things, or are you and William F. Boyd just plain stupid?"

"Kevin—," Hoshi said, rising from behind her desk.

I held up a palm and told her to keep quiet.

Audra Levy stood and tossed the magazine onto an empty chair. "I didn't even know this was your office," she said with indignation.

"Then just what the hell are you doing here?"

Hoshi's voice rang out from behind me. "Ms. Levy is here to see Jake."

"Jake?"

"I'm purchasing a condominium in Kakaako," Audra said. "I'm retaining Mr. Harper to review the contract."

"We don't *handle* real estate matters."

"*We* don't." Jake suddenly emerged from the conference room. "But *I* do."

I dipped my hand into the right pocket of my suit jacket and fondled my pill bottle. "What are you talking about, Jake?"

"We dissolved our partnership, son. Or have you forgotten already?"

"So now you're handling real estate matters?" I said incredulously.

"Real estate, wills and probate, divorce, adoption. I'm coming up on seventy, son. I can't be chasing after iceheads and gangbangers during my sunset years. I'm resuming a general practice, something I did in the old days back in Houston when the judges weren't being generous with criminal assignments." He smiled at Audra. "I'll be right with you, young lady."

"Do you not know who she is, Jake?"

"Pardon?"

"This is AUSA Audra Levy. She's working the Turi Ahina case with our friend Billy F. Boyd. So there might—just *might*—be a bit of a conflict involved."

"I apologize, Mr. Harper," Audra said, shaking her head. "I didn't know you worked with Mr. Corvelli or even shared office space. He's right; this would present a tremendous conflict of interest." She retrieved her handbag from the chair.

Then she turned to me. "I'm sorry, Kevin. I received a referral from my real estate agent. The Ahina case is Boyd's. I never saw a copy of your letterhead or I never would have shown up here."

Audra appeared distressed, and I immediately regretted raising my voice and barking accusations at her. I realized that my outburst was at least partly due to its being past time for my pills.

"You're Audra Karras, aren't you?"

She half-smiled. "So you do remember me from high school."

"I thought I did, but I didn't see a ring, so I wasn't sure."

She raised her hand, knuckles out, palm facing her. "No ring. I'm divorced."

I motioned down the hallway. "Why don't you take a seat in my office? Since you're already here, we might as well take the opportunity to talk."

"That's not necessary."

"No, please. I'd like to discuss the case and I don't trust the phones. And I'm sure as hell not stopping by DEA headquarters until this case is concluded."

Audra finally agreed, leaving me and Jake alone in the reception area with Hoshi.

"Sorry, son. I had no idea."

"I realize that. I never mentioned her name."

Just then the conference-room door swung open, and I heard a small boy's voice. "Miss Hoshi, do you have any more of those gummi bears?"

My heart nearly melted in my chest.

Jake stepped aside, and for the first time since shortly after Erin Simms slit her wrists, I saw Josh, a child I pulled from the Kupulupulu Beach Resort fire a long twelve months ago.

"*Kevin?*" Josh said. "I *knew* I was right. I *knew* this was where you worked!"

The boy ran toward me as fast as he could, and as I lowered myself on my haunches, he jumped into my arms.

I looked over the boy's shoulder past Jake, at a kind-looking couple in their late thirties, smiling deeply as they exited the conference room.

Jake shrugged at me, then smiled himself.

"An adoption I'm handling," he said. "Guess I'm just full of surprises today, son."

After meeting Josh's new family and assuring the kid we were still friends and that we'd see each other again real soon, I moved down the hallway to my private office, where I sat at my desk across from Audra. I began to tell her about my relationship with the boy, about the fire and the criminal trial that followed, but she stopped me midsentence by saying, "I read the book."

"The book?" I said, trying to regain my train of thought. It was now well past time for my Percocet and my mind was choked with fog.

"*Paradise on Fire* by Sherry Beagan. About the Erin Simms trial. The boy Josh was one of the main characters."

"Oh."

I didn't know what else to say, couldn't seem to figure a way to move on. Audra had read a nonfiction account of one of the most challenging and painful periods of my life, a story that depicted me as a cad, as a callous and calculating lawyer whose scheming didn't cease once he left the courtroom. It was more or less the portrait of a modern-day monster.

A sharp pain suddenly struck me like a fist in the gut. Perspiration formed at my temples. I needed my pills and fast. "Would you excuse me for a moment?"

I shot across the hall and entered Jake's office, quickly scanning the top of his desk. Empty as usual. I moved behind the desk and searched the drawers. No way I could wait forty minutes for the pills to kick in. I needed something to crush them. In Jake's bottom right-hand drawer I found a paperweight—an elaborate piece of glass art with a solid bottom. I fished the pill bottle from my jacket pocket, opened it, and spilled four pills onto the desk. I crushed them one at a time, keeping my eyes on the closed door. Then I reached into my back pants pocket, removed my wallet, and snatched out a $20 bill. I rolled the bill tightly then held it to my right nostril. I leaned over the desk and snorted the dust, cursing yet savoring the burn.

After cleaning up, I returned to my office, the drip still traveling down the back of my throat.

"Sorry about that," I said, sniffling. I felt like a racehorse, felt like grabbing a gun and running down to Chinatown to show Tam and the giant the type of haole I really was. "Now, where were we?" My fingers absently played with the file folders cluttering my desk.

"We were about to discuss your client Turi Ahina. And Orlando Masonet."

"Yes!" I said, slapping my desk. "Phase two of the plan is complete. We delivered the message to Masonet."

"How did you do that?"

I shook my head, pointed at the ceiling, and shook my finger, too. "No, no. That's something I don't share with you. Suffice it to say, we'll know if we can move onto phase three within forty-eight fours." I glanced at my watch. "Thirty-six hours to be exact."

"Boyd will be pleased."

The mere mention of Boyd's name caused me to deflate, to think of the last lawyer to truly get under my skin: a young state prosecutor named Luke Maddox. Maddox had made the Erin Simms trial personal, and somehow every matter I'd handled since felt the same way. That feeling could destroy a trial lawyer, could burn him into nothingness at a young age.

"How did you wind up with the US Attorney's Office anyhow?" I said, wondering briefly just how well and in what capacity she knew William F. Boyd.

"I clerked for a federal criminal court judge in the Eastern District right out of law school, and I guess I fell in love with the practice and wanted to be on the side of right."

I smiled, taking the jab in the spirit in which it was intended. She smiled back, but hers was more difficult to read. Whether it was friendly or flirty, from that moment on I couldn't take my eyes off her. With a mere twitch of her lips she'd gone from US attorney to human—a transformation I wouldn't have thought possible just an hour ago.

"I suppose that even the Justice Department finds itself on the side of right every once in a while," I said.

Audra shook her head but maintained a grin. "Sixteen years since high school and you haven't changed a bit, Kevin."

"Oh, I've changed. I've got the scars to prove it."

"Well," she said, rising out of my client chair, "let's save them for another time."

Abruptly I said, "How about tonight?"

"No. I have plans tonight. Besides, it is *not* a good idea for us to see each other socially."

"Who said anything about socially? We're going to have to communicate these next few days, and I already told you I have no intention of using the phones or going anywhere near your office building."

"Then let's discuss phase three of the plan now," she suggested, sitting herself back down.

"No can do." I stared at my watch. "I have a press conference scheduled in twenty minutes. Thanks to a strange twist of fate, I'm representing the governor of Hawaii in a murder investigation."

CHAPTER 15

Seamus slid a bottle of Longboard across the bar to me, then turned to close out Sand Bar's register.

"You know," he said, "since your law partner quit drinking, business is down forty percent."

"Jake feels terrible about that, but we're not partners anymore."

Seamus spun around. "No shit, Kevin?"

I explained the situation as best I could without going into details.

"So Jake has a general practice going now, is that it?" Seamus asked.

I took a pull of my Longboard. "That's what he tells me."

"Well, lad, that's convenient for me. Because without his business I'm going to have to file for Chapter Eleven. At least ol' Jake can handle my bankruptcy."

With that Seamus pushed a set of keys across the bar to

me. "Stay as long as you need. Just be sure to lock up when you leave."

"Thanks again for this."

"No problem. I set it up so that your lass can come in the back. See you tomorrow, then."

Once Seamus left, I went around the bar and retrieved the remote control for the television sets. I tuned in to KGMB and muted the volume. Soon as I did, Audra Levy walked in from the rear of the bar carrying a thin briefcase.

"Did I miss last call?"

I shook my head, motioned to the long line of top-shelf liquor bottles. "Pick your poison."

"Thanks, but I'll pass."

"I forgot, government lawyers never mix business with pleasure. Or pleasure with anything for that matter."

Audra took a barstool and pointed at the coffee machine. "Know how to work that?"

"Nope." I flicked it with my fingers but nothing happened.

"How about water then?"

I reached into the cooler and passed her a bottle of FIJI.

"How did the press conference go this afternoon?" she said.

I looked up at one of the television sets above the bar. "You'll get to see for yourself in about ten minutes. I'm sure it'll kick off the eleven o'clock news." I lifted the remote and turned up the volume a bit. "So, did you find yourself another real estate lawyer?"

"I did." She opened the briefcase on the neighboring barstool and removed a brochure. "This is where I'm buying."

I took the brochure from her. The front of the brochure read, *Welcome to Water Landings—Luxury Oceanfront Condominiums,* with an illustration of the proposed tower and a photograph of a beautiful Caucasian couple sitting hand-in-hand watching whitecaps roll over the Pacific at sunset.

"Ah, Exhibit A of the American Dream," I said, opening the brochure.

Inside I found a photograph of a stunning, nude Asian woman lying on her stomach, being massaged by a pair of clean, strong, masculine hands. Below the woman, whose buttocks were barely covered by a crisp white towel, the text read, *Contemporary. Vibrant. Urban. This is Water Landings—the calm, peaceful, contented life—a hideaway from the hustle and bustle, yet mere steps to downtown Honolulu. Your private oasis in the center of it all. No more early-morning commutes or late-night journeys home. You'll be close enough to walk to work. And while everyone else is sitting in traffic, you'll be relaxing in the Jacuzzi. Water Landings offers four hundred luxurious one- to four-bedroom, fee-simple residences with spectacular views.*

I set the brochure facedown on the bar. On the rear of the brochure was a thumbnail-size photo of the developer, Thomas S. Duran.

"Kakaako," I said. "I drove by this 'quiet oasis' last time I hit Restaurant Row. If memory serves, there were a couple hundred protesters marching around the construction site and sales office chanting slogans about preserving the waterfront and the need for affordable housing."

Even in the bleak light of the bar I could tell Audra's cheeks were burning. "There has been some controversy," she conceded.

Kakaako (pronounced *cock-a-a-co*), a commercial and retail district in Honolulu, stretched along the southern shore from

Ala Moana to Honolulu Harbor. The controversy wasn't restricted to the area around the proposed site for Water Landings; it had filled the pages of the *Honolulu Star-Advertiser* for the past several months. It was a bare-knuckle fight—and Governor Omphrey had been caught in the middle of it.

Kakaako remained public land, and the question was whether Hawaii's government should be selling it off. Particularly to T. S. Duran Properties.

A number of developers had vied for state-owned land in Kakaako, but T. S. Duran Properties came away with a contract, sparking accusations of kickbacks and dirty, backroom deals. Meanwhile, community activists—including the first lady of Hawaii—stated clearly that it didn't matter so much *how* the deal was done, but that the deal was done at all. A forty-two-story residential tower with units priced in the area of high six figures, they argued, was the last thing needed in Kakaako given the tragic shortage of affordable housing and an ever-shrinking southern waterfront.

Similar battles were being waged up North Shore, where longtime residents fought tooth and nail against urban sprawl, intent on keeping the rural areas of Oahu rural.

"There you are," Audra said, no small measure of relief in her voice as she pointed up at the television set.

And, yes, there I was. Standing in front of a bevy of microphones with Governor Omphrey and the first lady standing solemnly at my side.

I used the remote to turn up the volume.

"As you all know," I said at the podium, "Special Agent Neil Slauson of the Federal Bureau of Investigation issued a statement earlier today with respect to the FBI's investigation into the recent death of a young woman named Oksana Sutin at her Honolulu home in Diamond Head. As you also know, Special Agent Slauson offered very few details concerning that investigation, as the FBI is wont to do. As a result, there has been rabid speculation—beginning on local Hawaiian television stations and spilling over into the national cable news networks—as to why the FBI is involved in this case. Some have suggested, based on utter conjecture, that the FBI became involved in this investigation because a local public official has been deemed a prime suspect.

"I spoke earlier today with Detective John Tatupu, a veteran homicide detective with the Honolulu Police Department. Detective Tatupu, who is also assigned to this case to work in conjunction with the FBI, informed me in no uncertain terms that *no one* has yet been named a suspect in this case, let alone a public official. I am advised by Detective Tatupu that police and FBI are indeed seeking a 'person of interest'—obviously not the governor or any other public official—though that is all I am at liberty to say at this time.

"Now if there are any questions . . ."

A female reporter with the *Star-Advertiser* raised her hand. "Is it true that your client, Governor Omphrey, knew the victim?"

"Of course, I cannot divulge conversations with my client— with *any* client—since they are protected by the attorney-client privilege. However, I will say that I've spoken at length with the governor's chief aide, Jason Yi, and Mr. Yi informed me that Ms. Sutin and the governor may have been introduced briefly at a fundraiser held at the Blaisdell Center earlier this year."

Rolando Dias from the *Herald* was next. "Mr. Corvelli, a source close to this investigation says that fingerprints matching those of the governor were discovered at the victim's apartment. Can you confirm or deny?"

"A source close to the investigation?" I said incredulously. "Care to give me a name?"

Dias shook his head. "My source wishes to remain anonymous."

"Well, that's convenient. Do you happen to know which candidate this source is voting for this November?"

Light laughter from the crowd.

"I do not," Dias said. "Though I will add that he has proved a reliable source in the past and that he is in the employ of the Honolulu PD."

I stared Dias down in front of the cameras. "Well, perhaps your source is also in the employ of someone else, someone who is firmly in the corner of the governor's opponent. Have you checked your source's bank statements recently?"

Silence. Dias didn't respond.

"Might I remind you and everyone else, Mr. Dias, that Governor Omphrey was some seven thousand miles away from Honolulu on the evening this murder occurred, meeting with White House officials in Washington, D.C."

"Some might suggest that being in D.C. when the murder occurred is a very clever alibi," Dias stated.

"And some might suggest that you are a very clever reporter," I retorted. "But that doesn't necessarily make it so."

More light laughter, and I thought I also detected a few boos and hisses.

But Dias wasn't deterred by my comeback. "If there is no evidence whatsoever to suggest that Governor Omphrey was involved in the murder of Ms. Sutin, then why has the governor hired a high-profile criminal defense attorney such as yourself to speak for him?"

"Because if he hired a high-profile plumber, you guys in the media would suggest to the electorate that he was pretty stupid, wouldn't you?"

I ended the press conference on that note, and I also powered down the television in the bar, so as not to catch the post-press-conference analysis.

"Wow," Audra said, her brows lifting in surprise. "That was something. Did the governor have anything to say to you after you left the podium?"

"He asked me just what the hell I thought I was doing."

"How did you respond?"

"Truthfully. I told him, 'The more the story is about me, Governor, the less it is about you.'"

CHAPTER 16

A few minutes later Audra and I moved from the bar to a booth. Something about being in a bar after closing made me feel criminal. Still, I realized, I'd rather deal with a bad case of guilt than a bad case of death.

"So," Audra said once we were settled, "you handle many federal cases?"

"Jake and I took on a few CJA appointments. But there aren't many federal cases here in Hawaii to handle." I watched for her reaction. "That is, until recently."

Audra looked away, but in an empty bar there was little to look away at. "I suppose it's no secret, but Honolulu PD's Internal Affairs unit has had their hands full recently."

"So that's why the feds are getting their hands dirty looking for Orlando Masonet."

She shook her head. "Masonet has been on the DEA's radar for a long time. But it's just recently they realized he and his organization may be getting a good deal of cover from the

HPD, and very possibly authorities on the Big Island and Maui as well."

This hardly came as a shock, but I wanted to hear more, so I raised my brows and motioned with my hand for her to expand.

"In addition to meth," she said, "it's believed Masonet controls Hawaii's four G's—girls, gambling, guns, and ganja."

"Well, we both know how you feel about that last one."

She smiled. "I'm sorry about that, Kevin. I really am. It's been sixteen years; can we forget about it?"

I stared at her with my best poker face.

"And, no," she added, "I couldn't give a shit about weed. Personally, I think it should be legalized. I'm pretty sure most young AUSAs secretly do."

"But not Billy F. Boyd."

"No, not William. He's a complete asshole with absolutely no sense of reality."

"Some friendly fire," I said.

"Sure, I'll give you this. I can't stomach working with Boyd but I have no choice. I was transferred here from the Southern District of New York because of the upswing in federal cases in Hawaii. Not that I fought the transfer. I'd just gone through my divorce and I'd wanted to put as much distance between me and Marty as I could."

"But you kept the name."

"Just for the time being. In fact, I was going to ask Jake Harper if he could handle the name change along with my closing. I want to go back to being Audra Karras as quickly as possible. At the time, I just didn't want to deal with the extra hassle and explaining things away at the office."

"It's just a few forms. I'll prepare them for you and you can sign and file them yourself." I'd already looked into legally changing your name three years ago when I fled New York following the Brandon Glenn fiasco.

"Thanks," she said. "So back to the fabulous Hawaii Five-O. Word is, John Tatupu is one of the few cops on Oahu we can trust. That's why he's still on the Oksana Sutin case. Not everyone at HPD is dirty, of course, but there are enough bad apples that you wouldn't want to take a chance by sticking your head in the barrel and taking a bite."

"What exactly are we talking about? Protection bribes?"

"Protection bribes, sure. But it doesn't stop there. Dirty HPD cops are said to have alerted targets to raids by joint task forces, getting at least one federal agent killed and allowing countless gun- and drug-runners to get away. A few officers have been pegged as couriers, bringing meth in from Mexico and the mainland. Evidence—tens of thousands of dollars and more than that in drugs—has allegedly gone missing after it was recovered in successful raids. A number of officers have been accused of soliciting sex from female meth dealers and even a number of women who were simply pulled over on the freeway. And from what we understand, any time any gang offers any sort of competition to the Masonet Organization, members of that gang either go missing or are found dead off the shores of Wai'anae."

"And you think it's cops doing the wet work?"

She shrugged. "Who knows?"

I frowned. "But there haven't been any reports, any arrests involving police corruption, on Oahu in the past six years. Not since Ken Kamakana sued the department, prompting the last federal probe. Trust me, I've looked. I've searched every time I had to face an HPD officer on the witness stand over the past few years."

Audra nodded. "Since that probe a new set of rules apply. The dirty cops who weren't exposed in that probe laid down the law, constructed a new blue wall of silence that no one's been able to penetrate."

Blue wall of silence referred to a code among police officers that was similar to the Italian Mafia's omertà: the categorical prohibition of cooperation with authorities. The code was adopted by Sicilians long before the emergence of Cosa Nostra. Violation of the code was punishable by death.

"Why are you telling me all this?" I said.

But I thought I knew. Audra Levy—soon to be Audra Karras again—was lonely. Recently divorced. Recently transferred thousands of miles away from her closest friends. She didn't like Boyd, and me, well, she knew me at least casually from way back when.

But that's not what she said. "I admire you, Kevin. I know what happened three years ago following the Shannon Douglas murder. I know you were the one to discover the real killer and that it must have been difficult to turn her in. And I know why you're doing what you're doing for Turi Ahina, and I admire that, too. You're putting your life on the line for your client and friend. I don't know many lawyers who would do that."

I didn't describe for her the elaborate measures I'd taken so that I didn't get myself killed aiding Turi. This bar, for instance, was presently being watched from the outside by no fewer than four private security agents.

"And I read *Paradise on Fire*," she continued. "I know that you loved and lost Erin Simms. And that you saved that boy Josh's life not once but twice. And that you killed in order to protect him." Audra's eyes were moist. "What I said to you today, about having not changed in sixteen years, I couldn't have said something less true."

The horribly awkward moment was mercifully interrupted by the buzz of my cell phone. I reached into my pocket and pulled it free. Opened it without bothering to check the caller ID.

"Kevin, it's Scott," Damiano said urgently.

Quickly I rose to my feet, my stomach filling with dread. "What is it?"

"It's Turi."

Instantly I froze. Scott was watching Turi. He'd only call me if he lost his subject or if Turi was dead.

"He's been arrested. By the Honolulu PD."

"Arrested?" I immediately experienced a sensation of relief that would prove to be short-lived. "Arrested for what?"

"Murder. They're charging him with gunning down a cop in Pearl City."

'AUKAKE

(AUGUST)

CHAPTER 17

Scott Damiano and I sat on opposite ends of the tattered blue sofa in his twenty-third-floor apartment in Waikiki, watching a twenty-four-inch screen. He lived in the same building I'd vacated a few years ago, a renovated tower on Tusitala a couple blocks from the beach. Sitting there, I experienced a bit of nostalgia laced with envy. It was the first time I realized I missed living in the heart of Waikiki.

I also had a sick feeling in the pit of my stomach because, at that moment, Marcy Faith's bug-eyes were staring back at me from the TV.

"We're talking this evening about an American hero from our nation's fiftieth state," the odious legal-news pundit barked. Cable's worst commentator had started poisoning my pool of potential jurors weeks ago and wouldn't relent until well after any verdict was read.

"A hero who was struck down in the call of duty," Marcy continued. "An officer of the law who was gunned down on the dark streets of Pearl City. His name was Kanoa Bristol, and he was a detective with the Honolulu Police Department. Let's now go live via satellite to our affiliate in Hawaii. Jim Reynolds of KGSP. What do you have for us, Jim?"

Reynolds and his receding hairline filled the screen, the Honolulu Police Department's headquarters on South Beretania serving as the backdrop.

"Marcy, Kanoa Bristol was a thirty-eight-year-old detective in the Honolulu PD's Narcotics Intelligence Unit. He'd been with the department for just over seventeen years. Last month, while off-duty, near his home in Pearl City, Bristol was shot dead, police say, by this man—Turi Ahina, a lifetime Kailua resident with multiple arrests for drug possession and trafficking. Police assert that Detective Bristol caught Turi Ahina in the midst of an unlawful act—in all likelihood a drug transaction—and was attempting to apprehend the suspect when Ahina turned a gun on him and shot him twice, once in the chest and once in the throat. The forty-four-caliber bullet to the chest lodged in the Kevlar vest Bristol was wearing for protection, but the bullet to the throat killed him, police say, almost instantly."

"Oh, dear," Marcy said, a hand fluttering to her crimson lips. She shook her head, swinging the locks of her platinum-blond wig. Once she finally pulled herself together, Marcy asked, "What, if anything, did police recover from the suspect, Jim?"

"Police say they recovered an envelope filled with cash, Marcy. Somewhere in the ballpark of five thousand dollars. And a forty-four-caliber Glock was discovered in a sewer near the scene. There were no prints on the gun, but ballistics tests show that this was the weapon used to kill Detective Bristol."

"Oh, dear. Tell me, Jim. I'll brace myself. Did our American hero have any children?"

Reynolds bowed his head. "He did, Marcy. A spokeswoman for the Honolulu Police Department advises us that Detective Kanoa Bristol left behind a wife and two young children."

A familiar ominous tune boomed from the television speakers as Marcy Faith stared solemnly into the camera. "When we return, we'll bring you Vic Merriweather, a criminal defense attorney from Atlanta, and Anna Crane, a former prosecutor from Denver, to discuss the ongoing criminal case against Turi Ahina, the local thug who shot and killed this American hero in our nation's so-called paradise."

Scott snapped off the TV. "Our man still sticking with his story?"

I nodded. In the weeks immediately following the shooting, Turi insisted he didn't pull the trigger. "Gunshot-residue tests turned up negative."

Scott shrugged. "Gunshot residue can be completely washed off in a couple minutes. Hell, some guns don't release any residue at all."

I knew this through research on cases dating back to my days as a clerk at the Cashman Law Firm in New York. Scott Damiano spoke from personal experience.

I placed my hands behind my head, ran them down my neck and across my shoulders, trying to smooth out some of the tension. A lump the size of a golf ball protruded from the back of my shirt, and the pain was overwhelming.

"Neck still bothering you?" Scott said.

I nodded, flashes of pain accompanying every movement.

Scott leapt off the couch and disappeared behind me. For a moment I thought he was about to offer me a neck rub, and my pulse began to race. A neck rub initiated by anyone associated with the Tagliarini family typically involved a length of piano wire and ended with a whole hell of a lot less breathing in the room.

Instead Scott returned to the sofa with a business card. "Call, make an appointment."

I read the card. "Massage therapist?"

"Yeah, her name's Lian. She's great. Best massage in Chinatown."

"Chinatown," I mumbled, stuffing the card in my pocket.

Scott popped the top on a beer. "I still don't know how that fat bastard got by me."

"I'm only concerned with why."

Scott was charged with watching Turi Ahina's cottage in Kailua the night of the shooting. He and another guard with the private security firm I hired after Turi was bailed out of the FDC. Turi told Scott he was turning in for the night, then somehow slipped out of his cottage, jumped in an old, borrowed black Nissan Pulsar, and drove to Pearl City.

Scott didn't know Turi had left the cottage until the other guard on duty received a call from his boss, telling him Turi Ahina was on the news—for killing a cop.

Turi told me later that he drove to Pearl City to collect some money that was owed to him—the $5,000 police later found in his possession. But he couldn't—or wouldn't—tell me who had owed him money. "I only know him by face," Turi insisted.

The gun recovered by police in a nearby sewer was dusted for prints and came up clean. But I was still waiting on most of the prosecution's discovery. This morning I appeared before Judge Hideki Narita and filed a motion to compel. Donovan Watanabe stood in for the state and promised to have discovery for me later this week.

Experience had taught me that I could expect only one thing once discovery was finally turned over to the defense.

Surprises. None of them pleasant.

CHAPTER 18

I set a copy of this morning's *Honolulu Star-Advertiser* down on the dashboard of my Jeep. The governor had lost a few points in the polls but maintained a double-digit lead. Still, Omphrey wasn't leaving anything to chance. He was convinced that as the election grew closer, his critics would jump on his alleged ties to Oksana Sutin and attempt to implicate him in her death. Thus, the governor wanted me to handle this case as though he'd already been indicted. That meant a full independent investigation by the defense. Which was fine by me, since I was currently handling Turi's high-profile homicide case pro bono. And I still had to eat, still had to pay the rent.

So Flan and I sat quietly in my Wrangler, watching Oksana Sutin's ritzy apartment building in Diamond Head, waiting for one of its residents to exit. Knocking on doors in a murder case was not a proven strategy. Better to catch your witnesses offguard, on neutral turf. Preferably in a public place, where they were less likely to cause a scene or run away.

Since the governor couldn't—or wouldn't—tell us much about the deceased, the only way to learn the details of her life would be by hitting the pavement. Learning the details of a victim's life was the best and often the only way to learn the details of a victim's death.

"My father's flying out here tomorrow," Flan said out of the clear blue.

"All the way from New Orleans? What for?"

"To die, I guess."

That was one hell of a conversation-stopper. Flan's dad, Miles, was an eightysomething widower with no family left on the mainland. He had two daughters, but one went MIA once she married and the other had moved to France. Still, the flight from New Orleans to Honolulu seemed like a long way to go just to die. A man could die pretty much anywhere these days.

"You going to take him in like you did Casey?"

Casey was the younger of Flan's own two daughters. Up until last year he'd seen neither of the girls since they were babies. Casey was now eighteen years old and living with Flan after a fight with her mother, Flan's ex-wife, Victoria, back in New Orleans.

Unfortunately, Flan's unexpected leap back into fatherhood wasn't a story straight out of a fifties sitcom; it was more like a risqué reality show, complete with a glove box filled with used condoms, and Casey's footprints scuffing the ceiling of his ancient Ford. In her first few months in the islands, Casey racked up enough speeding and parking violations to pay down half the state deficit, and she was filching Flan's money and painkillers with the aptitude of a professional thief. Still, I had to hand it to him; Flan was hanging in there when few formerly estranged fathers would.

"Nah," Flan said. "Can't do that. Gonna have to put him in a nursing home."

"Your dad have any money?"

"Some. In fact, I was talking to Jake just yesterday about updating my dad's will."

A brand-new navy Jag passed us on the street, followed by a mint silver Porsche Carrera GT. Typical of these Honolulu neighborhoods just outside Waikiki. Diamond Head, Black Point, Kahala. All of the glitz and convenience with—at least ostensibly—none of the crime or noise.

"Here's something," Flan said, motioning with his chin to a shiny black Lincoln pulling up to Oksana Sutin's building.

Thanks to the Lincoln's tinted windows, we couldn't see in. The driver parked the car but didn't get out.

A few minutes passed before we realized why. The Lincoln was there to pick someone up. An interesting someone with an unbelievable body and dirty-blond hair all the way down her back. The driver did get out when he saw her. Walked around the rear of the car and let her slide that figure into the backseat. Then he got back into the driver's seat and drove away.

I started the Jeep and pulled away from the curb. I kept the Lincoln in sight while hopefully maintaining enough distance so that we wouldn't get made. Not that we were doing anything wrong. Not yet anyway.

The Lincoln kept a steady pace, obeyed all the laws. When it pulled into the Grand Polynesian resort, I pulled in after it. The Lincoln stopped in front of the main lobby, and a bellhop helped the young woman out. Then the Lincoln kept moving.

I asked Flan to take the wheel and I jumped out of the Jeep, nodded curtly to the bellhops, and followed the blonde inside. Meanwhile, Flan followed the Lincoln in the Jeep.

A few minutes later, while I was standing in the main lobby, Flan called my cell. "The Lincoln's parked. Looks like he's waiting on her."

"She went into the spa," I responded. "I'm going to catch her on her way out. If I keep her attention too long and you notice the driver getting antsy, send me a text. And if he makes his way over here, be sure to follow him inside. I don't want to be blindsided if we can help it."

I ended the call. Bought a copy of *Newsweek* at the gift shop and waited on a bench outside the spa. I read an article about the nation's tightest congressional races. It was only August and I was already sick of politics.

A little over an hour later I received a text message from Flan. The Lincoln was headed back to the front entrance of the main lobby.

I tossed the copy of *Newsweek* in the trash and bolted toward the spa. When I opened one of the double glass doors, a petite brunette was standing at reception, making her next appointment. I risked a bit of rudeness.

"Excuse me," I said, nearly muscling the brunette out of the way.

The tanned young woman behind the counter stared at me hard.

I ignored the looks from both of them and said, "I'm a driver. I'm here to pick up a young woman, a tall blonde, but I left my client list back at the garage. Am I too late?"

"Iryna?" the receptionist said.

I shrugged. "I'm sorry, I'd only recognize her last name."

The receptionist hit a few keys on her computer. "Kup-chenko."

"That's the one."

"She's still here. Would you like me to notify her that you're waiting?"

"No, no. I'm in enough trouble. I missed my last pickup by thirty minutes. I'll just wait out in the lobby. Please don't let her know I stopped in. I've got four kids, all under the age of two. If I lost my job in this economy . . ."

"I understand."

I stepped out of the spa, thinking, *Four kids, all under the age of two?*

I didn't have long to dwell on it. Two minutes after I left the spa, the blonde stepped back into the lobby, her skin glow-ing, hair shimmering, finger- and toenails ready to party.

"Don't I know you?" I said as she passed me.

She glanced at me but didn't stop, didn't slow. "I don't think so." Her Eastern European accent was thick and smoky.

"Iryna," I said. "Iryna Kupchenko."

That stopped her.

"You don't remember me?" I gave her the sad, hound-dog eyes. "I believe Oksana introduced us."

"I know no Oksana," she said, turning toward the exit.

I wrapped my fingers gently around her pencil-thin fore-arm. "Oksana Sutin. She lived in your apartment building in Diamond Head."

"I didn't know her," she insisted.

"Come on," I said, smiling. "Two beautiful, young Russian women living in the same building . . ."

"I am not Russian." She was growing irritated, her perfect cheeks tinged red. "I am Ukrainian. Now, if you will excuse me, I really must run."

I gripped her wrist a little tighter. "Please, just a few words." My cell phone vibrated in my pocket, but I ignored it.

"A few words about what?"

"About Oksana."

"I told you—"

Iryna's eyes flashed over my shoulder, then a firm male hand gripped the back of my neck, the same spot where the painful lump had formed, the exact area that carried all of my stress. It actually felt good. But the hard jab to my left kidney that followed, not so much.

I would've fallen to the ground but Iryna's driver held me up.

"Go outside to the car," he instructed her.

I heard Iryna's heels clip-clop across the lobby.

"As for you, Mr. Corvelli . . ." The driver's voice was gruff and accented, another import from Russia, Ukraine, Georgia, Romania, somewhere along the Black Sea. "You should be minding your own business."

"This *is* my business."

He wasn't impressed. Suddenly I felt the sharp tip of a blade through my shirt. "Ever get fucked in the ass with a hunting knife?"

No, but last year I did get fucked in the upper abdomen with a stiletto.

"This is your only warning," he said, parting the flesh at the bottom of my spine. "Stay away from the girls."

He swung my right arm around my back and lifted it up

until I heard a crack and felt a sharp pain flash from my elbow up through my shoulder. I swallowed a scream, and no one in the lobby seemed to notice. The knife stayed in my back.

Then Flan's voice emanated from behind my attacker. "I've got a thirty-eight Special aimed right at your balls, Yakov. Let the lawyer go or you're gonna have one hell of a worker's comp case. And let me tell you from experience, the settlement will *not* be worth the anguish."

The driver slowly released me.

"Now head out the door, get back in your Lincoln, and drive," Flan ordered him. "And if I see you near the lawyer again, you might as well have your nuts in a jar so you can simply hand them over to me. Because I promise you, you won't be going home with them."

The driver turned and scurried out the revolving door.

"Nice bluff," I said.

"Who's bluffing?"

I looked down and saw the .38 Special in Flan's rough hands. "Where the hell did you get that?"

Flan shrugged. "Found it in Casey's room."

CHAPTER 19

The next morning, after visiting the Trials Division of the Honolulu Prosecutor's Office for a brief sit-down and exchange of discovery with Hawaii's best-dressed prosecutor, Donovan "Dapper Don" Watanabe, I shot over to the county jail to meet with Turi Ahina.

"They treating you all right?" I asked him once we were safely seated in the confines of the concrete tomb they called an attorney-client conference room.

"Yeah, Mistah C. Fo' now."

I had petitioned the powers-that-be to keep Turi in a cell by himself for his own safety. But what Turi was implying—and what I knew to be true—was that eventually the wrong guard would be on duty at the wrong time. A simple "mistake"—a cell door left open, for instance—and Turi could get shanked in the gut while he slept. A tray of food that passed through the wrong set of hands and Turi could end up with a fatal food poisoning. And there was always the fallback: a shot through the back of the head, followed by the words "The prisoner tried to escape."

As long as Turi was inside, he wasn't safe.

"I'm not going to waive speedy trial," I told him. "I just informed Dapper Don and I sent a letter to Judge Narita. We need to get you in front of a jury as soon as possible and win you an acquittal. Stay in here too long and you're—"

"A dead man."

"Technically, the prosecution has six months to take this to trial. But Dapper Don said he'll be ready to go by October. That means you have to hang in and watch your back for another sixty days or so. It's the best we can do under the circumstances. Narita's not going to budge on bail since you were already out on bail on the federal drug charges when you were arrested."

Turi bowed his head.

I pulled his file from my briefcase and told him that it was time we discussed strategy. "If we're going in October, I need to get my witness list together now. So I'm going to ask you again, and I expect a straight answer. Who did you go to see in Pearl City on the night of the shooting?"

Turi shook his head in apparent frustration. "I already gave you one answer, yeah?"

"But I'm not buying it. And a jury's not going to buy it either. Some motherfucker on the street owes you five grand, and you don't know his name or where to find him? Bullshit."

Turi looked away from me.

"And you went looking for this son of a bitch who owed you that kind of money without going strapped? *Knowing* the entire Masonet Organization was gunning for your ass? Come on, Turi. Who the hell do you think you're fooling?"

Turi stared down at the table.

"Ballistics show the bullets were fired from a Glock. Same caliber you were carrying the night we went to Chinatown to see Tam."

"You think I own the only forty-four Glock ever made, eh?"

"No. But police searched your home in Kailua and didn't find a gun. They didn't find a gun in the Nissan Pulsar you borrowed. And they didn't find one on your person when you were arrested. So if the gun they recovered from the sewer isn't yours, then where is the gun you had on you in Chinatown?"

Turi finally looked me in the eyes. "Why you asking about that gun when you the only one who seen it? The police don't know I own it. Tam and his crew ain't gonna testify. So why you care so much, brah?"

"Because the more you lie to me," I said evenly, "the more difficult it's going to be for me to win your case."

"You think all your clients lie."

I let silence engulf the cramped room while Turi sat on the hard chair, hands in his lap, indignant.

Finally I asked, "Did you shoot Kanoa Bristol?"

His head shot up. "*Fo' real*, Mistah C? I say, 'Yeah,' and I'm in Halawa fo' life. That what you want to see?"

"It was your gun, Turi. The prosecution *knows* it was your gun."

"And how they know that, eh?"

I took a deep breath. "Because ballistics tests show that it was the same gun used to kill Alika Kapua."

Turi remained silent for a long while following the revelation. I remained silent, too. Because what was going through each of our heads was too damned difficult to discuss. Turi's saving my life three years ago in Kailua could cost him his own now.

"This doesn't mean a conviction," I finally said. "It just means a change of strategy."

Turi's voice cracked. "How you figure?"

"Kanoa Bristol was armed."

"Yeah, so? He was one cop."

"I think there were things you left out during our proffer session with AUSA Boyd and Special Agent Jansen," I said. "Like how the Honolulu Police Department offered the Masonet Organization protection. How dirty cops sometimes took out Orlando Masonet's competition."

Turi's throat looked as though he were swallowing an egg.

"You didn't tell Boyd and Jansen about HPD's dirty Narcotics Intelligence Unit because you were scared the blue would come after you. Isn't that right, Turi?"

He didn't confirm. He didn't have to.

"But they came after you anyway. Bristol didn't catch you in the middle of a drug transaction, did he, Turi?"

Turi twisted his large neck and shook his head.

"Bristol was off-duty but wearing Kevlar. He was going to silence you. This wasn't a botched arrest, was it, Turi?"

Turi finally spoke, though his voice was little more than a whisper. "Nah, Mistah C. This was no botched arrest. This was one hit."

CHAPTER 20

Late that night I was back in my Jeep, again outside Oksana Sutin's Diamond Head apartment building, this time with Scott Damiano sitting beside me. For the third time in the past half hour he asked if he could smoke a cigarette, and for the third time I said no.

"This is fucking boring," he said.

"I could use some boring."

Just as I said it, a long, white limo turned off Diamond Head Road and into the chic building's parking lot. I lifted a small set of binoculars I'd borrowed from Flan, who'd observed a familiar black Lincoln picking up an exotic brunette a few hours earlier.

This driver exited the limo and rounded the vehicle to greet a young woman dressed expensively and sexily, a lithe blonde with legs that went up to her neck. With the blue eyeliner and scarlet lipstick it took me a moment to recognize her. It was Iryna Kupchenko.

"Gimme those," Scott said, grabbing the binoculars from my hand. "Holy shit. And here I thought New York was the ass capital of the world."

I turned over the engine and waited for the limo to roll back onto the road. Then I followed.

The stretch limo didn't take us far. Just down the road to a breathtaking piece of property sitting right on the ocean in Black Point.

"So much for affordable housing and preserving the waterfront," I muttered.

I parked the Jeep on the road, and Scott and I crept toward the monstrous property on foot. We watched the limo pull out from behind a colossal yet ornate steel gate and turn back in the direction of Diamond Head. Which meant that Iryna Kupchenko was staying for a while. And who could blame her.

We silently climbed a hill opposite the property, and Scott held the binoculars to his face.

"Can't see shit. We're gonna have to go ring the doorbell."

He was right. Iryna wasn't talking, and I didn't want another blade pressed against my kidneys. If my suspicions were correct, we needed to identify the man she was visiting in order to get some answers. But ringing the doorbell probably wasn't the best way to do it.

I took the binoculars. "Over there." I pointed. "Think we can get over that part of the fence?"

"We don't have to. There's a door in the gate over there."

"I saw it. It's probably locked."

Scott shook his head. "Not locked enough."

Right again. Because after a mere three minutes of fiddling

with the lock with some small tools Scott carried in his pocket, he had us in.

Quietly we skirted the edge of the property. We stopped behind the cover of some tropical bushes and scanned the windows for some sign of life.

Scott motioned to the back deck. "There's an easy way in right there."

I shook my head. "We're already trespassing. We'll wait for the woman to leave then—"

I never finished my thought.

I couldn't.

The cold barrel of a handgun was being pressed to the back of my head.

Scott and I stood facing the ocean with our hands raised high above our heads. Behind us two men shouted questions at us in Japanese. I couldn't understand the questions, but their tone was universal. They sure as hell weren't inviting us in for Kona coffee.

I summoned what Japanese words I could. *"Watashi-wa bengoshi-desu,"* I yelled over the sounds of the Pacific washing onto the rocks.

Scott looked at me, startled. "What the fuck does that mean?"

"Means, 'I am a lawyer.' It's the only Japanese phrase I know besides 'the sushi was delicious.'"

Scott shook his head. "We can't just stand here, waiting for one of these assholes to get jumpy and accidently set his gun off."

"I'm open to suggestions."

Scott pursed his lips as though he were contemplating his next chess move. "How many men did you see?"

"Two."

"They both have guns?"

"Yeah."

Scott gave me no warning, so when I heard the words emanate from his mouth, I nearly pissed my pants. Literally.

"Hey, fuckheads," he said.

My stomach instantly dropped into my pelvis. Two men with guns pointed at our backs, and here was an unarmed wiseguy egging them on in a language they didn't understand.

"Hey, fuckheads," Scott shouted again.

I chanced a glance back and saw one of the men approaching us, pistol raised. I swung my eyes back onto the ocean and listened to his footfalls crush the grass behind us. I took deep breaths.

When the armed man was all but on us, Scott swung around, grabbed the man's wrist, twisting it quickly until it snapped. The man went to the ground, screaming in pain.

Scott raised the gun on the writhing fellow's friend as he rushed toward us.

"Whoa," Scott shouted. "Where the fuck you think you're going?" From the side of his mouth, Scott said, "Kev, tell this fucker to drop his gun."

"I don't know how," I reminded him, my pulse racing, my arms still slightly raised.

Scott shrugged. "Then tell him the sushi was delicious. I don't care. But if he doesn't drop his gun in the next five seconds, I'm gonna drop *him*."

Suddenly, on the upstairs deck, a Japanese man in a color-ful silk robe appeared, unarmed. "Taku," he shouted down, followed by something I couldn't make out.

Immediately the man standing directly in front of us dropped his weapon.

Scott backhanded the guy with the butt of the gun he was holding. The man dropped to his knees as blood spewed from his broken nose.

Scott pointed his index finger at the man on the upper deck. "We got questions for this guy?"

I glanced to the left and saw Iryna Kupchenko staring out at us from a high window. She looked scared. Sirens sounded in the distance and they were getting closer and closer.

I shook my head. "Let's save the questions for another night."

We darted off the property and made it safely back to the Jeep. I turned the key in the ignition, and we took off before the flashing lights came into view.

I sped back into Diamond Head, slowing only after we passed the building clearly occupied by at least two of Oksana Sutin's surviving associates.

"Mind if I smoke a cigarette?" Scott said, holding up a crum-pled pack of Camels.

I glanced at him as shadows played across his hard face, one eye clearly smaller than the other. "Go right ahead. Be my guest."

CHAPTER 21

"Choice of evils," I said. "That's the technical term for the defense. Section 703 of the Hawaii Penal Code."

Jake closed the door to the conference room and slowly took a seat across from me. "Justifiable homicide?"

I nodded. "Self-defense."

Jake appeared skeptical. "Killing a police officer?"

"Killing a hitman who happened to work as a police officer."

"You think a jury here in nirvana is gonna buy that, son?"

"With the right sales pitch, yes. If I can expose the corruption in the Honolulu PD from top to bottom and convince the jury that Kanoa Bristol set out to kill Turi Ahina in order to silence him, then they'll have no choice but to acquit."

"That's a tall order."

"Not if I can find me a whistle-blower."

Jake arched his brows. "Penetrate the blue wall of silence?"

"It can be done. Trick is to do it without ending up in a body bag."

"Well, where do you start?"

I pursed my lips. "AUSA Audra Levy-soon-to-be-Karras. She knows about the corruption and she doesn't seem to give a damn what Boyd or anyone else at her office thinks of her. If she doesn't know who the whistle-blower is, she'll be able to find out."

A rap on the conference-room door was immediately followed by the hellish squeak of its opening. Flan stepped inside with a file folder in his hand.

"I have a name for you," Flan said as he sat. "The john you saw at Black Point is Yoshimitsu Nakagawa. Forty-eight years old, owner and chairman of the Nakagawa Retailing Group, which boasts thirty billion dollars a year in sales."

Jake whistled. "Thirty billion a year? What the hell does he sell?"

"Slim Jims and slushies."

"Say again?"

"Slim Jims and slushies. His company owns eight thousand convenience stores in North America and twice as many in Japan."

"You mean—"

"Yes, I do," Flan said. "We have two dozen of 'em right here on Oahu."

"I'll be damned," I said. "We are in the wrong fucking business, Jake."

"You just figuring that out now?"

Flan said, "Mr. Nakagawa is a family man. A wife back in Japan, with six children, ages six through sixteen."

I sighed. "So we've got a glitzy Diamond Head building filled with Eastern European women who could easily pass as supermodels. And we've got Lincolns and limos transporting these ladies to five-star resort spas and to the summer homes of some of the world's richest and most powerful men."

"Which means?" Flan said.

I rose from my chair. "Which means it's time to have another talk with the governor."

After placing a call to Jason Yi and setting up a meeting with Governor Omphrey in the morning, I dialed Audra Levy's home number from my cell. I told her we needed to talk.

"About what?" she said.

"Not over the phone. Give me your address."

Ten minutes later I was in my Jeep on my way to her rented home in Ewa on the leeward side of the island. I made certain I wasn't tailed and I parked six blocks from her place, dodging the streetlights and creeping through the shadows before rounding her house and knocking on the back door.

"This is risky" was her only greeting.

"And much appreciated," I said, stepping past her.

Looking around Audra's modest apartment, at the typical wicker furniture and framed Walmart paintings that adorned most small island dwellings, it suddenly struck me: this was the first woman's home I'd been in since Erin Simms's. Well, aside from Oksana Sutin's, of course, but that didn't count because by then she'd been a corpse. And before Erin Simms's rented place of confinement in Kaneohe, the last woman's home I'd visited more than a handful of times was Nikki Kapua's. Nikki, who was now doing twenty-five to life on the mainland for murder. Aside from one-night stands in hotels and a brief fling with an artist in Kahala, in the past few years I hadn't gotten close to anyone who wasn't either dead or locked away in prison.

I sat on a rattan chair in the living area. "I need your help."

Audra remained standing, her arms folded across her chest. It was the first time I'd seen her dressed down, wearing anything other than the uniform of a government lawyer. In faded jeans and a yellow tank with bleach stains, she looked like someone else entirely, someone who could sit on a lanai and watch the sun set while holding a frosty bottle of Corona to her lips.

"In case you forgot," she said, "we're on different sides."

"No, we're not. Not us. Not now. You made it clear to me last month when we were at Sand Bar. We both want the truth to come out."

She smirked. "You've got to be kidding, Kevin. You think I'm going to help a cop-killer? You must be out of your goddamn mind."

"Maybe. But that's not the point here. The point is, Turi didn't murder Kanoa Bristol. It was justifiable homicide."

"*What?* How can you say—"

I stood and raised my palms. "Hear me out, Audra. Kanoa Bristol didn't happen upon a drug deal while he was off duty. He sought Turi out. Bristol was strapped and he was wearing a Kevlar vest. This wasn't a botched arrest. This was a hit on Turi Ahina. Turi shot and killed Bristol in self-defense."

Audra gaped. "The shooting took place a block from Bristol's *home*. What the hell was Turi Ahina doing in Pearl City to begin with?"

"I don't know yet. Turi won't tell me. But I intend to find out."

"This is ludicrous, Kevin. I need you to leave my apartment. Right now."

"I will. But first I need a name from you."

"What are you talking about?"

"How did the feds find out the HPD was dirty?"

Audra backed away from me. "No way. Get out."

"There was a whistle-blower, wasn't there? There *had* to be. Someone passed through that blue wall of silence, and I need to know who."

"You *know* I can't tell you that. I wouldn't only be risking my career, I'd be putting a man's life at stake."

My eyes bore into hers. "There is *already* a man's life at stake."

It was Audra's turn to freeze up.

"Please," I begged.

Her chest heaved in and out. "I'll put him in touch with you," she finally said. "I'll give him your number. But whether he calls you or not, that's up to him. That's the best I can do."

CHAPTER 22

"A prostitute?" Wade Omphrey said.

"To be perfectly honest, Governor, I'm not inclined to believe that you didn't know."

"I don't give a damn what you believe, Mr. Corvelli. The fact is I had no idea, and even as I sit here, I still have my doubts."

"So you never paid her a dime?"

"Of course not."

"And if the feds trace all of her assets, they won't find a link to you or Mr. Yi or any of your people."

"Certainly not."

My private office grew silent as the governor and I stared each other down across my desk.

Finally he said, "Where do we go from here?"

I leaned back in my chair. "Special Agent Slauson has been tight-lipped about the FBI's investigation since our meeting with him. We have to assume the FBI knows everything we

know at this point. Which means they're undoubtedly looking into her johns and her handlers."

"That is, if Oksana was what you say she was."

I ignored the insinuation. "Lok Sun is presumably still at-
large. Or else his arrest would be all over the news. Which
leaves us pretty much where we started. If you think Oksana's
murder is going to haunt you politically these next two months,
my office will continue its independent investigation."

"I don't *think* it's going to haunt me, I *know* it is. You've
seen my opponent. He's eleven points behind in the polls and
growing more desperate by the hour."

The part of me that handled my practice's finances had
hoped the governor would ask me to continue my investigation. The other part of me—the part that desired to live a
long, full life—had wanted Omphrey to call the whole thing
off and walk out of my office for good.

"This prostitution thing," Omphrey said, "this isn't going
to wind up in the papers, is it?"

"I can't predict the future, Governor. And I can't control
what other people do. If the issue arises, we'll exercise damage
control. Remember, no one's yet exposed any concrete evidence
of your affair."

The governor sighed. "Of course not, Counselor. This is
politics. Timing's everything. If the other side has anything,
they'll hold onto it and use it as their October surprise."

"I've requested a copy of Ms. Sutin's autopsy report, but since
you're not officially a suspect, they've ignored my request."

"We already know how she died, don't we? What can the
autopsy report tell us?"

"You'd be surprised."

My cell began vibrating somewhere beneath the clutter on my desk. I moved around a few file folders, legal pads, and bills before I finally found it. The caller ID read A.

"Excuse me, Governor," I said, opening the phone. "I need to take this."

Slowly he rose from his seat.

"Hold on," I said into the phone. To Omphrey I said, "Please have Mr. Yi drop off another check by the end of the day."

The closer we got to finding out who Oksana Sutin really was, the more dangerous this was becoming. At the very least I was going to be paid.

"Very well," Omphrey said. "Jason will also be dropping off a pair of invitations. I'd like you and Mr. Harper to be my guests at a fundraiser next weekend."

"Thank you. We'd be delighted."

I waited until he'd left my office and the door closed behind him before I raised the phone to my ear again. "Sorry for the delay."

"It's all right," Audra replied. "I've arranged the meeting for tonight at eleven p.m. at Chinaman's Hat."

I was about to thank her when the reality of what she'd just told me finally sank in. "Chinaman's Hat? You've got to be kidding me."

Audra wasn't kidding. "Come on, Kevin. You've lived in Hawaii a few years now. Don't tell me you can't swim."

CHAPTER 23

A half-moon lit the north end of Kaneohe Bay, the immense body of water that surrounds the offshore island commonly known as Chinaman's Hat. The island earned its unusual name because of its odd cone shape, which resembles the peasant's hat worn in rural China.

Chinaman's Hat sits 614 yards offshore from Kualoa Beach Park on the windward side of Oahu, which meant I would have to swim the equivalent of six football fields in the dark of night to meet my whistle-blower, who, for all I knew, might put a bullet into my head and let my body drift off to sea.

But, the way I figured it, I owed Turi at least that.

I stepped onto the empty beach wearing only a pair of swim trunks and a swim mask, not that I'd be able to see anything underwater. Everything beneath the surface would be pitch-black, and I didn't dare risk bringing an underwater flashlight. If I was followed, picking me off in the water would be as easy as shooting fish in a barrel.

I had made the swim to Chinaman's Hat once before. During the day, of course, when I was surrounded by other swimmers and kayakers who might save my life if something went horribly wrong. The bay was normally calm, but strong currents were not unheard of. And they invariably arrived without warning. Tourists often reported sharks in the bay, most frequently in the early morning, which suggested they entered the bay and sought their prey only in the dead of night. A comforting thought as I entered the water.

In the years since I'd arrived in Hawaii, I had indeed become a much stronger swimmer. I had become stronger in general, going so far as to maintain a regular workout regimen, including hundreds of sit-ups and push-ups, and miles of running and jogging each week. It had nothing to do with vanity or even maintaining a healthy lifestyle. But after being shot at, stabbed, and nearly beaten to death, I realized physical fitness could prove vital to my survival as a defense attorney.

Tonight it paid off. I made it to Chinaman's Hat in under forty-five minutes, even fighting against the current. I was tired, but not nearly as exhausted as I was when I swam here just a few years ago.

When I came ashore, I scrambled up the sharp rocks, wishing I'd worn a pair of reef shoes. I felt along and finally found a trail that led to the back of the island, where a small beach was surrounded on either side by tiny sea caves.

The silhouette of a large man stood against the moonlight.

"Glad you could make it, Counselor."

I immediately recognized the voice and could have kicked myself for not figuring it out sooner. It had just seemed too obvious. But I could have saved myself a lot of trouble simply by approaching John Tatupu on the streets of downtown Honolulu.

"Detective," I said, having already caught my breath.

"I'm sorry about the location, Corvelli, but I really saw no other choice."

"No worries. I swim six hundred yards just about every night."

"Twelve hundred," he said. "Unless you don't plan on swimming back."

The thought of sleeping on the island had crossed my mind, but I didn't tell him that. Instead I said, "We might as well get right to it then. What can you tell me about the Narcotics Intelligence Unit?"

Tatupu bowed his head. "The NIU was formed to investigate organized narcotics manufacturing and trafficking in the islands. But in practice, the unit quickly became just another arm of Hawaii's criminal underworld. The unit shared information with Orlando Masonet's people, tipping them off to raids and working with them to eliminate competing criminal enterprises."

"How the hell do they get away with it? From everything I've read, the unit reports directly to the chief of police."

"That's right," Tatupu said. "Chief McClusky knew exactly what was going on within that unit. McClusky got a cut just like everyone else. Eighteen months ago I threatened to expose him."

"Just as the Honolulu Police Commission was about to reappoint him."

"That's right. And in his place, we got Chief Edward Attea, a cop who's been dirty since day one. That's why I finally went

outside the department. The feds assured me that my identity would be kept secret and that no information I provided
them would be leaked."

The trade winds picked up, and I brushed off the chill, trying to decide how to ask Tatupu if he'd testify without scaring
him off. But first I wanted to know what the feds were doing
to clean up the NIU.

"Every step they've taken thus far has failed," Tatupu said.
"The unit is smart, tough, and extremely careful. The feds
tried placing an undercover agent in the unit, and he disappeared. They tried recruiting criminal informants with sweet-
heart deals, but everyone's too scared. Better to live in prison
than die on the street, they say."

"What about Internal Affairs?"

Tatupu shook it off. "Counselor, this corruption runs far
deeper than just the NIU and the chief of police."

"You're saying the *entire* department, including IA, is on
the take? Forgive me, John, but I find that hard to believe."

"Let me put it this way, Counselor. Ice is a billion-dollar-
a-year industry in the Hawaiian Islands. A *billion* dollars a year.
And that's not counting money from prostitution, gambling, or
selling guns and other drugs. I'm not exaggerating when I tell
you, I don't know a single cop on Oahu besides myself who has
ever turned down an envelope."

"How do you know all this? You have to have some concrete evidence I could use to corroborate your story. Where's
your proof?"

Tatupu frowned. "Counselor, you see a carton of milk in
the refrigerator that expired three months ago, you don't need
to open it up to know that it stinks."

"So there's nothing to back you up?"

"The feds hinted that there was a dirty cop who had recently decided to come clean and cooperate, but I don't know who that cop is. For all I know, the feds were blowing smoke up my ass so that I'd keep talking."

I sighed. "What do you know about Orlando Masonet?"

Tatupu shook his head. "Same as you, Counselor. I've heard hundreds of stories and read dozens of different descriptions of him, but I don't know anyone willing to say they've actually met him. The feds have a voluminous file, complete with a sixty-page psychological profile, but not a single photograph. He's a ghost."

I gazed out over the calm waters. "Kanoa Bristol," I said quietly. "Was he one of the bad apples?"

Tatupu nodded. "Rotten to the very core."

It was time for the moment of truth. "Will you testify, John?"

He hesitated. "Without finding Masonet I'm useless to you at trial. No one's going to take the word of a washed-up cop with not a single friend in the entire department."

"But we can try."

Tatupu took a step forward and looked me in the eyes. "I'll feed you any information I can, just as I'm doing tonight. But I can't go any further than that. Corvelli, it's common knowledge around the department that you already have a target on your back. I can't let you put one on mine, too. I have a family, Counselor. I have kids."

"And is this the Hawaii you want to see your *keiki* grow up in, John?"

"If I do anything more, Corvelli, I may not see them grow

up at all." Tatupu turned toward the water and started walking away.

"Is that why you're not working the Bristol homicide case, Detective? Because you're scared?"

Tatupu spun back around. "I'm not working the Bristol homicide case because I'm not assigned to the Homicide division anymore. After your little press conference for the governor, Corvelli, in which you mentioned my name and stated that I provided you information on a pending investigation, I got transferred to the Auto Theft division. So if someone steals your Jeep Wrangler, Counselor, you be sure to let me know."

CHAPTER 24

The rear door to Oksana Sutin's apartment building in Diamond Head wasn't locked enough. Neither was the front door to Iryna Kupchenko's fifth-floor apartment. By 1:00 a.m. Scott and I were both inside, sitting in the darkness in perfect silence.

In New York, an apartment as lavish as this would surely have been protected by an alarm. But not here. Not in paradise. Here people felt safe, shielded. Even though just weeks ago a young woman was violently murdered in this very apartment building.

A few minutes after 2:00 a.m., as Scott and I were taking in the magnificent view of the night Pacific, we heard a key turn in the door. We both stood and took our prearranged places in the apartment. We didn't want to frighten her. And if she wasn't alone, we didn't want to get ourselves killed.

As soon as she entered, Iryna Kupchenko flipped on a lamp and locked the door behind her. We waited for her to drop her handbag onto the couch, then I—the less imposing of the two of us—stepped forward.

"Don't be scared," I said softly. "We just want to talk."

Iryna started like a cat whose tail just got stepped on. She spun toward the door.

"Whoa," Scott said, moving toward her. "Easy now. This isn't the way it's going to go."

She faced us again, a tear trickling down her cheek. "I will call the police," she said, her accent every bit as thick and smoky as it was outside the spa.

"I don't think you want to do that," Scott said with a patronizing smile.

"We saw you in the window at Yoshimitsu Nakagawa's house at Black Point," I added. "Unless you want to spend the night downtown explaining to cops what you were doing there, I suggest you take a seat and answer our questions."

"These questions, what are they about?"

I pointed to the couch. "First, you sit down."

Iryna stepped tentatively toward the couch, then straightened her short skirt and sat, careful to keep her knees closed. "Now you tell me. What do you want to know about?"

"Your friend." I watched her eyes dance as I said it. "Oksana Sutin."

"She is dead."

"We know she's dead. We want to know why."

Iryna appeared perplexed. "How should I know this?"

"You worked together."

"I am unemployed."

"Maybe as far as the State of Hawaii is concerned, but not as far as we're concerned." I took a step toward her, placed one foot onto the couch next to her. "You don't have to tell us anything about yourself or your business. We only want to know about Oksana. Let's start with this. In the four weeks before her death, how many men did she see?"

Iryna responded without hesitation. "One."

"One? And who was that?"

"Her boyfriend. Mr. Omphrey."

"The governor," I said.

"Yes. He was the only man she had seen in months."

"Was he paying her?"

"No."

"She was seeing him for free?"

"I did not say that."

"What *are* you saying?"

"I am saying only that as far as Mr. Omphrey knew, they were a couple. I do not know any more than that."

Scott suddenly piped up. "So you're saying while she was seeing this guy, she wasn't hooking? Wasn't doing any other guys on the side?"

"No. She remained faithful."

"How do you know that?" I asked.

"Because she told me so. And because she would not lie to me."

"She confided in you?"

"What is *confided*?"

"She told you things about herself, about her relationship, that she wouldn't tell anyone else?"

"Yes, if that is *confided*, then she confided me."

"Was she using drugs?"

"Not at the time she died, no. Not for at least the last three weeks."

"But before that?"

"Before that, yes. She used cocaine every day."

"Why did she stop using cocaine three weeks before she died?"

Iryna looked from me to Scott and back, then gulped and said softly, "Because she was pregnant with Mr. Omphrey's child."

A chill suddenly ran up my spine. Before I could utter another word, a beeper went off somewhere in the room.

"It is in my purse," she said. "If I do not look at it, my driver will know something is wrong. He will come up here and he will kill you both."

I picked up her handbag and tossed it to her. She opened it and retrieved a pager. Then she turned back to me. "It is a client." She placed the pager back in her bag and removed a small brown vial. She twisted the cap off and dumped a small pile of white powder onto her fist and inhaled it. After one more bump, she recapped the vial and placed it back into her handbag and stood up. "If you gentlemen will excuse me now, I have to go to work. I expect you will not be here when I return."

She stepped to the door, opened it, and left without looking back.

"What do you think?" I said to Scott.

"A gorgeous prostitute with a gram of coke? If it's up to me, I say we stay."

"It's not up to you, Scott."

CHAPTER 25

Sitting along the north shore of Pearl Harbor is Pearl City. Tourists won't find any lengthy descriptions of the city in a travel guide nor any elaborate brochures touting its beaches or nightlife. Pearl City is simply a middle-class town with a diverse makeup, thirty thousand souls with a median income of $60,000. Pearl City's greatest claim to fame is its Little League team, which won the Junior League World Series a few years back.

But Flan and I weren't in Pearl City to catch a baseball game this morning. We were here to investigate the crime scene in the case of *State versus Turi Ahina*.

I pulled my Jeep to the curb and told Flan, "This is the street."

Kolohe Street was lined with average ranch-style houses and ended in a cul-de-sac. A dead end, so to speak. As I exited the Jeep, I grabbed a file folder full of photographs from the backseat.

"Turi claims Kanoa Bristol shot first," I said. "But nothing in discovery corroborates that fact."

"You think he's lying?"

I shrugged. "Wouldn't be the first time Turi's lied to me."

"Did he tell the police that Bristol shot first when they arrested him?"

"He told them nothing. I taught him well."

We walked down the street, side by side, Flan examining one of the photographs I'd just handed him.

"Turi claims Bristol's bullet struck a car parked in the cul-de-sac," I told Flan. "A navy Honda Civic with a Jesus fish on the bumper and a KEIKI ON BOARD sticker in the rear window."

Flan shook his head. "There's nothing like that in these pictures."

"I know. And I showed Turi the photographs, but he insists."

"It's not possible. These photos are time-stamped. They were taken just a few minutes after the shooting, as soon as police arrived on the scene."

"That's what I told him. But Turi's not budging on this."

"How about Bristol's gun? Did Ballistics run tests?"

"Of course," I said. "Bristol's gun came back clean. At least that's what it says in discovery."

"But our forensics expert has the right to examine the weapon himself, right?"

"Right. But if what Turi suggests is correct—if police went so far as to alter the crime scene—what chance do you think there is that the weapon they hand over to us will be the same weapon Kanoa Bristol was holding the night of the shooting?"

"Where does that leave us?" Flan said, once we'd reached the end of the street.

"We have to find a navy Honda Civic that once had a bullet lodged in its bumper." I pointed to the house Turi claimed the Honda was parked in front of. "And that's where we have to start."

The man who answered the door was in his midfifties and didn't seem too pleased to see us. His face was long, his head topped with a buzzcut. When he barked, "What can I do for you?" I pegged him as former military.

I introduced myself and Flan. "We're trying to gather some facts about the shooting that occurred here a few weeks ago."

"Well, you're going to have to gather them somewhere else, Mr. Corvelli. I wasn't around here that night."

"May I ask where you were that night?"

"I was in Waipahu, visiting a lady friend."

"And your lady friend," I said, glancing back at his mailbox, "what is her name, Mr. Guffman?"

"I don't see how that's any of your business."

"I'm just trying to avoid having to subpoena you at trial," I said affably. "We can do this in front of a judge, but frankly, I don't want to waste your time, or mine."

Guffman sighed. "Her name is Meredith. Meredith Yancy."

I smiled casually, said, "See? That's about all I need. And your first name?"

"Max."

"Well, thanks, Max. I appreciate your assistance." We turned to leave. "Oh, by the way, was anyone else in your home that night?"

"I live alone."

"I see. And what kind of car do you own?"

Guffman hesitated, searched Flan's eyes, then mine. "I don't own a car. I take the bus."

"Where do you work?"

"I work from home. I'm a marketing consultant for companies on the Web."

"Did you know Detective Bristol?"

Guffman shook his head. "Just in passing."

I made a show of looking over at his garage. He followed my eyes but didn't say anything.

I reached into my pocket and fished out a business card. "If you hear anything or remember anything that might be relevant to this case, would you do me a favor and give me a call?"

"Sure."

Guffman snatched the card from my hand, turned, and closed the door before I could say another word.

I turned to Flan. "What do you think?"

"I think I'd like to have a quick look in his garage."

CHAPTER 26

No Honda Civic sat in Max Guffman's garage, but it sure as hell had room for one. Everything in the garage was neatly stacked on the sides to allow space for a car, and oil stains dotted the floor. Which suggested Max Guffman was lying.

Hawaii has no statewide Department of Motor Vehicles, so we checked with the county. No vehicle was registered in Max Guffman's name. Not now and not ever. But he did have a driver's license, and it had been renewed only last year.

Flan and I drove back to Pearl City later in the day, after most people had returned home from work, and canvassed the area, asking if anyone was familiar with a navy Honda Civic with a Jesus fish on the bumper and a KEIKI ON BOARD sticker attached to the rear window. Not one person answered yes.

And I didn't believe a single one of them.

"Why would the car have been parked in the street instead of in the driveway?" Jake asked when Flan and I returned to the office. Since he'd gone dry, Jake had been putting in odd hours, but not wanting to head home alone was something I understood all too well.

"Maybe his lady friend—this Meredith Yancy—was visiting him and not the other way around," I suggested. "Maybe her car was in the garage."

Jake swiveled his chair to gaze out the conference room windows. "What about the ear-witness?"

The ear-witness, one Mrs. Doris Ledford, was a seventy-two-year-old widow who told police she heard two gunshots then "ran" to the window, only to see an obese man bolting from the scene.

"Mrs. Ledford didn't answer the door," Flan said. "Her neighbor across the street said she flew to Arizona a couple weeks ago to see her grandkids. The neighbor didn't know when she'd be back."

"My bet is she won't be back in Hawaii until jury selection," I said.

Jake sighed and swiveled his chair back around to face us. "That leaves finding the Honda Civic."

I turned to Flan. "Make a list and check every repair shop on the island. It's a longshot, because if the HPD went to these lengths to cover this up, then they're going to know how to keep a mechanic who does bodywork quiet. But we've got to try. Bring a wad of cash, and if you get any bites, wave the bills in front of them."

"Your best bet may be the junkyard," Jake said.

"Are you volunteering?"

"Hell, no."

"Then I guess you've got that one, too, Flan."

"Where are we with the governor?" Jake asked.

I stood from my chair, suddenly anxious. "Iryna Kupchenko told us that the victim was pregnant. And that Wade Omphrey was the father. That closes the issue on motive. But the feds are clearly hanging back until they can lock down Lok Sun. But if news of Oksana Sutin's pregnancy leaks, Omphrey's opponent isn't going to need the Pharmacist behind bars to beat the governor in November."

"Where does that leave us?"

"Pretty much back where we started. Iryna Kupchenko suggested that *someone* was paying Oksana Sutin to lie down with the governor, and if that's true, we need to find out whom. That means finding out exactly where these girls came from, who brought them here, and who is now renting them out as party favors."

"And just how do you plan on doing that?"

"By having another chat with Iryna Kupchenko."

CHAPTER 27

When I got home that evening, I was exhausted. I went to the mailbox, retrieved a handful of envelopes, unlocked the door, and stepped inside. As usual, Grey Skies greeted me immediately. I bent low, ignoring the sharp pain radiating from my neck down my back, and ran my hand through his long soft fur. I listened to him purr, then checked his food dish. Empty as usual. Skies was a big eater and he was always ready for a fresh dish of Science Diet by the time I arrived home from work. I fed him, then fed myself four Percocet and a small loaf of taro bread.

I sat on my mattress with a bottle of Longboard and flipped through the mail. An invitation from my law school alma mater for a ten-year reunion went right into the trash. Seven thousand miles seemed a bit far for a few hours of drinks with old friends. Letters from two separate school lenders followed. Then I found an unusual five-by-seven-inch manila envelope in my hand. I checked the envelope for a postmark but there was none. No return address. Whoever left this envelope dropped it right into my mailbox.

When I opened the envelope, I found a single DVD with no writing on it. I turned it over in my hand, staring at the spot where my TV had been. Then I remembered someone telling me that I could watch DVDs on my laptop computer. So that's what I did.

With the laptop sitting on the granite counter in my kitchen, I popped the disc in. I listened to the disc spin and whir and waited until an image appeared on-screen.

The image was grainy, as though captured by a hidden camera. I swallowed hard when I recognized the wet bar in Oksana Sutin's apartment.

I heard a man's voice offscreen. "Can I pour you a snifter of brandy?" Omphrey's voice. A few moments later Omphrey himself appeared on-screen. Just a glimpse of his profile, then he turned his back to the camera to pour the drink.

"No, Wade," a heavily accented young woman's voice called from offscreen. "No brandy. I can't take alcohol, remember? Just tea."

The governor slipped a hand into his pocket and pulled out a small vial. "That's right. No problem, honey. I'll gladly make you some tea. Go take your shower. Your tea will be ready by the time you get out."

There was a time lapse. I stared intently at the computer screen until my eyes burned fiercely. Pain inched up my neck. For nearly sixty seconds no people were visible, no words were spoken off camera.

Then a scream.

I jumped as though I were in a theater as Oksana Sutin literally fell into the scene. Dressed in the same sheer nightie I'd seen her in that night at the crime scene.

On the floor, her face and neck stiffened first, then her arms and legs began to spasm. The spasms grew continuously worse, but Oksana remained awake and alert, shrieking loudly and incessantly.

My own body trembled in its entirety, but I couldn't look away from the screen. I stood motionless, on the verge of sick, my head suddenly pounding like a piledriver at a construction site.

Oksana's body jackknifed back and forth for what seemed an eternity, every muscle violently contracting simultaneously. It was easily the most gruesome thing I'd ever seen. The screams were far worse than any I'd ever heard emanate from a horror movie.

My legs suddenly threatened to collapse beneath me. I was sweating profusely and felt faint. But I gripped the granite countertop and somehow willed myself to remain conscious.

At least until Oksana Sutin stopped screaming.

Some several minutes later the shrieking finally ceased. Oksana's dead eyes stared at me through the computer screen, her face forever frozen in a grimace.

I remained in front of the computer screen for a long time, staring back into Oksana's eyes. Wishing they would blink, hoping they would close.

Knowing they never would.

CHAPTER 28

I didn't mention the DVD when I arrived at the office the next day. On my way to Honolulu, I had stopped at the Kapolei branch of the Bank of Hawaii, where I kept a safety-deposit box for just such things. For evidence I didn't yet know what to do with.

Flan caught me as soon as I walked through reception. "I spoke with Meredith Yancy this morning."

I listened but the fog in my head wasn't yet ready to lift.

"She corroborated Guffman's story, said they were together at her apartment in Waipahu the entire night of the shooting. But get this—she opened the door carrying a *keiki*. Her fifteen-month-old grandson, Kyle."

"*Keiki* on board," I said.

"Exactly. Her daughter and son-in-law are both military, living in Mililani. I asked her if she and Max got to spend a lot of time with her grandson, and she said, 'Oh, yes. Max and I always take him to the beach.' Then I asked her if she had a car, and she got real quiet. She said no, she doesn't have a driver's license. I checked with the county and she was telling the truth."

"So Max is the one taking her and Kyle to the beach."

Flan nodded. "In his Honda Civic, I think. After I saw Meredith Yancy this morning, I drove back to Pearl City and broke into Guffman's garage again. And guess what I found in one of the boxes?"

"What?"

Flan reached into his pocket and pulled out a piece of plastic meant to look like metal.

I took it from him and studied it. "A Jesus fish."

A few minutes later the conference room door opened and Jake stepped out, leading an old man by the wrist. I took a good look at him. The old man closely resembled Flan, but appeared every bit as dead as Oksana Sutin did in the video I endured last night. I shivered again just thinking about it.

"Kevin," Flan said, "I'd like you to meet my dad, Miles Flanagan."

"A pleasure," I said.

Miles stuck out his hand, and I hesitated.

"Don't worry, lad," he said. "Natural causes ain't contagious."

I took his hand, and it felt like loose bones in a Ziploc bag. "How was your flight?"

"I would've been more comfortable traveling in a coffin."

"Ah, you flew coach."

"Damn right I did. How's an old man like me gonna fly

first-class? I got two daughters who ran out on me and a wife who went and died on me. All I have left is my son, Ryan, here, and he's a victim of the devil herself."

I nodded, smiled a little. "Victoria."

"Oh, don't get me started on that cunt, lad. Ryan here married her 'cause he had his head up his ass. Thought he'd won himself a fucking trophy." Miles shook his head from side to side, exercising the flesh on his throat. "Marry ugly I always say. I did."

Flan frowned. "Dad!"

"No, it's the truth, Ryan, and you damn well know it. Your mother, she was a saint, but she broke more mirrors than Hurricane Katrina."

I kept myself from laughing.

Miles continued, "But at least she treated me right. Forty-four years and never once a word about divorce. Never once threatened to take away my kids." He turned to Ryan. "But yours, that Victoria. She may have had the tits and ass of a Greek goddess, but she was every bit as evil and mean as Hades himself. And if I had the strength back in New Orleans, I'd have put her in the ground and buried her so deep that even fucking BP couldn't have found her."

I didn't know what to say.

Fortunately Jake stepped in. "Well, it was a tremendous pleasure meeting with you, Mr. Flanagan. Your son promised to take me over to Nanakuli to visit you once you get settled in."

"It's a fucking death house, that place," Miles said.

"Yes, well," Jake said, "we'll all be heading there someday." He looked from Flan to me and smiled. "Some of us sooner than others."

CHAPTER 29

The governor was dressed in a bright blue aloha shirt with yellow flowers, a lei draped around his thick neck. When I sat across from him at the conference table, he clenched his teeth and told me I'd better make this quick. "I have to return to the festival. I'm scheduled to begin a speech in less than an hour."

"Fine," I told him. "Let's get right to it then. Oksana Sutin was pregnant."

"Excuse me?"

"With your child."

Omphrey seemed to deflate, the headful of steam released in one great sigh. "Who told you this?"

We were alone in the conference room, Jason Yi sitting just outside in reception. I'd told the governor no more games, no more aides. Yi wasn't the governor's wife and he could testify against him if called by the prosecution.

"A confidante who lived in Oksana's building," I said.

"What is her name?"

I ignored the question. "She said that you and Oksana were exclusive for the few months you were together. But she suggested someone was paying Oksana nonetheless."

"That's complete bullshit."

"Then what was her source of income? How did she manage the rent in Diamond Head?"

"I told you, we never discussed those things. For me to do so would be to open a door that can't always be closed."

"What do you mean?"

Omphrey drew a deep breath. "The mistress of a powerful man, Mr. Corvelli. More often than not, they want things. Once you start giving, you can't stop. And eventually, someone follows the money and you're exposed."

"So that's why you never asked—"

"Exactly. Rule one, never discuss money. Rule two, never discuss your wife."

I regarded him as I sat back in my chair and crossed my right leg over the left. "Rule three, kill them when they become inconvenient."

Omphrey's mouth opened wide but no sound emanated from his throat.

"I received a package in my mailbox last night, Governor. It contained a DVD, two scenes apparently captured by a hidden camera in Oksana's apartment."

Omphrey remained silent.

"In the first scene, you're standing in front of her wet bar, asking if you could pour her some brandy. She reminds you she can't drink and asks instead for some tea. You tell her to go ahead and take a shower while you make the tea. Then you reach into your pocket and fish out a small brown vial, which, if this case goes to trial, will be said to contain strychnine."

"What the hell are you *saying*!"

"In the second scene," I said calmly, "which it will be suggested occurs just a couple weeks later when you were in Washington, DC, Oksana falls to the floor and goes into violent convulsions. When the convulsions finally stop, Oksana Sutin is dead."

"Jesus Christ," he said in an apparent panic. "I'm being set up."

"Let's not jump to conclusions, Governor."

"What do you mean? What other explanation is there?"

"First off, did you know Oksana was pregnant?"

"Of course not."

"Yet you knew she couldn't drink."

"She'd been sick. She was taking antibiotics."

I leaned forward. "Let's put the pregnancy aside for the moment. The tea you prepared for her that night, describe it."

"Black tea, very strong. The leaves came in a bag like the coffee beans you buy at Starbucks or in a supermarket."

"And the vial? It's only on-screen for a moment, but it appears to contain a white powder. Strychnine, as you may know, also takes the form of a white powder."

Sweat budded on the governor's ample upper lip. "It wasn't poison," he finally said. "It was cocaine."

"Who did you get the coke from?"

"From Oksana."

"You said directly to Special Agent Slauson that Oksana didn't dabble in drugs."

"She didn't," the governor said in a huff. "I did." A brief pause. "I *do*. And Oksana procured the cocaine for me from one of her friends."

Had Scott and I not seen Iryna Kupchenko pull out a similar vial to do a fist bump or two before she left to meet her client, I wouldn't have believed Governor Omphrey. But as it was, I did. At least about the cocaine. I didn't tell the governor that Iryna said Oksana Sutin used cocaine every day up until the time she found out she was pregnant with Omphrey's child.

"I'm fucked," Omphrey said, seemingly on the verge of tears. "My life is over."

"These things can be explained away at trial, if it even comes to that."

"Fuck trial. This fucking disc you found is going to be released to the press, and it's enough to end my political career *and* my marriage. It has me in Oksana's apartment, obviously for an affair. And it shows me pulling a vial of blow from my pocket."

I reached behind me and tried to loosen the unyielding tendons in the back of my neck. With the governor's drug use already on the table, I was tempted to reach into my own pocket and pull out the bottle of Percocet. I could crush a half dozen, and Wade and I could have ourselves a little pity party and wash away our troubles in a narcotic haze.

"If you *are* being set up, Governor, which this evidence *does* suggest, then I think it's time to consider who might be behind this."

Omphrey gaped. "Who the hell do you *think* is behind this? My opponent. That fucking scum-sucking bottom-feeder would kill his own mother to take my office from me."

The governor's challenger, whom I'd voted for in the primary and would vote for again in the general election, was John Biel, a candidate running on such issues as Hawaii's declining education resulting from budget cuts, the governor's failure to lower taxes on working families, his vetoing of the civil unions bill passed by the state legislature, and of course the environment. I couldn't quite envision the sixty-four-year-old candidate murdering pregnant prostitutes with strychnine to frame an incumbent.

"I think it would be best if we expanded our list of possible suspects, Governor. Surely, someone in your position has made other enemies over the course of your political career?"

"We all make enemies, Counselor." Omphrey suddenly stood up. "Find me the motherfucker responsible for this, and I can assure you that your enemies in the state prosecutor's office will quickly find themselves back in Los Angeles." As he stepped past me, he smiled and addressed the stunned look on my face. "Oh, yes, Mr. Corvelli, I read *Paradise on Fire*. I know all about how Luke Maddox tried to win a conviction in the Simms trial by planting stories in a pyromaniac's head. And I know how you turned things around to win your client an acquittal. How you took a knife in the gut to save the boy. That took some brass balls. That's what I look for in a lawyer, Mr. Corvelli. That's why I hired you."

CHAPTER 30

That evening Scott and I sat across from Oksana Sutin's building in a rented black Hummer, watching a black Lincoln idling in the parking lot. I was behind the wheel while Scott rested in the passenger seat holding a Walther PPK.

"Where did you get that?" I asked.

"Chinatown." He narrowed his eyes as he looked at me. "Speaking of Chinatown, did you go see my massage therapist yet?"

"Not yet."

"Go see her. Lian will take care of that problem with your neck."

"Speaking of problems, any word from back East?"

"Nah. If Pop and my brother, Chris, are still alive, then the feds are hiding them good. Cashman called me last week. He said Nico Tagliarini's men are scouring Brooklyn looking for me."

"No one knows you're here except Milt?"

Scott shrugged. "Someone always knows something."

The black Lincoln finally pulled out of the parking lot onto Diamond Head Road in the direction of Kahala. I waited a bit then started the engine and followed.

"What was the alias listed on your Eastern District indictment again?"

Scott chuckled. "Scotty Two Dicks."

"How the hell did you get that name?"

"'Cause my first hit, right, Nico told me to go out and whack this *stronzo* who ripped him off and to bring back his dick. So that's what I did. Only Nico had been fucking with me. So there I was, standing in a room full of wiseguys with a prick in my hand. When the laughing died down, I asked Nico, 'Well, what do you want me to do with this?' Nico stared at me for like two minutes straight, then said, 'What the fuck do I know? Now you got a backup. Hey, everyone, say hello to Scotty Two Dicks.'

"Few days later Nico sees my brother, Chris, in the steam room, yada yada yada. Nico comes out and declares that Chris is hereafter to be known as Chrissy Half-Cock."

"Harsh."

Scott shrugged. "I guess. But he was still better off than Benny Brown Dick. Benny earned that name during a ten-year stretch at San Quentin."

As soon as the Lincoln turned off the main road, I killed my lights, and Scott readied his weapon. The door to Iryna Kupchenko's apartment was now dead-bolted and she was accompanied by an armed driver at all times. So Scott and I unfortunately had no choice but to get creative.

"This is as isolated as it's gonna get," Scott said. "Let's do this."

I gunned the engine and jumped into the lane reserved for traffic heading in the opposite direction. I passed the Lincoln on the left, then immediately swerved in front of the Lincoln and slammed on the brakes.

The Hummer's tires screeched. The Lincoln's tires screeched. The Lincoln struck the Hummer from behind and the impact flung me hard into the steering wheel. I spent a moment thinking I'd cracked a few ribs and resented Scott for suggesting we disconnect the airbags. Fortunately, my adrenaline quickly diffused the pain and prepared me for the next phase of the operation.

"Ready?" Scott said.

"Ready."

I threw off my seatbelt as Scott did his, then we opened our doors and leapt from the Hummer, Scott with a pistol in his hand, me with a blackjack.

I stepped over to the rear door on the Lincoln's driver's side and swung the blackjack at the window, smashing it to pieces just as the butt of Scott's pistol did the same to the window up front on the passenger's side.

I heard Iryna scream as Scott hollered, "Don't you move, you cocksucker," to the driver. I opened the door and grabbed Iryna by the forearm as Scott got into the Lincoln. I dragged her gently toward the Hummer, then stuffed her inside, telling her to climb over the console into the passenger seat. I climbed in after her, turned the key in the ignition, and started to drive, leaving Scott and the Lincoln and its driver behind.

"What the fuck are you doing?" Iryna was yelling at me. "You are going to go to jail for this, you bastard!"

I remained silent. I knew that no one in her position—a

prostitute with no visa—would possibly chance going to the cops.

"What in hell do you want from me?" she cried.

"Answers," I said with feigned calm. "Just some answers."

"What we all hope for is to make it to United Arab Emirates," Iryna said, taking a drag off a long, thin cigarette and ashing out the window as we drove. "To somewhere where there is money, like Dubai or Abu Dhabi. Some of us make it there or to Bahrain or Qatar. But most of us are not so lucky."

I steadied the Hummer and glanced at Iryna, who for some reason looked thinner than when I'd first seen her. Or maybe she just appeared more fragile sitting next to me in this motorized monstrosity.

"Where were you taken from?"

"I was not *taken*." Anger seeped into her thickly accented voice. "Nobody grabbed my hair like a caveman and dragged me onto a ship. I was brought here."

"Okay, where were you brought here from?"

"From Odessa. It is a city in southern Ukraine. We girls, we go down to the port at night and stand around and wait for a car. When a car comes, we pose in the car's headlights as the pimp leans into the window and negotiates price. Usually two of the two or three dozen of us are chosen. We hop into the car and get driven away. Far away from Odessa. And, believe me, this is a good thing."

I believed her. I'd read an article in *Time* not too long ago about the international sex trade, how Odessa had become a hub for women from the poorest parts of Eastern Europe following the collapse of the Soviet Union. Women from Russia, Ukraine, Romania, and Moldova fled their homes to cross the Black Sea from Odessa to the Arab states and Western Europe.

But they weren't forced and didn't need to be. After decades behind the Iron Curtain, these women were entirely ignorant of the outside world and desperate for opportunities. The process was completely voluntary. These women weren't fed lies or manipulated through trickery. They knew precisely where they were going and what they'd be doing when they got there.

Still, only someone with the hardest of hearts wouldn't feel sorry for them.

"So, who is it who brought you to the United States, to Hawaii?"

Iryna shook her head and smirked. "You must be so crazy. Because you do not seem so stupid."

"I've been beginning to think I'm a bit of both these past few weeks. But I'm something else too, Iryna. I'm tenacious. I *will* get my answers, even if it means you and I have to drive around this island nonstop the next five days and nights. Even if costs me twenty grand in gasoline because this goddamn Hummer gets a quarter of a mile to the gallon. And if all else fails, I'll drive us right to the federal building in Honolulu and put you into the hands of my good friend in Immigration, Special Agent Marc Dalton."

Iryna shrugged her stick-thin shoulders. "If I tell to you this name, Mr. Corvelli, you might as well shoot me."

"I don't think so." I turned past a sign for downtown Honolulu. "From what I've read and from what you've told me, having you hauled back to Odessa would be a far worse punishment than killing you."

"You are right on that," she said, sighing.

"So what's it going to be, Iryna. Just a name and I'll never tell a soul where I got it."

Her chin dropped into her chest. "He is German-Irish," she said quietly. "He calls himself Gavin Dengler. I have met with him just yesterday, so he is still somewhere on the island."

"Gavin Dengler," I said aloud. "Okay, I'm going to pull over now. When I do, you're going to give me a complete description of him. You're going to tell me where I can find him. Then I'm going to drive you home. If your answers are entirely truthful, I promise you'll never see me again."

She swallowed hard and swiped at a tear. "That is something I can promise you, too."

CHAPTER 31

On the evening of the governor's fundraiser, I grudgingly dressed in an Armani tuxedo and rented a stretch limo to pick up Audra at her house in Ewa. When she opened the door, my mouth nearly dropped, but I kept things in check by smiling and saying nothing more than the obligatory "You look beautiful."

But beautiful didn't do Audra Karras justice. With her maiden name back in place she looked every bit as stunning as she did during our senior year of high school. Dressed in a backless black dress, she lit up the night the way few women could. Even our driver, unsmiling until then, cracked a joke about getting her home by midnight, before his black stretch limo turned into a bright orange pumpkin.

When we arrived at the Grand Polynesian resort in Waikiki, I took Audra's hand and led her through the main lobby toward the Grand Ballroom, all the while smiling for the cameras. Since Justice Ingraham had stayed Turi Ahina's federal case pending the state trial, there was no longer any reason Audra and I couldn't be seen together.

We were standing at the open bar, retrieving our first drinks, when Scott Damiano tapped me on the shoulder. Jake, still suffering from a terrible case of sobriety that began more than a year ago, had declined the governor's invitation. So I invited Scott, who cleaned up significantly better than Flan.

"Tremendous, Scott," I said, eyeing him in his tuxedo. "You look terrific."

"Kevin, I'd like you to meet my date, Chloe."

Chloe held out her hand, and I took it. She was thin at the waist, with gigantic fake breasts, wearing a tight black dress that more than just accentuated them.

"Haven't we met before?" I said.

"Maybe. I'm a dancer."

"Oh," Audra said, stepping in. "Where at?"

Chloe didn't hesitate. "Striptopia on Kapiolani Boulevard right here in Honolulu."

"Oh," Audra said again.

"Well," I said to Chloe, "if I haven't seen you dance yet, I'll be sure to drop by to see you soon." She smiled as I turned back to Scott. "Well done."

"Hey, Kev, you told me this crowd was classy. I wasn't gonna just head into Waikiki and grab the first two-bit hooker I found."

When I turned back, I was surprised to see Audra and Chloe had gone off on their own, chatting like old school pals. "Well, I guess that means it's you and me, Scott. Let's grab some cocktails and I'll introduce you to the governor."

"Looks like I'm running with a much different crowd than

I did back in Brooklyn," Scott said as we stepped up to the bar. "Seems I'm heading up in the world."

I glanced around the ballroom, at the tanned Botox faces, the men wearing too much hairspray, the women too much makeup and jewelry. To me it looked more like a costume party than a $500-a-plate fundraiser.

"Don't be so sure of that," I said.

Full tumblers in hand, Scott and I merged through the crowd until I spotted the governor. Omphrey stood with another man, much taller with the unmistakable look of money. On the governor's other side stood his wife, Pamela, Hawaii's first lady. She was dressed to the hilt, complete with her best fake authentic smile.

"Kevin," the governor said cheerfully. It was the first time he'd ever called me by my first name. "So glad that you could make it. Of course, you know my wife, Pamela. And this gentleman is Mr. Tommy Duran. He's a major land developer here in the islands."

I reluctantly shook Duran's hand. He was handsome with dimples on either side of a rich, round face and one on his chin. His tux fit him like a glove, while diamond cufflinks peeked out from under his jacket sleeves. He had dark brown hair and matching eyes. I pegged him for about fifty, but he could well have been older; money often disguised age as much as a rubber mask.

"Nice to meet you, Kevin," Duran said during the too-long, too-firm handshake.

I introduced them all to Scott Damiano, who gave them each a "How ya doin'?" before offering his left hand.

Before another word could be said, we were surrounded

by three more beautiful women—Audra, Chloe, and Tommy Duran's wife, Holly.

When Audra heard the developer's name, she glowed. "I'm purchasing a unit at Water Landings in Kakaako."

I watched for Pamela Omphrey's reaction, but there was none.

"Really?" Duran said. "Well, congratulations. Let's all hope we'll meet no more opposition from the Land Use Commission."

The governor turned toward his wife as he tried to avoid Duran's gaze. All of a sudden all of us were quiet.

Finally, between sips of champagne, Duran asked Audra what she did for a living.

"I'm a federal prosecutor," she said.

"Really? And just what are you doing nuzzling up to a criminal defense attorney? Is he that good in bed?"

Duran laughed alone, coaxing awkward smiles from each of us. Audra's cheeks, meanwhile, burned red.

"We're just friends," I said.

"If you'll all excuse me," Omphrey said politely, "I have to run around and scare up some votes."

Duran, too, excused himself and his wife. Scott escorted Chloe and Audra to the bar, promising to bring me back another highball. Which left me alone with Pamela Omphrey.

"Quite a man, your husband," I said to fill space.

"Sometimes," she said, bowing her head. "But then, as a criminal defense attorney I'd imagine you've seen the worst of the worst."

I knocked back a bit of my Ketel and club. "Certainly no worse than a politician's wife must have seen."

"How is it that all lawyers loathe politicians and vice versa when all of you attended law school?"

"Don't get me wrong," I said. "I loathe lawyers, too."

Pamela grinned. "So, is my husband still going to be a politician come November?"

"You know I can't speak to you about the investigation, Mrs. Omphrey."

"Who said anything about the investigation?" she said without looking at me. "I already know all I need to know about Ms. Sutin. I know she was a harlot. I know that she was a drug addict. I know that my husband was fucking her. And I know that Wade was in Washington when she was murdered. I know he didn't kill her."

I didn't say anything.

"No, my question wasn't a legal question, Mr. Corvelli, it was a political one. Do you think my husband will win in November? With all this shit that's going on?"

"The governor has my vote," I lied.

"Mine, too." She sighed, then took a sip of her martini. "Just when I'm sure my husband was born without a spine, he finally stands up to someone like Thomas Duran."

"On Kakaako?"

She finally looked me square in the eyes. "Kakaako is really just the tip of the iceberg. What Duran really wants to get his hands on is the North Shore. But not on my watch. I swore, if Wade ever caved on the Waimea Valley project, I'd divorce him."

"I read about the public hearing."

"You realize, it's not just about keeping the country *country*," Pamela said. "It's the environmental impact of ocean pollution from septic systems and construction sediment runoff." She smiled mirthlessly. "But of course, all that doesn't fit on a bumper sticker."

"No. Nor does it fit neatly into a four-second sound bite."

She nodded. "I suppose that's something politicians and lawyers can agree on: the dreadfulness of the modern media."

"Nothing brings people together like a common enemy."

"Nothing else brings people together, period. Not these days. Even tragedy possesses a brutally brief shelf life. And what's more tragic than what we are doing to this planet, Mr. Corvelli?"

Even in the dim light of the banquet hall, I could see a wall of moisture forming in front of Pamela's eyes.

"If it's any consolation," I said, "many people here in the islands, myself included, appreciate you standing up for the environment. This country could use more first ladies like you."

"It's a rare pleasure to hear that. Thank you."

Hours later, after a dinner that included seafood cakes and a whole-tomato salad, grilled mahimahi, Kona lobster, and steak, with pineapple shaved ice for dessert, Audra and I said our good-nights to Scott and Chloe and the Omphreys and the Durans, then exited through the lobby to our waiting limousine.

"To the young lady's house in Ewa first, sir?" the driver called back to me from the front seat.

Audra looked at me. "I'm up for a nightcap if you are."

I hesitated. I was tired, due for another few Percocet, and my life was complicated enough. But finally, before I could change my mind again, I loosened my tie, opened the top button of my tuxedo shirt, and said, "To Ko Olina please." I glanced at my watch. "And we'd better hurry because it's almost midnight."

CHAPTER 32

When we arrived at my villa in Ko Olina, Grey Skies didn't greet me at the door. He liked strangers even less than I did but was usually enamored of beautiful women. I checked his food dish and was surprised and concerned to see that it was full. But I found him a moment later, fully awake and content, lying on my bed in the living room.

"Just move in?" Audra said.

"Moving out actually."

"When?"

"Don't know yet. Probably after Turi's case is over."

"That's a long time to sleep in the living room, isn't it?"

"Not really. I've already been doing it for months."

I went immediately to the liquor cabinet. "Scotch? I have several single malts. I'm going to have a glass of Glenlivet myself."

"No scotch for me. Do you have anything else?"

I checked the fridge but I was fresh out of Kona Longboards.

My liquor cabinet was filled with nothing but scotch. Then I remembered the bottle of red wine that had been hiding in plain sight on my kitchen counter since my last female visitor.

"Red wine? Seventeen eighty-seven Château Lafite," I joked. "Either that or a cheap bottle of Merlot I shoplifted from ABC."

She smiled as she leaned over to pet Skies. "Merlot is perfect."

The bottle had been opened by the previous guest. I popped the cork back out and poured a few ounces into a wineglass.

"Don't you like red wine?" she asked as I handed her the glass. "Aren't you Italian?"

"Actually I'm allergic to it. That and grape juice. Doctors tell me it's the sulfites."

"That's too bad. You're missing out. You can't even have a single glass?"

"Not unless you want to see me wake tomorrow morning with bright red blotches all over my body."

She scrunched up her features. "Who says I'm going to be here when you wake up tomorrow morning?"

For a moment our eyes met.

"I've gone my whole life being presumptuous," I said. "Why stop now."

Audra took a sip of her wine and sat on the bed. I took a gulp of my scotch and contemplated sneaking away for a Percocet.

"So where do you plan on moving to after the trial?" she asked.

"I'm not sure yet. A few places around the globe have crossed my mind."

"You mean, you're leaving the islands?"

"I've given it a lot of thought, and I think it's time."

Audra fell silent. So did I. We sat there staring out my

sliding-glass door at the full moon. If I left the States, it would mean leaving the law behind. And that sounded right. I often imagined myself tending bar on the outskirts of Rome or waiting tables at a world-class restaurant in Madrid. A job I could leave behind when I went home.

Finally I shut off my fantasies and excused myself to the bathroom.

Soon as I made it there, I ripped my bottle from the medicine cabinet, uncapped it, and dumped four pills in my hand. As I swallowed them, one at a time, I stared at myself in the mirror. I was thirty-four, hurtling toward thirty-five. Not a single gray hair, but the lines on my face were undeniably more defined. My thoughts these days were turning more and more toward my own mortality. And not just because I recently had a gun pressed to the back of my head.

How long can I keep running? I wondered.

By not settling down I imagined I was somehow fending off time. But the calendar said differently. For a male lawyer who drank heavily and popped Percocet for emotional pain, thirty-five *had* to be considered middle age. Oddly, it both pained and comforted me to know I was halfway through life.

Suddenly I heard a glass shatter, followed by a woman's scream. I booked out of the bathroom and rushed into the living room.

There I found Audra lying on the hardwood floor, her body shuddering in pain.

I glanced down at the broken wineglass lying next to her and knew immediately what had happened. Panicking, I reached for my cell phone and dialed emergency services.

"Nine-one-one operator," a female answered. "What's your emergency?"

I knelt next to Audra, my whole body trembling. "A woman in my home has been poisoned."

"Poisoned with what, sir?"

I swallowed but my mouth was dry of saliva. "Strychnine, I believe."

"Who am I speaking to?"

I gave her my name, rushed through my address. Every word I spoke was an effort.

"Kevin, are you the one who poisoned her?" the operator asked.

"Of course not," I roared over Audra's shrieks.

"All right, sir, I'm going to need you to calm down for me. Help is on the way. But in the meantime, I need you to keep her as quiet as possible, since any loud noise will increase the violence of her spasms."

I talked soothingly to Audra, told her to relax, that everything would be all right. I reminded her how beautiful she looked tonight, how she'd soon own a home smack-dab in paradise. I asked her to calm herself, but even as I said it, her convulsions grew worse.

"It's not working," I cried into the phone. "What else can I do for her?"

"Do you have any tranquilizers in the house?"

"Benzos, sure. All types."

"Any Valium?"

"The generic. Diazepam."

"Good. Get those and place a few under her tongue. Not too many or you'll depress her respiratory system."

I tossed the phone next to Audra on the floor and raced back to the bathroom and snatched a bottle filled with diazepam, which had been prescribed to me by my shrink, Dr. Damian Opono, immediately following Erin Simms's suicide. I'd taken a few but had little use for them on top of the Percocet.

When I returned, Audra's convulsions had grown even worse. I opened the bottle and spilled several pills into my hand, then I cradled her head in my lap and did my best to get the pills under her tongue.

"Are you still there, Kevin?" came a far-off voice.

I stared at my phone on the floor a few feet away.

"Kevin? Are you there?"

I didn't respond to the 911 operator.

She heard the sirens coming from outside my villa and told me to hang on, help was only a few seconds away.

With Audra's head in my lap, I rocked back and forth, humming.

I don't remember precisely what happened next, except that I darted downstairs to let the paramedics in. Then I begged them to save Audra's life.

KEPAKEMAPA

(SEPTEMBER)

CHAPTER 33

When I stepped into the conference room on the fourteenth day of September, Jake and Flan were already huddled together with the contents of two files spread across the long mahogany table. One was labeled *Oksana Sutin Investigation*, the other *State versus Turi Ahina*.

"Does this mean what I think it means, Jake?"

"The partnership papers are drawn up, awaiting your signature, son."

I sighed with relief. *"Mahalo,"* I said, as I took a seat. "I'm going to need you to second-seat me at Turi's trial next month. I'm not going to be able to handle this one on my own."

"Well, Josh Leffler's adoption is going smoothly, and Miles Flanagan's will is drawn up, so you're looking at a free man. I'd be honored to stand at your side, son."

"All right," I said. "Let's start with the governor."

Governor Omphrey was losing some ground in the polls with rumors about his affair and possible involvement in the murder of Oksana Sutin spreading around the island like the flu. The *Honolulu Star-Advertiser* had him eight points up with a margin of error of plus-or-minus four. The governor was growing uncomfortable. He wouldn't survive an October surprise.

"Priority one is finding Lok Sun," I said, the name dripping like acid from my tongue.

The strychnine in the red wine was meant for me, no question about that. No one could have known that Audra Karras was coming back to my villa with me following the governor's fundraiser. Nor could anyone have known that I was allergic to red wine; it wasn't something I advertised. And the timing was right. The poisoning immediately followed my conversation with Iryna Kupchenko, who after that night had either gone underground or gone missing.

I had considered that the bottle might have been poisoned before the night of the fundraiser, but evidence suggested that someone had been in my villa that evening. Most notably, a memory stick that had been sitting in my laptop had disappeared and the hard drive had been erased. On both were documents that contained copious notes on the Oksana Sutin murder investigation, including the name Gavin Dengler. At that point I hadn't mentioned the name Gavin Dengler to a single person. So if I had died of strychnine poisoning that night, the name would have been gone for good.

Flan said, "How do we go about finding the Pharmacist when we don't even know what he looks like? The feds can't nail him down; what makes you think we can?"

"Chances are he's lying low in Chinatown. That's not a large area to cover."

"Not if you're Charlie Chan," Jake said. "But if you haven't noticed, the three of us are all Caucasian."

I leaned back in my chair. "We don't need a Chinese detective. We've got lawyers, we've got guns, and we've got money."

"You plan on busting up an entire city?"

"Just a few square blocks of it, for now."

"What's our second priority?" Flan said.

"Finding Gavin Dengler. Oksana Sutin's apartment building has been quiet as a morgue these past couple weeks. No Lincolns, no limos, no nothing in or out. So we start with the devil we know—Yoshimitsu Nakagawa."

Jake chuckled. "Something tells me we're not gonna have much luck bribing a billionaire, or hauling him into court, for that matter."

"The thing about billionaires," I said, "is that they typically have a lot to lose."

I stared out at the Koolau Mountain Range, a thick rainbow stretching across its highest points.

"Lok Sun, Gavin Dengler, and Yoshimitsu Nakagawa," I said, pushing aside the *Oksana Sutin* file. "That takes care of the governor. Now let's move on to Turi Ahina."

One week after Audra was released from the Queen's Medical Center, Turi found his way to the infirmary with a busted eye socket. He'd been attacked in his cell in the middle of the night while he slept. The guard charged with making certain all relevant doors were locked was currently on paid leave. I raised all kinds of hell, but it got me as far as I expected. Bottom line was, I needed to get Turi acquitted of the state charges or he wouldn't make it to Thanksgiving.

Since the attack on Turi in jail, my dreams about Brandon Glenn and his rape and murder at Rikers Island had increased, and I'd been losing night after night of sleep.

I looked at Flan. "Where are we with the Honda Civic?"

"Nowhere. Still no luck finding the car. I paid a visit to Meredith Yancy's daughter and son-in-law in Mililani, and they deny any knowledge of the existence of a Honda Civic owned by Max Guffman. If you ask me, they had been trained to say exactly that. I didn't believe either one of them."

"Any luck locating Mrs. Doris Ledford in Arizona?"

"Negative. I got a phone number for one of her kids living in a suburb of Phoenix. He said, yes, Mama had come to visit briefly. But only on her way to Nevada. Apparently Mrs. Ledford won an all-expense-paid trip to fabulous Las Vegas just before she left Hawaii. The son had no idea what hotel she was staying at and he hadn't been given a telephone number."

Jake said, "Sounds like the prize came courtesy of the HPD."

I frowned. "That leaves us with Detective Tatupu. I need to convince him to testify." I pulled part of Turi's file toward me. "Even with a busted eye socket, Turi's not talking about what he was doing in Pearl City in the first place. That means we have to pound the pavement again and find out for ourselves."

Flan rose from his chair. "Is that where you want to start today?"

I thought about it then nodded. "Sounds like as good a place as any."

CHAPTER 34

We expanded our search of Pearl City, covering as much of the five square miles and nine thousand households as we could in a day. Still, we barely scratched the surface. No one admitted to recognizing Turi Ahina other than when they saw him on television. It killed me that we would be coming back here all week, taking up time that should have been used to prepare Turi's defense. But after Brandon Glenn, I wasn't going to take anything for granted.

"I don't see the point," Flan said as the sun began to set over Kolohe Street. "Why waste our time helping him if he won't even help himself?"

My mind was already on the areas that bordered Pearl City, Aiea to the east, Waipahu to the west.

"It's frustrating," I said. "But that's what criminal clients do. They lie and keep secrets from their lawyers. And more times than not it comes back to burn them in the ass."

Flan sighed, leaned on my Jeep, and spread out his hands. "But *why?*"

I leaned next to him, folding my arms across my chest, staring down at the pavement. "In most cases, I'd say it's because they've learned from experience that they can't trust anybody. They've been fucked over their entire lives, usually beginning with their parents. As they got older, they were fucked over by people they thought were friends. By the time they make it to me, they think getting fucked over is just another side effect of humanity. Why tell their lawyer the truth when their lawyer's just going to bend them over a barrel in the end?"

I reached into the Jeep and pulled out a pair of prescription sunglasses and placed them on my face to mute the sunset. "Sometimes clients think they know better than their lawyer," I said, "but that's rare. Deep down they know the law is every bit as complex as medicine, and the government's a cancer that's going to get them sooner or later." I shrugged. "But with Turi, I don't know, Flan. Whatever he's hiding from me, he has his reason. And you can bet that whatever that reason is, it has nothing to do with his own best interests. Turi's protecting someone. And if I'm going save him, I have to find out who."

We got into the Jeep, and I drove Flan back to the office, where his jalopy was waiting for him. I took the elevator upstairs to our office and found Hoshi still sitting behind her desk at reception, staring intently into her computer screen.

I glanced at my watch. "What are you still doing here?"

She looked up, startled that someone was there. "Oh, hi, Kevin. I'm sorry, I didn't realize you were coming back to the office tonight."

"Just need to grab a Red Bull, then I'm picking up Scott in Waikiki and heading into Chinatown."

"How did the search go today?"

"About as well as expected. No one admits to knowing Turi, no Mrs. Ledford, and certainly no navy Honda Civic with a bullet hole in its bumper."

"With a Jesus fish and a KEIKI ON BOARD sticker, right?"

"Right," I said, smiling. "You've been eavesdropping, I guess?"

She smiled back. "In case no one's ever told you this, Kevin—your voice travels a bit."

"I guess it does at that."

"So I noticed you're not on Facebook. But you do know what it is, right?"

I shrugged. "I've heard of it. Why?"

"Well, it's a social-networking site. People post messages about what they're doing and stuff."

"And what are these people doing?"

"Oh, it could be anything. Eating pizza, going for a drive, walking their dog."

"Sounds exciting."

"Not always," she said. "But that's not the point."

I looked at my watch. "Well, what is the point, Hoshi?"

"People post pictures all the time. You know, so their friends can see. But not every Facebook friend is someone you know in real life. You can just type in someone's name and send them a 'friend request.' Most people don't even pay attention to who they're friending. They just click to confirm and are excited to boost their number of friends."

"Sounds like the exact opposite of how I live my life."

Hoshi giggled. "Yeah, kind of. But back to what I was saying. I send out friend requests all the time. And I don't usually get turned down. Especially by guys."

"And?"

"And so I friended a guy named Brian Haak."

"Why does that name sound so familiar?"

"Because he's married to Karen Haak, Meredith Yancy's daughter."

"Okay, I'm with you so far."

She waved me forward. "Come around my desk."

When I got there, I leaned over her shoulder and peered at the screen. She used the mouse to click on her own Facebook profile, then she moved the mouse to the area labeled FRIENDS.

"Here he is," Hoshi said, pulling up Brian Haak's profile.

His profile stated that he was married to Karen Haak, that they had one child named Kyle. It listed Brian's birthday and his current city as Mililani, Hawaii. He was a Christian who voted Republican. He was a marine and his motto was "Get some," whatever the hell that meant.

Hoshi dragged the mouse over to a link that read PHOTOS. She scanned through a number of albums before finally saying, "Here it is. I downloaded it. But I wanted you to see the real thing."

She clicked on a photograph and I immediately recognized both of the faces. Max Guffman and his lady friend, Meredith Yancy, who was holding an infant, presumably Kyle. The picture appeared to have been taken in the parking lot of Kualoa Beach Park.

"Well, I'll be damned," I said.

Parked a few feet behind them was a navy-blue Honda, with a Washington State license plate I couldn't make out. On the rear bumper a silver Jesus fish hung lopsided across from the word CIVIC, and just a few feet north, pasted onto the rear window, was a diamond-shaped, blue sticker that read KEIKI ON BOARD.

"Hoshi, if I wasn't such a bad man, I'd kiss you."

Hoshi grinned up at me—a bit devilishly, I thought—and said, "I don't think either of us is ready for that quite yet."

CHAPTER 35

Scott Damiano and I were on Nuuanu Street by the time darkness fully fell over Chinatown. We stood in the shadows as Scott finished a cigarette, no words spoken by either of us. A light drizzle fell onto the street, soon followed by a full rain. It seemed fitting that the skies would open up as we searched for Lok Sun. I wouldn't have been terribly shocked if the seas rose, if the earth trembled and swallowed us whole. This was how surreal my life had become.

Scott flicked the cigarette onto the wet sidewalk, and we left our nook and stepped into the downpour. Since it seemed impossible to learn anything significant about the Pharmacist, I decided to learn as much as possible about the drug. Through speaking with our forensics expert, Baron Lee, I absorbed a number of pertinent facts about strychnine, which could well aid us in our investigation.

First, the substance occurred naturally in the tree known as *Strychnos nux-vomica*, which was native to India and other tropical places, including Hawaii. Although small doses of strychnine were widely used to treat stomach ailments before World War II, it had no modern uses in Western medicine. However, *Strychnos* continued to be used in Chinese herbal medicine, particularly in the treatment of cancer.

Unfortunately, the Chinese pharmacies we were interested in weren't listed in the *Paradise Yellow Pages*. So I went on the Internet and found a few relevant Chinese symbols that might assist us in tracking down a pharmacist in Chinatown.

"There," I said, pointing to a second-floor window marked with several Chinese symbols.

"See?" Scott said, following my finger. "I would've guessed that read 'unisex hair salon.'"

"Never mind that. Just get your gun ready."

I tried the downstairs door. It was locked, but not nearly enough to keep Scott Damiano out. I watched the street while Scott played with the tumbler.

"Got it," he said ninety seconds later.

We stepped into a dank, dark hallway that smelled like a Dumpster parked behind a cheap Chinese takeout.

"You have enough bullets?" I said as we crept up a flight of creaky wooden stairs. "Because if the stench is any worse up there, I'm going to ask you to put one in the back of my head."

"Just say when," Scott said a little too deadpan.

As soon as we reached the second landing, we were greeted by a hideous centipede, no less than eight inches in length, moving like a bullet across the short hall.

"*Christ,*" Scott said, keeping his voice low. "If we come across one any bigger than that, I'm shooting it."

"Be my guest," I said softly. "No one here will mind. The

Chinese consider the centipede one of the five evils of the natural world."

"What are the other four?"

"The snake, the toad, the scorpion, and the gecko. They're each said to symbolize corruption."

"Why the gecko?"

I looked at him. "How the hell should I know?"

Three doors were on the second landing, one in the front and two on either side in the rear. We moved toward the door that would open to the room with the Chinese symbols on the window.

I gave the door a light rap. Then I stepped back and let Scott do his thing.

"Last time I broke into a pharmacy it was for Oxys," he said from his knees as he worked the lock.

"Well, let's see how this one goes and maybe we'll try our hand at a Longs Drugs on the way home."

By the time I finished my sentence, Scott was already in. He opened the door, and we stepped inside. The walls of the creepy little hole were lined with shelves, lined with small, colorful boxes, presumably filled with medicinal herbs. Jars everywhere, some filled with strange-looking berries, others with what looked like animal parts. The stench nearly brought me to my knees.

This was no traditional Chinese pharmacy. I'd been to a few of those in New York's Chinatown during law school, when my stomach was in constant distress. This looked more like something out of a horror movie.

"Look at this," Scott said, picking up a small jar of white powder.

"Careful with that."

He twisted the lid and stuck his index finger into the jar, then touched his finger to the tip of his tongue.

"What the *hell* are you doing?"

"Relax, Kev. It's Yunnan Baiyao. The Vietcong used it to stop bleeding during the Vietnam War."

"How the hell do you know?"

"Nico Tagliarini used it on a gunshot wound when Danny Flakes winged him in the Bronx."

"Danny Flakes?"

"He had bad dandruff," Scott said.

"Had?"

"Oh, yeah. He's gone. They found his body on the side of the road right off the Throgs Neck Bridge the next day." Scott stuffed the jar into his pocket. "This shit's expensive. You can't find it in the States."

"Do your Christmas shopping later. Right now we're looking for strychnine. And if you find it, don't touch it. And sure as hell don't put any on your tongue."

The small space had too many items. I worried we'd be here all night and find nothing. Worse, I didn't imagine that Chinatown had many of these underground pharmacies in its three-block radius.

Forty minutes after we entered the place I was ready to give up. I glanced over my shoulder and saw Scott playing on his cell phone.

"What are you doing? We don't have time for you to be sending text messages to Chloe."

"It's a fucking iPhone," he said as though that cleared everything up. "I'm on the Web. Come here, look."

He handed me the phone, and I studied the picture on the screen. Then my eyes moved over the jar Scott was pointing to. The jar was filled with flattened seeds covered with red hairs radiating from the center of the sides.

I studied the screen on the iPhone again. The caption read: STRYCHNOS NUX-VOMICA (SEEDS).

"Well, I'll be damned," I said.

CHAPTER 36

"Take care of the lock," I said to Scott. Then I stepped back into the shadows of the dark hallway to watch him play.

Instead of reaching into his pocket for his tools, he lifted his right foot and kicked the door in with a thunderous bang.

"Go ahead," he said. "I'll be right back."

I didn't even hesitate to step inside the apartment alone. My mind was locked in, conscious that the son of a bitch who lived here was complicit in attempting to poison me, and complicit in killing Oksana Sutin and very nearly Audra Karras.

From invoices in his store, I already knew his name.

Zhi Zhu, a middle-aged Chinese man, blew out of a back bedroom dressed in his nightclothes, a dirty white tank top and boxer shorts. When he saw me, he froze, then attempted to retreat.

I rushed him, grabbed him by the shirt, and threw him hard against a living-room wall before he could utter a word.

His head snapped back and his eyes temporarily rolled back in their sockets. Then he became fully alert.

"Where is Lok Sun?" I shouted into his face.

He closed his eyes, his mouth contorting into a cry. "No speak," he muttered. "No speak English."

"Let's see if I can't give you your first language lesson." I rammed my knee into his groin.

He screamed, tried to go to the ground, but I held him up against the wall.

"Where is Lok Sun?"

"No know," he cried. "No know no Lok Sun."

I jabbed him in the mouth with my right fist. "Try again, you piece of shit."

"No know! No know!" he screamed as blood flowed down his chin. "No know no Lok Sun!"

My right hand went to his throat and held there, my fingers threatening to squeeze. "Who did you sell the strychnine to?"

"No sell strychnine! No sell strychnine!"

I buried my left fist into his gut this time.

"Plea! Plea!" he cried. "No have no strychnine! Never! Never!"

Scott's voice suddenly boomed from behind me. "Is that so?"

Scott crossed the room, pushed me aside, grabbed Zhi Zhu, and tossed him onto the ancient couch standing lopsided in the living room. I waited for Scott to pull his gun, but he didn't. Just got right into Zhi Zhu's face, hovering over him.

"Ten seconds you have to tell us where to find Lok Sun," Scott said to him.

"I tell your friend, I no know no Lok Sun!"

"One," Scott said.

"You waste your time!"

"Two."

"I no know Lok Sun! You crazy man!"

"Three." Scott reached into his pocket.

"I already call police!"

"Four." Scott pulled out a small plastic bag.

"Police be here any second."

"Five," Scott said, waving the plastic bag in front of Zhi Zhu's face.

"What! What that?"

"Six." Scott split the Ziploc with his finger.

"Fuck you!" Zhi Zhu said.

"Seven." Scott tilted the bag over the man's mouth.

"Plea no! Plea no!"

"Eight." The flattened seeds began to descend toward the top of the bag.

"No know! No know no Lok Sun! Plea no!"

"Nine," Scott said, just as one of the flattened seeds breached the top of the bag.

"All right! All right! I tell! I tell!"

Scott pinched the top of the bag, a seed still dangling over Zhi Zhu's mouth. With his other hand Scott gripped the man's jaw, ready to hold his mouth open if necessary.

"Lok Sun," Zhi Zhu cried. "He stay in abandon building cross the street. Used to be big whorehouse. He no there tonight, but when he there, he protect by men with guns!"

Zhi Zhu continued weeping as Scott carefully rezipped the plastic bag, returning it to his pocket.

Then Scott stared into Zhi Zhu's red, puffy eyes. "I'm not scared of men with guns. I'm not scared of anything." Scott stood up and smiled at me. "Except maybe centipedes. Those fucking things are disgusting."

CHAPTER 37

The next morning Flan and I returned to Pearl City. Political signs sprouted from front yards like weeds, a constant reminder that the election was less than two months away. We were inching ever closer to October and whatever surprise awaited the governor then.

This morning in the Jeep we passed an inordinate number of signs to reelect Dave Iokepa to the State Senate.

"Why does that last name sound so familiar?" I said, easing on the accelerator.

"I questioned a young lady named Mindy Iokepa a few weeks back."

"Where does she live?"

"A couple houses over from Max Guffman."

"What did she say?"

"Same as everyone else. Didn't recognize Turi except from TV. Knew Kanoa Bristol only in passing."

"You have an iPhone?" I said.

"A what?"

"Never mind."

I pulled the Jeep over and plucked my cell phone out of my pocket. I dialed the office and waited for Hoshi to answer. When she did, I asked her to pull up the Web site for Dave Iokepa. "See if it says anything about his *'ohana.*"

A few seconds later she informed me that Dave Iokepa had a wife named Diane and a daughter named Mindy.

"Thanks." I ended the call and turned to Flan. "Mindy Iokepa is the state senator's daughter. Notice anything unusual when you spoke to her?"

Flan shrugged, then shook his head. "No, she was polite. The conversation was a little rushed because she was carrying her baby."

"Did you speak to her husband?"

"No husband. I asked. She lives alone and doesn't see the baby's father."

"Boy or a girl?"

"A baby girl."

I sat back and thought about it. "Think we can get the kid's birth certificate?"

Flan smirked. "Doubt it. Not here in Hawaii. Remember the flap over President Obama's? We'd need the mother's signature."

I closed my eyes tight, leaned back, and thought about it some more before I said, "Or the father's."

That evening I went to see Audra at her home in Ewa. Since her near-death experience at my villa, she'd become reclusive, frightened, rarely leaving her house. She'd taken a leave of ab-

sence from work at the US Attorney's Office. She only ate food
that came out of manufacturer-sealed containers, and even
then, only if she opened the container herself. She'd lost weight,
at least fifteen pounds, reducing her to practically nothing. She
stood five foot six and couldn't have weighed more than a hundred pounds.

"I found him," I said, as I sat next to her on her sofa. "He's
living in an abandoned brothel in Chinatown."

Her eyes, perpetually tired since her release from the hospital, widened. "Did you contact the FBI?"

"Not yet."

"Not yet? Why not?"

"Because," I said, gently placing a hand on her slender fore-
arm, "eliminating Lok Sun doesn't eliminate the real threat.
Handing the Pharmacist over to the feds at this point is like
handing over a murder weapon without knowing who pulled
the trigger."

She pulled her arm away from me. "And what if it was
Wade Omphrey?"

It was a legitimate question, one I hadn't given much thought
to. What lengths would I go to, to protect the governor, a man I
had no respect for and didn't like, but who was nevertheless my
client? If it turned out Omphrey had hired Lok Sun to kill Oksana Sutin, would I allow Lok Sun to flee the country, knowing
that he'd ultimately lead the feds to the governor if he was caught?
Would I permit Lok Sun to run even after what had happened to
Audra in my own home? No, I didn't think so. But that didn't
mean I'd have to turn Lok Sun over to the FBI either. After all,
justice didn't always need to derive from the courts.

"I'll cross that bridge when I come to it," I said.

"How did you come by this information anyway?" she said, her anger evident in the hue of her cheeks.

"We found his source of strychnine. A man named Zhi Zhu."

"And this source, this Zhi Zhu, what's to keep him from running to Lok Sun and warning him you and your mob friend are coming?"

I felt a rush of contempt in my chest. "My mob friend," I said evenly, "is more dangerous than Lok Sun could ever be. And Zhi Zhu knows this. He learned it firsthand."

Audra sank deeper into the sofa. She remained perfectly silent for a few moments, then appeared to calm and changed the subject. "Do you ever find yourself wishing you did things much differently since graduating high school?"

"How could I? I don't even remember who the hell I was back then."

She frowned. "You were Kevin Corvelli."

"No. Kevin Corvelli is twice as old as that guy. He's wiser, better equipped to make decisions. That kid, he did the best he could with what little life experience he had. I feel sorry for him, actually. It's unfair that seventeen-year-olds are expected to make decisions that will impact their thirty- and forty-year-old selves. Get arrested, it follows you to college and beyond. Choose a major, chances are you're stuck in something you hate for the rest of your life. Go to law school, and you're shackled to the practice because of mountains of student-loan debt. It's an unforgiving world. We do the best we can. There's not enough time for regret."

She leaned over, rested her head on my shoulder. "So, when exactly do our decisions start to matter, Kevin?"

I turned my head, stared into her eyes, and experienced a warmth in my stomach I hadn't felt in months. My lips brushed against hers as her soft hand traveled up the length of my neck.

"In the morning," I whispered as our cheeks touched, and we both shut our eyes. "Our decisions begin to matter tomorrow morning."

CHAPTER 38

The time had come in Turi Ahina's case to move from investigation to trial preparation. The investigation wouldn't truly end until the verdict was read, but our trial date was coming up fast, with jury selection scheduled to begin in early October.

So Jake and I sat in the conference room staring blankly at a table blanketed with filled legal pads, photographs, pleadings, motions, police and autopsy reports, witness statements, copies of the Hawaii Penal Code and the Hawaii Rules of Evidence, and a single birth certificate from the Department of Health.

By now I was eating Percocet as if they were Tic Tacs, but they didn't alleviate the ferocious pain at the base of my neck. So I started adding ibuprofen, and before I knew it I'd developed a peptic ulcer and needed to include Nexium, Zantac, and Prilosec to my daily regimen of pills.

"Hoshi's preparing the subpoenas," I told Jake. "We'll have Flan serve them next week."

"How about pretrial motions?" Jake said.

I shrugged. "There's no confession. The only issue is the gun used to kill Kanoa Bristol. That's coming in, and we don't care if it does. No prints, no gunshot residue on Turi's hands or clothes. Dapper Don can't introduce the fact that this weapon was the same weapon that killed Alika Kapua. Judge Narita would throw him out of court. Besides, there's no proof Turi was the one who shot Alika Kapua three years ago."

"Unless you testify."

I stared at Jake, suddenly struck with what I hoped was an irrational fear. What if, after this trial—after we admitted that the weapon used to kill Kanoa Bristol belonged to Turi—the prosecutor's office came back and obtained an indictment against Turi for the murder of Alika Kapua?

It was as though Jake read my mind. "You sure your 'choice of evils' strategy is the way to go in this case, son?"

Since justification was not considered an affirmative defense in Hawaii, I wouldn't need to disclose our intention to use it before trial. Thus, neither Narita nor Watanabe knew it was coming. Which also meant I had time to change strategies if necessary.

Jake voiced his reasons for such a change: "As you said, there were no prints on the gun, no gunshot residue. You have one witness, a seventy-two-year-old woman, who claims she saw an obese man scampering away in the dark following gunshots. I don't doubt for a minute you could shred her like a piece of paper on cross-examination. And that's really all they got on our man."

"Except a dead officer," I said. "And no one else for us to point to."

Jake shrugged. "Dapper Don would still have a hell of a

tough time proving his case beyond a reasonable doubt. Hell, Narita might grant our motion to dismiss after Dapper Don finishes his case-in-chief. The evidence simply doesn't support a conviction."

"And what about the Honolulu Police Department?" As soon as I said it I regretted it.

"You know as well as I do, that's not our problem. You can't use Turi as a pawn to prove police corruption."

My eyes narrowed. "Is that what you think I'm doing?"

Jake shook his head. "Not unless you've grown a conscience since the Erin Simms trial and are suddenly more concerned with exposing the truth than winning an acquittal."

"And what if I know I can do both?"

"*Know* is an awfully strong word for a trial attorney. You can't predict what twelve idiots in a jury box will do any more than you can predict what voters will do four years from now in the next election."

I released my breath, unaware until then that I'd been holding it. "This is beginning to sound as though we're playing role reversal, Jake."

He winked at me. "Maybe we are."

CHAPTER 39

We knew where Lok Sun was, but getting to him was another story, Scott Damiano or not. So I hired a set of eyes to watch the Chinatown brothel and decided to approach this from the other side, by finding the pimp Gavin Dengler. Finding Dengler would put us one step closer to discovering who paid Oksana Sutin to have an affair with Wade Omphrey, Hawaii's own unwitting Client Number 9. And discovering who paid Oksana Sutin to sleep with the governor might just lead us to the party who paid Lok Sun to murder Oksana Sutin. My best guess was that they were one and the same.

The easiest way to locate Gavin Dengler, I figured, was to question one of his johns. The only john we knew by name was Yoshimitsu Nakagawa, the billionaire from Japan. Only I didn't want to deal with Nakagawa's bodyguards again—at least not while they were armed. So we'd have to catch Nakagawa somewhere men with guns presumably weren't allowed.

Somewhere Nakagawa would be hesitant to cause a scene. I decided we'd drop in on his next business meeting.

Armed with subpoenas and my translator Hoshi, I parked the Jeep at Ala Moana Center and walked across the street to one of Honolulu's most recognized business locations, a seventeen-story work of art in the Kapiolani Corridor.

Getting past security proved a hell of a lot easier than anticipated. A quick, innocuous fib about a meeting with a patent lawyer whose name I snatched from the building directory, and Hoshi and I were given visitor passes and a code to reach the top floor. Try that in New York these days and you could very well walk out of a building in handcuffs.

When we reached the top floor and exited the elevator, we walked to the end of the hall, where we could see into a mammoth conference room. I recognized Nakagawa right away. He was standing before a group of Japanese businessmen, presumably giving a presentation.

"Perfect timing," I said, pulling an envelope from my inside suit jacket. "Hoshi, you wait here. I'll be out in ninety seconds."

I marched toward the conference room and swung open the glass door, prompting every man in the room to cast his eyes on me.

"Pardon me for the intrusion," I said. "Mr. Nakagawa, I need to have a word with you."

Nakagawa seemed to recognize me, too. He turned to his colleagues and said something in Japanese, then followed me back to the door, eyeing the envelope in my hand the entire time.

"What is the meaning of this?" he said in perfect English as soon as we entered the hall.

I waved Hoshi away. Turned out, I wouldn't need a translator after all.

"My name is Kevin Corvelli, and I'm a lawyer. I have a few quick questions for you and then you can return to your meeting."

"Forget it," he said harshly. "Leave now before I have you thrown from the building."

I held up the envelope. "This is a subpoena. You can answer my questions here or I can haul your ass into federal court. It's your decision."

He smirked. "I would like to see you try, Mr. Corvelli. I retain an army of lawyers who will have your subpoenas quashed faster than you can have them signed. Now, if you will excuse me, I have *important* business to attend to."

He started back toward the conference room.

"More important than your wife and six children back in Japan?" I called out to him.

Nakagawa immediately stopped and turned to me. "Are you threatening me, Mr. Corvelli?"

"That all depends on how much you value your family, your name, and your reputation, Mr. Nakagawa."

Nakagawa moved toward me, a fresh fire in his eyes.

"On the positive side," I said, "I'm sure your twenty-four thousand convenience stores will sell a hell of a lot of newspapers when your face graces the front page above the fold, along with a provocative headline linking you to an international sex scandal."

"Do you know what billions of dollars could do to a man like you, Mr. Corvelli?"

I shrugged. "It could just about pay off my student loans."

"Go ahead. Make light. You have no idea who you are fucking with. But by all means, give it your best shot. Risk your life. Make your accusations. It will still be my word against yours."

"Not quite. It will be your word against mine—and the photos."

I could hear Nakagawa grinding his teeth as he surveyed my face to determine whether I was bluffing.

"Surely, Mr. Nakagawa, you don't think my friend and I were on your property just to examine your yellow hibiscus bushes. Though they were quite beautiful, they weren't nearly as intriguing as the specimens *inside* your house—specifically, the white flowers with the long stems."

The billionaire stood silent for a long while.

"If you'd care to see the photos, I could send them to my friend at the *Star-Advertiser*. I'm sure you'll find captioned copies on your front doorstep first thing in the morning."

"*Enough,*" he said abruptly. "What do you want to know about?"

"The girls."

"They are not mine," he said flatly. "I rent them out."

"I figured as much. What I want to know is who you rent them out from."

Nakagawa scanned the hall. "I make a phone call."

"To whom?"

"A man with a German-Austrian accent."

"Gavin Dengler," I said.

Nakagawa nodded.

"Where does he live?"

He shook his head. "That, Mr. Corvelli, I do not know."

"Give me the phone number."

Nakagawa unbuttoned and then reached into his suit jacket and pulled out an elaborate handheld device. His thumbs flew over the device like a child playing a video game. When he was finished, he showed me the screen.

I took the number down on the envelope.

"I can order a girl direct from Dengler by calling this number?"

"You need a code," he said, growing frustrated. "And a referral."

"You're my referral. Unless you want to do this in court. Now, what's the code?"

"He will ask for a number, a letter, and a name. The number is ten. The letter is *O*. And the name is Sam."

I took it down: *10. O. Sam.* "How much do these ladies run?"

Nakagawa looked me up and down, his thin lips curling in a sneer. "More than someone like you can afford."

CHAPTER 40

I made the call from a prepaid cell phone that night at Scott's apartment in Waikiki.

Five rings, then a voice with a German-Austrian accent answered, "Number?"

"Ten."

"Letter?"

"O."

"Name?"

"Sam."

"Who referred you?"

"Yoshimitsu Nakagawa."

"What would you like?"

"A redhead, tall and thin."

"No redheads," he said. "These girls are not from fucking Scotland."

"A brunette then."

"I have one brunette, five-feet-nine, fifty-two kilograms. From Moldova."

"How much?"

"Ten thousand for four hours. Five up front."

"Do you take Discover card?"

"This is not time for fucking joke. You want her or no?"

"Yes."

"Give me address."

I gave him Scott's address and the apartment number.

"She come up, you give her half. She go back down, give to her driver. He count, then she come back up and stay four hours. Before she leave, you give her second half of money. If you damage her, you give to me whatever money I lose. Understood?"

"Understood."

"One hour," he said, then the line went dead.

An hour later Flan and I were seated in my Jeep, waiting in the dark for a limo or a Lincoln or whatever. Scott Damiano was upstairs with $10,000 in cash and a grin that made me question whether this was the right plan.

"This is bullshit," Flan said for the fourth time. "Damiano's up there waiting for a gorgeous brunette, and I'm down here sitting in a Jeep with you. I've been with the firm for years; he's been here for a few months. I have seniority. How the hell does—"

"He's been instructed not to touch her,"

Flan glowered at me.

"Well, that's what he's been instructed," I said. "Remember, these girls are being exploited."

"Yeah, by everyone but me," Flan mumbled.

Mercifully, a black Lincoln turned onto Tusitala before Flan could utter another word. We watched as a tall brunette I'd never seen before exited the vehicle and sauntered toward the entrance of Scott's apartment building. She was dressed as if she had some place to go.

"Scott's probably going to have to move after this," Flan said.

"He's only got a month or two left on his lease."

Less than ten minutes later the brunette stepped outside and hurried back to the Lincoln. She stuck her head in the window and handed the driver one of the two envelopes I'd given to Scott. Once she was safely back inside Scott's apartment building, the Lincoln pulled away.

We followed the Lincoln, but we didn't have to follow it far. Just to the newest, most luxurious, most expensive hotel in Waikiki.

Owned by the most recognizable entrepreneur in recent history, the Aloha International Hotel on Saratoga Road towered over its neighbors.

I parked the Jeep across the street.

"Think that's where we'll find Gavin Dengler?" Flan said.

"Seems about right, doesn't it?"

Flan jumped out of the Jeep and followed the Lincoln on foot into the garage.

I sat alone, thinking about Oksana Sutin, about Iryna Kupchenko, about the nameless woman now sitting in Scott's apartment a few blocks away. Lawyers thought they had it hard, worrying about where the next client would come from, how much they'd get when they settled the next case. Senior associates at large law firms shrank behind their desks when their bosses crossed the halls in front of their offices, afraid of getting chewed out, of having another motion for summary judgment dumped in their laps. And it wasn't just lawyers, it was everyone in the working world. Legitimacy was constantly being taken for granted.

And on the other side, power was constantly being abused. Pimps such as Gavin Dengler, businessmen such as Yoshimitsu Nakagawa, they were all the same. Exploiting whoever could be exploited, whether it was renting out a woman or throwing a blue vest at a single mom and having her ring up imported garbage for minimum wage. Sometimes it seemed those with the right to complain were the only ones who never did.

I had seen the worst of humanity when I practiced law in New York, but somehow it seemed worse that all this happened here in paradise. A dirty cop in Queens never caused me to bat an eye. Here in Hawaii it seemed a far worse crime.

I popped a Percocet and waited for it to kick in, waited for that warm feeling to rush over my brain, to lighten my thoughts, improve my mood. To shut out the rest of this horrible night.

By the time the pill kicked in, Flan was back in the passenger seat of my Jeep.

He said only two words: "Penthouse suite."

CHAPTER 41

By the end of the month, the bulge in the back of my neck had gotten to be too much. With Turi's trial less than a week away and an October surprise looming in the governor's race, my body was beginning to break down. So I finally broke down and made an appointment with Scott's massage therapist.

On the last day of September, I drove my Jeep into Chinatown and parked in a garage. The big, hard sun felt good on my face, especially since I'd spent the last few days holed up in my office preparing for Turi's trial. The only two people who apparently spent more time inside than I did were Lok Sun and Gavin Dengler. Both the hotel and brothel were being watched around the clock. Lok Sun had his men and Gavin Dengler had his women run errands. But neither man could be found leaving his residence and walking the streets.

I double-checked the address before I stepped into the massage parlor. An older Asian woman greeted me as though I were a regular customer. She came around from the counter and immediately took my suit jacket. The waiting room was so small there was barely enough room to turn around.

"You here to see Lian, yes?" the woman said.

"Yes, I have an appointment."

"Good, good. You like. She take care of all your stress."

"Is it that noticeable?" I said, forcing a smile.

She smiled back but didn't reply, and it struck me that her English vocabulary was probably limited to those words she used every day.

A few minutes later a beautiful, young Chinese woman appeared in the doorway, dressed in a long, black silk robe. "You come."

I followed her into another small room with a narrow massage table sitting in the center.

She handed me a white towel. "You undress. I be right back."

I undressed and wrapped the towel around my waist, then lay on my stomach on the table. The lighting was dim, and a few moments later a soothing melody permeated the room. I tried to relax. I lay there for a few minutes, my eyes closed, my shoulders feeling a little less tense already.

Thank you, Scott. I wasn't a massage man. I'd never had one before, at least not professionally. I wasn't sure what to expect, but I was already relaxed by the experience.

Lian reentered the room and I kept my face buried in my arms on the table. She got right into it, working the muscles between my neck and shoulders. Slowly, using oils, she worked her way down my spine.

"Your muscles very tight. You carry your worries in your neck." Her voice sounded vaguely familiar.

As she worked, thoughts of Turi's trial tried to trespass, but

I pushed them back. In my mind I muted the governor's voice as he attempted to concern me about the polls and John Biel's October surprise. I didn't need to decide just now whether I'd move from Hawaii following the verdict. All I had to concentrate on for the next hour was relaxation.

After about twenty minutes Lian instructed me to turn over. Holding the towel tight above my middle, I did. Before I could open my eyes, she placed a warm, wet towel over them.

Lian worked on my chest, then moved onto my arms, gently massaging my biceps. Her hands ran over my heart as though she wanted to make certain it was still beating. She stopped at my abs. "How you get this terrible scar?"

"You'll have to read the book."

Wordlessly, Lian continued, moving her hands back up my chest then down over my stomach until her long, lithe fingers reached the towel. Then, slowly yet suddenly and without warning, one hand dipped inside the towel.

Wait a minute, I thought as the blood rushed to my groin and I swelled.

My heart pounded and the pain instantly returned to my neck. This was *not* what I ordered.

When she turned to gather more oils, I lifted the towel from my eyes and looked over at her, only to find that she'd disrobed as well. Down the length of her back, from her shoulders down to her perfect round ass, was a familiar image: a rare bird escaping from its cage. Lian was the girl from Tam's bar.

"Lian . . . ," I said.

She turned, exposing small pert breasts and a neatly trimmed—

Suddenly the door burst open.

"Police!" a man shouted, raising his gun. "Hands in the air."

My jaw dropped, my heart tried to beat its way out of my chest. As I rose off the table, my towel dropped to the floor. It didn't matter. Seconds later my naked body was hurled to the floor right next to it. My face was held down against the dirty linoleum as an officer planted a knee in my back and slapped on cuffs.

"You're under arrest for solicitation of prostitution. Anything you say can and will be used against you in a court of law . . ."

As I listened to him read me my Miranda rights, I realized exactly what was happening. My realization would be confirmed the moment they dragged me through the front door onto the street, where the photographers would be waiting. The police were undermining me and, by extension, any message I might have for Turi Ahina's jury. *Look at Kevin Corvelli,* they were saying. *A criminal just like his clients.*

To add insult to injury they refused to allow me my clothes. They covered me with nothing but Lian's sheer robe, then shoved me in my sore back until we reached the front door.

When the door opened, the big, hard sun hit me in the face again, accompanied this time by microphones and cameras. Every reporter on Oahu had apparently been tipped off.

The reporters hurled unintelligible questions at me as the police led me slowly toward the waiting prowl car.

"Looks like you're famous again, Counselor," one bastard cop whispered in my ear as another opened the car's rear door.

Enjoy it now, I thought as they shoved me inside, *because next week, I'm taking this whole fucking city down, starting with the police department.*

'OKAKOPA

(OCTOBER)

CHAPTER 42

"Ladies and gentlemen of the jury, my name is Donovan Watanabe, and I will be representing the people of the state of Hawaii during this trial. Today I am charged with the task of prosecuting the defendant Turi Ahina for committing the atrocious act of felony murder against an officer of the law with the Honolulu Police Department—veteran narcotics detective Kanoa Bristol of Pearl City."

As Dapper Don settled into his opening statement, I made certain to look each juror in the eye from my vantage point at the defense table all the way across the aisle. I instructed Turi to do the same, with the one eye that wasn't bandaged, but to be careful not to intimidate and not to smile. "Look earnest," I told him. "Show the jury that you're taking these charges very seriously, but that you're confident that the truth will come out."

Dapper Don continued, "My opening statement will be brief. *Why?* you may ask, when this is such an important case, a case in which a law enforcement officer was viciously gunned down while trying to uphold the law. *Why* will the attorney charged with the awesome responsibility of making certain that justice is done for Detective Bristol, for his family, for the citizens of Pearl City, and for all of Hawaii be brief in his opening remarks? The answer is simple and it is simply this: this is a simple case.

"As it is said in the parlance of our times, this case is open-and-shut. And after all the evidence is presented to you, you will know beyond any reasonable doubt that the defendant Turi Ahina committed the crime in question, the crime of murder. And he committed it in cold blood."

Jury selection had taken only a single day. I'd led with the simple question "Have you ever heard of the cable news legal pundit Marcy Faith?" I watched half the room and gave the other half to Jake. We were looking for the slightest smile, the tiniest sparkle in the eyes that said, "Yup, that's my girl." When we found it, we attempted to have that juror removed for cause. If that failed, we exercised one of our valuable peremptory challenges.

"The evidence that will be presented to you," Dapper Don said to the jury, "will also be simple and clear-cut. The evidence will show that at around eleven o'clock on the evening of July twenty-third of this year, Detective Kanoa Bristol, while off duty, came upon the defendant engaged in a criminal act, specifically a significant illegal drug transaction, and that Detective Bristol attempted to engage and interfere with that transaction, and for that reason Detective Bristol was shot twice, once in the chest—a bullet stopped by the officer's Kevlar vest—and once in the throat, the latter proving fatal. Furthermore, the evidence will prove beyond any shadow of a doubt that the man who fired those bullets into Detective Bristol is sitting in this courtroom today and will do so until this trial is over. That man is seated at the defense table, and his name is Turi Ahina."

Dapper Don pointed an accusatory finger at Turi, who did not look away. In the prosecutor's eyes I saw a raw passion I hadn't seen from him when I faced him during the Gianforte trial. At issue here, however, was a dead law enforcement officer, and Donovan Watanabe, it seemed, was taking this case personally. His normally calm, cool demeanor had all but evaporated. Without question, Dapper Don was out for blood.

"What is this evidence? you ask," Dapper Don continued. "Firstly, you will hear the testimony of Mrs. Doris Ledford, a young woman of seventy-two." Here he smiled and the jury smiled with him. "Mrs. Ledford will testify that while in her home at eleven o'clock that night, she overheard two *bangs* that sounded like gunshots, and she hurried to the kitchen window to discover what the sounds were. She will testify that when she looked out that kitchen window, she saw clearly an obese man running fast as he could down the street, away from the scene of the shooting."

Turi rolled his eyes, and I warned him to watch his body language in front of the jury.

"But what do he have to call me *obese* for, eh?" Turi shot back in a whisper. "There are ladies here in the audience, yeah?"

Watanabe said, "You will hear from the detective who was in charge of investigating this homicide, this murder of his fellow officer. Detective Ray Irvine will testify regarding every part of the investigation, from first response, to the gathering of evidence, to apprehending the suspect, and beyond."

Dapper Don walked over to the evidence table and lifted the clear plastic bag that held the alleged murder weapon.

"As you can plainly see, police recovered the defendant's gun. Not far from the spot where police would recover the defendant himself. Now, make no mistake, this defendant is not dumb simply because he committed such a terrible crime and got caught. No, this defendant was wise enough to wipe his fingerprints off the gun and to take measures to avoid, or possibly clean up, gunshot residue to help conceal his crime. The defense will attack, attack, attack on these issues, as though the defendant should be rewarded for being crafty. And Turi Ahina *was* crafty, just not crafty enough. And, as you will learn, just not fast enough either."

Dapper Don turned his meticulous frame and looked at me as though he were about to throw down the gauntlet. But this was a challenge I had long ago accepted, and now I had no intention of backing down. Not even following my arrest for prostitution. That case—the case of *State versus Kevin D. Corvelli*—remained pending, at least in court. But certainly not in the press. In the press I, like any criminal defendant, was guilty until proven innocent.

". . . and next you will hear from the Honolulu Police Department's ballistics expert, Denis Ritchie . . . ," Dapper Don was saying.

But I had stopped listening. When the prosecution's opening statement was concluded, I'd have to make an immediate decision: whether to rise and give my own opening statement today, or to delay it until the close of the prosecution's case. The pro of opening now was that the prosecution's entire case-in-chief would be colored with suspicion, looked at through the spectacles of possible police corruption. On the downside, I'd be locking myself permanently into the choice-of-evils strategy.

"You may have heard of my adversary, the celebrity defense attorney Kevin Corvelli," Dapper Don said out of nowhere. "So respected are his skills that he presently represents our governor."

"Objection," I said, rising to my feet. "There's no relevance here, Your Honor."

"I agree," Judge Narita said. "Sustained. The jury will disregard that last statement. Mr. Watanabe, move on."

"Your Honor," Dapper Don said, nodding, then turning back to the jury. "My only point is that Mr. Corvelli is exceedingly good at his job. I read once a line in a play; the line read, 'The law is a sort of hocus-pocus science.' Well, ladies and gentlemen of the jury, Mr. Corvelli is perhaps the world's premier illusionist. And because of that, I feel I must caution you to keep your eyes and minds on the actual evidence at all times."

I started to stand to object, then thought better of it and sat down. Let him go that route, I decided. In a few minutes I'd be able to show the jury myself that I hid no rabbits in my hat, that I was just a man, a lawyer like any other.

". . . and at the conclusion of this case, ladies and gentlemen, I will return to this rail to summarize the evidence introduced during this trial and ask you to return a verdict of guilty on the charge of murder in the first degree."

"Thank you, Mr. Watanabe," Judge Narita said from the

bench. Then he turned to me. "Mr. Corvelli, would you care to give your opening statement now, or would you prefer to reserve it?" In more crass terms, shit or get off the pot, Counselor.

Lay your cards on the table.

CHAPTER 43

"Ladies and gentlemen of the jury," I said, "this case is *anything* but simple. That Mr. Watanabe doesn't understand this fact is a sad truth, and it speaks volumes about the rift between the Honolulu Police Department and the Office of the Prosecuting Attorney. Because I am certain, knowing my adversary as I do, that had he challenged what he was told by police, had he dug deeper, Mr. Watanabe would have been both astonished and appalled at what he unearthed. And he would not be sitting here today trying to convict my client Turi Ahina of a crime he did not commit."

I lifted my arms and let the jury peer up the sleeves of my navy suit jacket. "Look closely. No aces, no playing cards whatsoever, up my sleeves. I'm no magician, no illusionist. I don't use smoke and I don't use mirrors, except to dress myself in the morning and sometimes fix my hair. I assure you, ladies and gentlemen, I want what *you* want out of this trial. And that is a fair and just verdict."

I gazed behind me at the gallery, at the sea of dark shirts, just about the entire HPD observing this trial from the pews. In the front row sat the widow Dana Bristol, glaring at me as though I'd put the bullets in her husband myself.

"The evidence I am going to introduce to you during this trial is going to shock you. Over the next few days and weeks, you are going to learn through testimony and physical evidence that the Narcotics Intelligence Unit of the Honolulu PD was—and *is*—engaged in criminal conduct that includes the receipt of protection bribes; the planting, removing, and altering of evidence from *this* very crime scene; and most pointedly, murder and attempted murder."

The gallery broke out in nervous, outraged chatter, and a few choice words were shouted above the din. Narita slapped his gavel as I continued.

"Attempted murder," I repeated, only louder. "You will learn through testimony and physical evidence that Detective Kanoa Bristol was *not* trying to apprehend a suspect when he was shot and killed on a dark street in Pearl City. No. Detective Bristol was trying to *execute* an innocent man."

I raised my voice to a shout as I pointed in the direction of the defense table while keeping my eyes locked on the faces in the jury box. "Let me say it again so that it is clear: *Detective Kanoa Bristol attempted to execute my client Turi Ahina.*"

The courtroom erupted, but I did not lose stride. Over the roar of the gallery I shouted, "This was *not* a botched arrest as the Honolulu PD would have you believe." With my fist, I pounded on the jury rail as I allowed my face to glow red with rage. "*This. Was. A. Hit.*"

Donovan Watanabe leapt from his seat. *"Objection, Your Honor.* Mr. Corvelli is now making argument."

"Overruled," Narita said with a surprising urgency. "If Mr. Corvelli cannot back these claims up, then he will suffer the ramifications."

"Rest assured, Your Honor," I said above the chaos, "these are not baseless allegations. These are provable facts." I spun back to the jury as the gallery finally quieted down. "How will I prove them? I will prove these allegations by showing you how evidence in this case was *manipulated* and *eliminated.* How witnesses were *coerced* and *intimidated* and even *bribed."*

I took a step back from the rail and leveled my tone. "You, ladies and gentlemen of the jury, will come to understand during the course of this trial that, on the evening of the twenty-third of July, Turi Ahina faced what the law calls a 'choice of evils,' and that Turi Ahina shot and killed Detective Kanoa Bristol in self-defense."

I paused to allow time for my words to sink in. "Ladies and gentlemen, the shooting of Kanoa Bristol on the night of July twenty-third was justified and *necessary* to prevent an innocent man from being assassinated. A man who was a threat to the Narcotics Intelligence Unit and the Honolulu PD as a whole. A man who had been arrested by the federal government and asked to divulge illicit information about how a multibillion-dollar criminal enterprise was permitted to run with impunity throughout the island. The reason being, of course, that the criminal organization in question was being *protected* by numerous members of the Honolulu police force, including Detective Kanoa Bristol."

Narita had to silence the crowd yet again. Once he did, I addressed every piece of evidence Dapper Don Watanabe had set forth in his opening. The eyewitness testimony, the so-called murder weapon, and the weapon found on the detective's body, which the prosecution asserted was never fired that night. I addressed the number of bullet casings found at the scene, and the $5,000 recovered from Turi's person following his arrest. I touched on each point once, and then again.

"You, ladies and gentlemen of the jury," I said a half hour later in closing, "will deliberate on one of the most important cases in the history of this state.

"*You* will put an end to the insidious corruption that currently plagues our island paradise.

"*You* will shed light on this dirty unit of this dirty police department in this otherwise idyllic city in this otherwise idyllic state.

"At the conclusion of this trial, *you* will say not guilty, and by saying not guilty, *you* will be saying to these dirty cops, 'No more.'

"No more."

CHAPTER 44

Once Judge Narita adjourned the proceedings for the day, I gathered my files, and Jake and I made our way up the aisle, looking straight ahead all the way. Eyes from both sides of the aisle bore into us like lasers. We met Scott and Flan outside the courthouse, and the four of us pushed through the tide of reporters and walked silently back toward the office together.

We didn't make it a block before my cell phone started vibrating in my pocket.

"Mr. Corvelli, it's Jason Yi. The governor needs to see you right away. It's urgent."

I feigned surprise. "I just finished making my opening statement in an important trial. My partner and I are heading back to the office to prepare for the state's first witness."

"The governor knows about the trial. That's why he needs to speak to you. He'll be at your office in twenty minutes."

Yi didn't allow for a response. During my protest I realized I was speaking into dead air.

"They're waiting for you in the conference room," Hoshi said.

I glanced at my watch. The governor must have been parked outside my building when Yi called because only six minutes had passed since Yi hung up on me.

"Want some backup?" Jake said.

"No, I'll handle this."

I opened the conference room door and found the governor flanked on either side by his wife, Pamela, and Jason Yi.

Omphrey dispensed with the greetings. "What the fuck are you doing to me, Corvelli?"

I took a seat across from the trio. "Care to elaborate?"

Omphrey's hands clenched into fists on the table. "Alleging widespread police corruption in Honolulu twenty-eight days before the election? My opponent has already issued a statement condemning my leadership. You're *sabotaging* me."

"So you are aware of the corruption, Governor? Is that what you're telling me?"

"I'm aware of *no such thing*."

"Then issue a statement through your press secretary, or better yet, schedule a press conference and explain to the people of Hawaii that you are launching a full investigation into the allegations set forth during the Turi Ahina trial."

The governor slammed his right fist against the table. "This isn't some fucking game," he shouted. "*Crime* is my issue. You've seen my ads. Crime and no new taxes, that's all I have. That son of a bitch John Biel is beating me up on education, on the environment, on the economy. If the Honolulu Police Department is smeared, I'll lose this goddamn election, and if I lose this goddamn election, Corvelli, I'll—"

"You'll what, Governor?" I said calmly.

His jowls were shaking, his doughy cheeks had turned red. Pamela and Yi had each placed a hand on his shoulders. "*This*"—he pointed a finger at me—"is a conflict of interest. I'll have you disbarred."

"There's no conflict, Governor. I represent you in an open murder investigation. It's not my job to see that you're reelected, only to make certain you don't go to prison for Oksana Sutin's death. My investigators and I have laid our lives on the line the past few months attempting to discover who was behind her murder. If you don't like the job we've done, then fire me and get the hell out of my office."

The conference room fell silent.

After a full minute, Pamela Omphrey finally said, "What has your investigation revealed?"

I looked at the governor. "I'm not at liberty to discuss the investigation in front of anyone but your husband, Mrs. Omphrey. Unless he says it's okay and waives privilege."

Pamela stared at her husband.

Omphrey said, "Wait outside, dear." To Yi, he said, "Jason, escort the first lady to the reception area."

Once the door had closed behind them, he turned to me. "Go."

"We know where Lok Sun is. We also know the location of Gavin Dengler, who was Oksana Sutin's employer during the time you were together."

"Her employer?"

"Her pimp."

"How many times do I have to *tell* you, Cor—"

"We believe she was acting as a spy, Governor."

Omphrey froze, his Adam's apple traveling up and down his throat like a broken glass elevator.

"A spy?"

I leaned forward. "You said you never asked her about her life or her work while you were with her, right, Governor? That's common enough for someone with your bloated ego. But I'll bet she asked about your life, about your work. That's why the affair lasted months and meant more to you than just sex, isn't that right, Governor? You like talking about yourself and Oksana Sutin was the perfect sounding board—long legs, large breasts, and as mute as a carp."

Omphrey gaped, his mind no doubt working more than it had at any given time in the past four years.

"So what did you discuss with her, Governor?"

His eyes moved back and forth across the table as though he were watching a tennis match. "Everything," he mumbled. "Everything."

CHAPTER 45

Doris Ledford looked well for a woman of seventy-two. No doubt her recent vacation to the mainland—first to visit her grandchildren in Arizona, then to fabulous Las Vegas for buffets and slot machines—had done her some good. The spots where her cheeks had once been were rosy, she wore makeup, and her hair was dyed a bright orange that made you think that at any minute she'd bust out the balloon animals.

After less than an hour of direct examination, during which Doris Ledford positively identified Turi Ahina as the obese man "running like the wind" from the scene of the shooting, Donovan Watanabe turned the witness over to me.

"Don't confuse the issue," Jake warned me before I went up to the podium. "We can't prove the police arranged for her to win a trip to Vegas after the shooting, so let it go. Focus on what we do know."

I nodded, reassured Turi, then took my place at the podium.

"Good morning, Mrs. Ledford."

She bowed her head politely, then looked over at Dapper Don as if to ask, *Was that okay?*

"Mrs. Ledford," I said, using the voice I reserved for children and the elderly on the witness stand, "would you please tell the jury, before that evening, how many times in your seventy-two years had you heard the sound of gunshots being fired?"

Her eyes widened, her left hand went to her mouth. "Never."

"Earlier, Mrs. Ledford, on direct examination, you testified that you heard two gunshots, is that correct?"

"Yes, two."

"And would you please remind us how much time passed between the first shot and second shot you heard on that evening?"

"No time at all," she said. "It was one bang right after the other."

"And that was why, as you said earlier, the shots sounded a lot like firecrackers to you, correct?"

"Yes, that's right. Just like firecrackers."

"Let me backtrack just a bit, Mrs. Ledford. When you first heard these bangs, these gunshots that sounded like firecrackers, were there any lights on inside your house?"

"Inside?" She thought about it, her eyes drifting toward the ceiling. "Yes, in both the living room and in the kitchen. Both those lights were on."

"And to refresh the jury's memory, the kitchen window is the window you went to after hearing the gunshots, right?"

"Yes, the kitchen window. That's correct."

I pretended as though I needed to consider my next question before asking it. Frankly, I wanted this witness to think

I was dumb. I wanted her to let her guard down, not to worry about being tricked. If possible, I would have liked her to feel sorry for me, the ignoramus that I was.

"Mrs. Ledford, did you shut the kitchen light off before you went to the kitchen window to look outside?"

"No, I didn't."

"Weren't you afraid?" I said gently.

"I guess I didn't really think about it."

I nodded to her as though I understood. "Maybe because you thought the sounds were nothing but firecrackers?"

"Yes, I suppose that could be the reason."

I scratched at my scalp, a puzzled look across my face. "Just so that we're sure, Mrs. Ledford, if you were mistaken about the nature of the sound, could you possibly be mistaken about how many shots you heard?"

The witness shook her head. "I don't think so, no."

"Though you did testify that the shots came one right after the other, correct? Could it as well have been three shots fired consecutively, one right after the other, as opposed to just the two?"

She scrunched up her face. "No, I'm pretty sure it was just the two."

I don't think so, I'm pretty sure—it was enough ammunition for my closing, at least for now.

"Immediately after looking out your kitchen window, you dialed 911 from your kitchen phone, correct?"

"I certainly did."

"Please remind us what you told the Emergency Services operator, Mrs. Ledford."

"I told the operator that I heard something that sounded

like firecrackers, and that I ran to my window and saw an obese man running like the wind down the street."

"During that telephone call, you never mentioned how many sounds you heard, did you?"

"No."

"You never mentioned the number two, correct?"

"Or any other number," she said.

"Because at that point, you still didn't know it *was* gunfire that you heard, isn't that right?"

"That's right, I guess."

"Understandably, you thought it was firecrackers, right?"

"Right."

"Firecrackers are fairly common in Hawaii, aren't they, Mrs. Ledford?"

"Yeah, sure, the kids set them off all the time."

"And firecrackers are fairly easy to obtain here in Hawaii, aren't they?"

"Too easy," she conceded. "The Honolulu City Council didn't pass a ban until a couple years ago. I know because I went to the public hearings. But the kids had plenty of time to hoard the firecrackers before the ban went into effect. They still stick those M-80 things into mailboxes all the time in Pearl City. Everywhere else on the island, too, I'd bet."

"And you had called 911 before when children set off firecrackers along your street, hadn't you?"

"Well, they could set our damn houses on fire, so yeah, sure."

I walked over to the defense table and took a long sip of ice water.

When I returned to the podium, I said, "You testified earlier,

Mrs. Ledford, that while you were on the phone with Emergency Services, you looked out your window a second time, correct?"

"Correct."

"Was your kitchen light still on?"

"Yes. I can't walk around in the dark. I'll fall and break my hip."

"And the kitchen curtains, you testified, were open?"

"Yes, they were open. I don't close them until I go to bed."

"You were still unafraid at this point, then?"

"I guess."

"What did you see when you looked out the window this second time?"

"I saw a man lying in the street."

"What did you say to the 911 operator when you saw this man lying in the street?"

"I screamed, 'Oh, dear God,' and I told the operator what I had seen."

"This man you saw lying on the ground, did you describe him for the operator?"

"No."

"Did the operator ask for a description?"

"She asked me a few questions, like, 'Is he moving?' And I told her I couldn't tell."

"Could you have described the man to the operator if she'd asked you to?"

"I don't know, not really, I guess."

"Could you have told her if he were white or black or Hispanic or Asian or something else?"

"No, not at the time," she said. "Later I learned he was white."

"Could you have told her if he was heavy or thin?"

"No."

"Could you have told her if he had facial hair?"

"No."

"How far was this man from your window, Mrs. Ledford?"

"I'd guess about a hundred feet."

"And he was just lying there and yet you couldn't describe him?"

"That's what I just said. I *couldn't* describe him."

"Maybe part of the reason was that the street was dark?"

"Very dark. One of the streetlights has been out for six months already."

"And your kitchen light was on, that couldn't have helped, right? It creates somewhat of a mirror effect with the window."

"That's right."

"Remind the jury to what you testified earlier—how far away was the man you saw 'running like the wind' away from the scene?"

She hesitated, suddenly upset with herself. "About thirty yards, I think I said."

"So, in other words, about ninety feet?"

"Yes."

"Yet you testified earlier that you got a perfect look at him. Under the same conditions—it was dark, your kitchen lights were on. Yet you were able to point at my client today and say, 'That is the man I saw,' correct?"

"That's correct," she said meekly. "Your client has a very distinctive feature."

"And what feature is that?"

"He's obese."

I let her words hang in the air before I continued, "What steps did you take after you saw the man lying in the street?"

"I closed my kitchen curtains and shut all the lights."

"Because by then you were scared, right? By then you realized you weren't dealing with an M-80 in the mailbox but rather something much more serious."

"That's right. I was scared then."

"How long after you closed the kitchen curtains and turned off the lights did the police arrive at the scene?"

"Not long at all. Almost immediately."

"And how long after the police arrived at the scene did they come to your door?"

"Again, almost immediately."

"Did the police ask you what you witnessed?"

"Yes, of course."

"What did you tell them?"

"I told them that I heard gunshots and—"

"But that wasn't the truth, was it, Mrs. Ledford? You actually heard what you thought were firecrackers. You realized they may have been gunshots only *after* you saw the man lying in the street, correct?"

"Um, yeah, that's right."

"So what did you *actually* tell the police about the noises you heard?"

"That I thought I heard firecrackers, but I don't see what you're trying to get at because surely they were gunshots."

"Sure, Mrs. Ledford, what you heard were probably

gunshots, not firecrackers. But you didn't *think* that they were gunshots until after you saw the body, and you didn't *know* that they were gunshots until you were actually told so. Am I right?"

"Yes, that's correct."

"What precisely did the police tell *you*, Mrs. Ledford?"

"That the man lying in the street was an off-duty officer and that he had been shot twice."

"And you hadn't told the police how many gunshots you heard—or that you had heard gunshots at all—up until they told you this, correct?"

"Yes, that's correct."

"Only *after* the police told you that the officer had been shot twice did you say that you heard two shots, right?"

"Well, the police officer said, 'You heard two gunshots, ma'am, correct?' and I said, 'Yes.'"

"Didn't you find it odd that the police were telling *you* how many shots you heard?"

"No, I mean, I don't know. They weren't telling me, they were asking me."

"I see. The police were *asking* you in the same way that I am questioning you, leading you, suggesting to you the answers. So, I ask you, Mrs. Ledford, are you certain that you heard only two shots that night?"

"I believe so, yes."

"Mrs. Ledford, you *believe* in a god, you *believe* in ghosts, in dragons, in werewolves, in Santa Claus, in the tooth fairy. You do not *believe* in the number of gunshots you heard."

"Objection," Dapper Don shouted. "Counsel is making argument."

"Sustained."

"Mrs. Ledford, the shots you heard were fired in rapid succession, yes?"

"Yes."

"And you had never heard gunshots before in your entire life, correct?"

"Correct."

"So *three* gunshots may have possibly been fired that night, isn't that right?"

"It's possible, yes. But the police only found two bullets."

"Or so they would have *us* believe, Mrs. Ledford."

I withdrew that last statement before Dapper Don could complete his objection.

CHAPTER 46

After court, I picked up two cheeseburgers at Cheeseburger in Paradise in Waikiki and drove to Audra's home in Ewa. We ate in silence at her dining room table, then she offered me a gin and tonic.

"What, no wine?"

She didn't smile. She poured me a Bombay Sapphire and tonic and set it on the table. "So how's your case going?"

"The state put on its first witness today, a seventy-two—"

"No, I mean *your* case. The prostitution charges."

It was my turn to not smile. "You know it's bullshit. I had no idea I was walking into a rub-and-tug. I went in for a massage to try to thwart the constant pain in the back of my neck."

Audra shrugged. "Have you spoken to the prosecutor?"

"Of course not. Why would I do that?"

"It's your first offense. They'll probably offer you a plea to a petty misdemeanor and slap you with a five-hundred-dollar fine."

"It's *already* a petty misdemeanor. But that's beside the point. I'm not pleading guilty to anything. I didn't *do* anything."

"What do you say to your clients when they tell you that?"

I almost told her that my clients were liars, that the truth was irrelevant, that trials were all about what could be proved. In my head, a thousand voices seemed to shout at me all at once, each of them protesting their innocence, just as I had to Audra a moment before.

"Look," I said, massaging my temples, "can we talk about something else?"

"Sure. What do you want to talk about?"

"You."

"What about me?"

"When you return to work, are you going back to the US Attorney's Office?"

"Of course, why wouldn't I?"

I shrugged. I wasn't sure why I asked. What would have possibly changed her in the past two months? Did I think she was suddenly going to switch sides and ask to join my firm as an associate?

"Do you plan on staying in Hawaii?" I said.

"Yeah. How about you?"

I took a pull off my drink. "How about me, what?"

"Are you staying in Hawaii after Turi's trial?"

"No," I said, though I hadn't given the matter much thought in recent weeks. But then, I'd made my decision to leave Hono-lulu when I decided to expose its entire police department, hadn't I? I couldn't stay here in the islands. Not if I wanted to live. Bullets are bad for my health.

"They finally broke ground on Water Landings," she said after a few moments of awkward silence.

"Congratulations," I said, my mind flashing on the brochure still sitting at home on my kitchen counter. "No more protesters?"

"Some. But most of them moved up to the North Shore. That's where the next big fight is taking place."

"The Waimea Valley project," I said, leaning back. "Pamela Omphrey told me that if the governor caved on that issue and allowed development to go forward, she'd divorce him."

Audra shrugged. "He may not be in office long enough to cave."

I frowned. The governor remained seven points ahead with less than a month to go before the election. Of course, you couldn't script October. Not in baseball, and certainly not in politics.

"What's John Biel's stance on the Waimea Valley project?" I finally said.

"He's generally against any further development on the North Shore, but he's been uncharacteristically quiet on the Waimea Valley project."

"Who's the developer on that project?"

"Who else? T. S. Duran Properties." The name dripped off her tongue like sour milk. Meeting Tommy Duran in person had no doubt diminished some of the excitement surrounding her first home purchase. "So, is Detective Tatupu going to testify at Turi's trial?"

"Not unless I can prove the corruption at the department independently. Then I have a shot at him. He won't bury the HPD himself, but I get the feeling he'd be more than happy to put the final nail in the coffin."

She shook her head as her mouth contorted into a frown. "How are you going to prove that Detective Bristol intended to kill Turi when there's no physical evidence whatsoever to suggest that?"

"By showing the jury where that physical evidence went, and how."

"You're *truly* going to suggest to the jury that the police, one, removed a bullet casing from the scene; two, removed the vehicle that the bullet had lodged into and brainwashed the owner of that vehicle to say that vehicle never existed; and three, destroyed Bristol's service weapon and handed over a false weapon to the defense so that it would look as though Bristol never fired a shot."

I pursed my lips. "Among other things, yes."

"Solely by crossing the lead detective on the case?" she said incredulously.

"That's right."

"And when is this scheduled to happen?"

"Tomorrow morning."

Audra folded her hands and rested her chin on top of them.

"What are you thinking?" I said.

"I'm thinking I might actually leave the house tomorrow morning. This is going to be something to see."

I took a hit off my gin and tonic, thinking about how much I hated gin.

"You wouldn't mind my being there, would you?" she said.

"Just be sure to get to the courthouse early tomorrow morning," I cautioned her as I stood to leave. "Or else you won't get a seat."

CHAPTER 47

The next morning Donovan Watanabe called Detective Ray Irvine to the witness stand. Irvine didn't look like a cop, but then again, neither did Kanoa Bristol. Both were big men with heavy, thuggish faces, both in their late thirties, though either could easily have passed for fifty. I supposed they didn't look like cops because they weren't cops, not really. Hell, knowing what I did, I should have been surprised that they still looked human.

On direct examination Dapper Don took Ray Irvine through his illustrious career as a Honolulu police officer, from his days patrolling Waikiki on bicycle through his years as part of the Narcotics Intelligence Unit, right up until his promotion to Homicide earlier this year. What wasn't mentioned was that Irvine was only promoted to Homicide after John Tatupu was transferred to Auto Theft, following the press conference held on behalf of the governor by yours truly.

Once Irvine's credentials were exhausted, Dapper Don led him through the crime scene as Irvine purportedly found it.

The body of fellow officer Detective Kanoa Bristol was discovered immediately upon arrival. Irvine himself checked his longtime friend for a pulse. But it was too late. Two bullets had struck Bristol, one in the upper left part of the chest, the other in the throat. The first bullet had lodged into Bristol's Kevlar vest, the second went out through the back of Bristol's neck.

"I immediately instructed my team to seal off the area," Irvine testified. "Once that was accomplished, we immediately began the investigation."

"What was the first step you took with respect to this investigation?" Dapper Don said in his usual cerebral tone.

"I made a preliminary survey of the crime scene."

"And what did you discover during that preliminary survey of the crime scene?"

"Using a flashlight, I found two bullet casings approximately twenty-five feet away from Detective Bristol's body."

"Anything else?"

"Not during that preliminary survey, no."

"What was the next step you took in this investigation?" Dapper Don asked.

"Immediately following that preliminary survey, I walked across the street and rang the doorbell of Mrs. Doris Ledford, the woman who had called Emergency Services."

"And did Mrs. Ledford answer the door?"

"Yes, she did."

"What happened next, Detective?"

"Mrs. Ledford invited me inside, and we sat in her living room, where I asked her a series of questions regarding what she heard, what she observed, and what she did in response."

"Were any other officers present inside the house?"

"No, not at that time. It was just me and her."

"What did Mrs. Ledford tell you?"

I objected, claiming the answer called for hearsay, though I knew this testimony wasn't being offered for its truth. I just wanted to remind the jury of that, and fortunately Dapper Don did that for me before Narita could overrule.

Continuing with the witness, Dapper Don asked, "What did you do based on the information Mrs. Ledford provided you?"

"I put out an APB—that's an all-points bulletin—for a man fitting the suspect's description."

"What was the description given?"

"A heavyset, possibly obese, man, possibly of Hawaiian or Samoan descent."

"Briefly moving back to your conversation with Doris Ledford, Detective, did you at any time in the conversation suggest answers to the questions you were asking her?"

"Of course not."

"Did you at any time ask leading questions?"

"No, sir."

"Thank you, Detective." Dapper Don bowed his head in apology. "Now, returning to the crime scene. After issuing the APB, what did you do?"

"I went back outside. By that time, officers were collecting evidence and photographing the crime scene. I then met with the chief medical examiner, Dr. Charlie Tong. Just about two minutes into our conversation, I received a radiocall informing me that a man meeting the suspect's description had been pulled over in an old, black Nissan Pulsar just a few blocks away. I instructed the officer to hold the suspect and informed him I would be there shortly to ask questions and determine whether there was probable cause to make an arrest."

"What happened next?"

"Before I could leave to meet the suspect, an officer at the crime scene informed me he'd made a discovery."

"What was that discovery?"

"A forty-four-caliber Glock found under a sewer grate on the far curb, approximately seventy feet from the victim's body."

After entering the Glock into evidence, Dapper Don next took Detective Irvine to the scene of the arrest. Irvine stated that Turi Ahina met the description of the suspect provided by Doris Ledford. So Irvine immediately informed Turi Ahina of his Miranda rights, then asked Turi what he was doing in the vicinity. Turi refused to answer any questions and asked for his lawyer, Mr. Kevin Corvelli. Turi was cuffed and placed in the backseat of a patrol car. Irvine then conducted a search of the Nissan, wherein he discovered an envelope filled with cash. Five thousand dollars to be exact.

When I reached the podium to cross-examine Detective Ray Irvine, I suddenly froze like a fly on a windshield in the middle of winter in upstate New York. The only weapons I had to break this dirty cop to pieces were my words. No physical evidence, no corroborating witnesses. It would be like attacking a tank with stones, like killing a man using a water gun filled with nothing but water. I glanced over my shoulder at Audra and remembered her words from last night, her incredulity. Then the double doors to the courtroom swung open, and

John Tatupu stepped inside. I swelled with confidence again as he nodded in my direction.

Dapper Don rose from his spot at the prosecution table when he saw Tatupu enter the courtroom. Tatupu was on my witness list, and at Dapper Don's request, Narita would have ordered Tatupu excluded from the courtroom so that he couldn't hear the testimony of other witnesses. Strategically, it would have been the smart move, even if Tatupu didn't listen to, or later offer, a single word of testimony. Just by being present in the courtroom Tatupu would serve as a silent witness, unnerving Ray Irvine on the stand. But Dapper Don had known Tatupu too long, worked with him on too many cases, knew that Tatupu was as honorable a cop as any he would ever meet. So instead of objecting, Dapper Don sat back down and waited for me to proceed.

"Detective Irvine," I said without greeting him, "prior to your recent transfer to the Homicide division, you were a member of the Narcotics Intelligence Unit, or NIU, were you not?"

"I was. For nine years."

I hesitated. By merely mentioning a single name I was about to open a door that could not be closed. Once I asked the next question, Donovan Watanabe could have a field day on redirect, asking Irvine questions about Turi Ahina's criminal past that could never have otherwise been asked. My next query was the quintessential double-edged sword.

"During those nine years, Detective, were you involved in an ongoing investigation into the operations of a criminal drug syndicate known as the Masonet Organization, so named for the head of that organization, Orlando Masonet?"

"Objection, Your Honor," Dapper Don said from his seat. "Exceeds the scope of direct."

"Judge," I countered, "Mr. Watanabe had Detective Irvine detail his time in the Narcotics Intelligence Unit. I am merely asking the detective about one specific investigation."

Narita took his time making a decision. "I'll allow it."

On the stand, Irvine swallowed visibly. "Yes, I was involved in the investigation into the Masonet Organization."

"How long were you involved in that investigation?"

"All nine years of my service with the NIU."

"And in those nine years, Detective, were any arrests made in connection with that investigation?"

"There were numerous arrests made, yes."

"Approximately how many members of the Masonet Organization were arrested during your involvement in that investigation?"

Irvine shifted on the witness stand. "It's hard to say. When we conduct a raid on a meth lab based on, say, an anonymous tip, we don't always know who is at the top of the food chain. It may be Masonet, it may be someone else entirely. The individuals we arrest aren't always forthcoming. But if I had to venture a guess, I would say dozens. We arrested dozens of members of the Masonet Organization over those nine years. Possibly hundreds."

"So, what you are saying, Detective, is that during your nine years as part of the Narcotics Intelligence Unit, dozens, possibly hundreds, of Masonet Organization members were arrested, yet the syndicate itself continued to operate illegally. How is that?"

Dapper Don objected to the question, but Narita overruled him.

"Most of the arrests we made were of small-time dealers. We were unable to penetrate the upper echelon of the Masonet Organization. Partly because the NIU was poorly funded; we didn't have the money or manpower to conduct the surveillance an adequate investigation required. And partly because of an apparent code of silence among the organization's members. The suspects we interrogated either immediately clammed up and asked for their lawyer or insisted that they knew nothing about the organization and were only doing their job, just as a Wal-Mart cashier may know nothing about the management of the corporation beyond their individual store. We also suspect that members of the Masonet Organization are reluctant to talk for fear of retribution."

"Members of the Masonet Organization, you're saying, are quite possibly afraid that they might be executed if they reveal information to authorities or testify against other members of the organization, correct?"

"That's what we suspect, yes."

"To your knowledge, has Orlando Masonet himself ever been arrested here in the state of Hawaii?"

"He has never been arrested here, no."

"During the course of your investigation into the Masonet Organization, Detective, did you ever become aware of the existence of a clandestine methamphetamine superlab in Waialua, known to some as the Tiki Room?"

"Yes, I became aware of the lab shortly before my transfer from NIU to Homicide."

"Did the Narcotics Intelligence Unit ever formulate plans to conduct a raid on that lab?"

"Yes, we did. Following several days of surveillance."

"And was a raid in fact conducted on the Tiki Room by the Honolulu Police Department?"

"No, one was not."

"Why not?"

"Because the US Drug Enforcement Administration beat us to the punch."

"To your knowledge," I said, "was the NIU or anyone at HPD made aware of the plans for the federal raid on the Tiki Room prior to the DEA's raid being conducted?"

"No, we were not informed."

"Isn't that unusual, Detective? Isn't it customary for federal and state law enforcement agencies to combine their efforts and intelligence to conduct such raids together?"

"That's been my experience."

"Was there any effort made by the DEA to form a joint task force with the NIU?"

"Not to my knowledge, no."

I feigned surprise. "Despite the lengthy investigation of the Masonet Organization by the NIU, there was no request from the feds for information or intelligence before the DEA conducted this dangerous raid in Waialua?"

"No, there was not."

"Why do you suppose that is, Detective?"

Dapper Don rose to his feet. "Objection, Your Honor. Calls for speculation."

"Sustained," Narita said.

"Could it be, Detective," I said, slightly raising my pitch, "that the Honolulu Police Department was not informed of the DEA's plans for this raid on the Tiki Room because federal agents feared that members of the HPD, specifically the Narcotics Intelligence Unit, of which you and Detective Kanoa Bristol were a part, would tip the Masonet Organization off as to the raid, thereby placing the lives of federal agents in further jeopardy?"

"Same objection!" Dapper Don was on his feet again, eyes narrowed, teeth clenched. "Your Honor—"

"The objection is sustained," Narita said. "Mr. Corvelli, tread carefully."

"Of course, Your Honor." I stepped back from the podium, gathered my courage. "Detective, at some point after the DEA raid on the Tiki Room was conducted, did you become aware of the raid?"

"Yes, later the same day."

"And were you made aware that individuals suspected to be members of the Masonet Organization were arrested by the DEA during that raid?"

"That's correct."

"And was one of the suspects arrested during the raid of the Tiki Room the defendant in this case, Mr. Turi Ahina?"

"Yes, that's correct."

"Did you discuss the arrest of Turi Ahina or any of the other suspects apprehended at the Tiki Room with any other member of the Narcotics Intelligence Unit in the days immediately following the raid?"

Irvine hesitated. "Maybe just briefly."

"Did you discuss the arrests with Detective Kanoa Bristol?"

Irvine shook his head. "Not that I recall."

"At any time, did Detective Bristol convey any fear regarding the arrest of Turi Ahina by the DEA?"

"I don't quite understand your question."

"Well then," I said, "did you yourself experience any fear regarding the arrest of Turi Ahina by the federal government?"

"Of course not. Why would I?"

I stepped in front of the podium and spoke clearly so that every member of the jury could follow my words.

"Well, Detective, let me put it this way. Did you at any time fear that Turi Ahina would cooperate with federal authorities and reveal the NIU's association with the Masonet Organization, and the HPD's ongoing protection scheme that permitted Orlando Masonet and his syndicate to continue to act with impunity in these islands?"

"*Objection*," Dapper Don roared. "Assumes facts not in evidence."

"Sustained!" Narita shot at me. "Counselor, you've been warned."

"Detective," I said without pause, "did you personally ever accept money from Orlando Masonet or his organization in return for protection and intelligence, such as tips on when and where raids would be conducted?"

"*Objection!* Argumentative," Dapper Don said, still standing from his last objection. "Mr. Corvelli is stating conclusions and asking the witness to agree with him."

"I'm doing no such thing, Your Honor."

"The objection is sustained," Narita said. "Mr. Corvelli, if you wish to avoid a contempt citation, you will cease what you are doing *right now*."

"Isn't it true, Detective, that following Turi Ahina's arrest by the DEA and subsequent release on bail, members of the Narcotics Intelligence Unit, including you and Kanoa Bristol, fearful that Mr. Ahina would cooperate with federal authorities, *conspired* with the Masonet Organization to *assassinate* Turi Ahina?"

"*Objection!*"

"Sustained!" Narita rapped his gavel. "Mr. Corvelli, you are now in contempt of this Court."

I didn't relent. *Let Narita throw me in fucking jail.*

"Isn't it true, Detective, that Kanoa Bristol was chosen to *be* that assassin? That he attempted to *execute* Turi Ahina that evening in Pearl City, and that you and your team did everything in your power *to cover it up?*"

A rap of the gavel, an eruption in the courtroom, then Narita called for a recess and ordered, "All lawyers to my chambers. *Now.*"

CHAPTER 48

I wasn't placed under arrest. And Watanabe's appeal for a mistrial was denied. I wrote a check for my contempt citation and assured Judge Narita that I would back up every allegation I'd made with hard evidence and corroborating testimony. In other words, I lied. Not that it mattered. An hour later we resumed proceedings and I took another crack at cracking Detective Irvine. I asked whether he or any of his team removed evidence from the Pearl City crime scene, specifically a bullet casing from Detective Bristol's service weapon. I asked whether he or any of his team had discovered a bullet in the bumper of a navy-blue Honda Civic parked at the end of the cul-de-sac. I asked whether he or any of his team had the Honda Civic removed from Kolohe Street, whether the owner of that Civic, Max Guffman, was bribed or otherwise coerced to say that the Civic never existed. I asked whether he or any of his team switched out Bristol's service weapon for another so that it appeared that Bristol never fired a shot. I asked him why in his experience

Detective Kanoa Brostol would have been wearing a Kevlar vest while off duty at that time of night.

And I got nowhere. Detective Ray Irvine proved much more slippery than I ever anticipated.

Later, after Narita adjourned for the day, Jake and I sat in the Lawyers Room at the courthouse.

"Mind taking the state's ballistics expert tomorrow?" I said, loosening my tie. "I think this judge and jury have seen enough of me for a while."

"I'll handle Denis Ritchie, son. I'll handle Charlie Tong, too. ME's not going to have much to add in this case."

It was late, and we were the only two lawyers in the room. "So what did you think?" I said.

"It was either brilliant or it was a disaster. Maybe both."

I leaned back in the plastic chair, took a sip from a warm can of Diet Pepsi. "Wouldn't be my first brilliant disaster."

"You need John Tatupu. And you need one of the feds."

"The feds will deny everything. All I have is one shitty Queen for a Day agreement signed by Boyd. Besides, we don't know that they have anything besides what Tatupu told them. And even that will be struck down as hearsay."

"Maybe the feds have conducted more of an investigation than we think. Maybe they have photos and wiretaps. For all we know, they may be waiting for this trial to be over to indict half the department."

I thought about it. I thought about what Tatupu had told me at Chinaman's Hat, that the feds had hinted that a dirty cop had recently decided to come clean and cooperate. If there *was* an ongoing investigation into the HPD's corruption, it wouldn't be the DEA doing the investigating. It would be the FBI.

"Slauson," I said aloud.

"You might be able to make a trade," Jake said.

I was thinking the same thing. "The location of Lok Sun for Slauson's testimony at Turi's trial."

"Problem is, soon as Slauson knows that you know where Lok Sun is, he doesn't have to bargain. He can simply arrest you for obstruction of justice and haul you before Platz, who will lock you up until you talk. Platz will probably have you share a cell with SoSo."

I had been receiving letters from SoSo just about every other day since mid-August. SoSo blamed me for the additional fifteen years Justice Platz slapped him with at his sentencing. It was my fault, SoSo said, because I should have warned him that insulting the judge could have negative ramifications. At the conclusion of each letter, SoSo promised that he would visit me at my home the very day he left prison. SoSo had a new lawyer working on his appeal, and his lawyer was confident that his conviction and/or sentencing would soon be overturned and SoSo would be a free man. Luckily for me, SoSo's new lawyer was Mickey Fallon, one of the dumbest attorneys ever to be spit out of an American law school. And that was truly saying something.

"By the same token," I said, "if I can prove Slauson has information relevant to Turi's trial, I can subpoena him."

"Sounds like a Mexican standoff," Jake said. "Only there's no way you can prove Slauson has information without having someone on the inside. And I highly doubt Flan can pull off impersonating a federal agent."

"I don't necessarily need an agent. Just a member of the Justice Department."

"A lawyer?"

"A lawyer," I said.

"She'll never go for it."

Jake was right, but then again, you never know until you try.

"Not a chance," she said before I could even finish the question.

We were seated in the back of Big City Diner at Ward Center, out of earshot of any other patrons. We had just seen the latest Seth Rogen movie, and until this point in the evening she'd been in a great mood.

"Just hear me out," I said. "All I need to know is whether there is an official investigation into corruption at the Honolulu Police Department, and if so, what evidence the feds have."

"What am I supposed to do? Walk into FBI headquarters, flash my badge, and demand to see the file? It doesn't work that way, Kevin, and you know it."

"I know exactly how it works, Audra, and all I'm asking you to do is have a frank discussion with Special Agent Slauson. Before Turi was arrested for shooting Bristol, you told me the feds knew everything—about the protection, missing evidence, police couriers, solicitation of sex. You even implied they knew about cops performing Masonet's wet work."

"It was all rumor and conjecture, Kevin. I haven't seen a shred of physical evidence."

"That doesn't mean there isn't any. If Tatupu squawked and the feds did nothing, they'd be derelict in their duty, and Slauson doesn't seem like the type of guy who sits on his ass and waits for something worse to happen."

"But if Slauson didn't engage the US Attorney's Office, that means the investigation is ongoing, and there is no way he or any other agent is going to speak to me about an investigation that's still pending."

"He will if you have something to offer him."

She stared at me for a moment, then said, "How dare you, Kevin."

I held up my hand. "Easy. Not sex. I'm talking about the location of Lok Sun."

Her eyes fell on the half-eaten portobello-mushroom sandwich in front of her.

I knew right away. *"Fuck,"* I muttered under my breath, looking down at my own empty plate. "You've already told him, haven't you?"

"What choice did I have?"

"I trusted you."

"I'm a prosecutor."

"So what are they doing?"

"They're watching him, just like you. You know how the feds work. They don't move in until they have enough evidence for a conviction. Right now, all they have is the Pharmacist's MO and Zhi Zhu's testimony."

"They arrested Zhi Zhu?"

"It was all very quiet. Zhu's back on the street as though nothing's ever happened. And if Lok Sun contacts him again for more strychnine, he's agreed to wear a wire."

"When are the feds moving in?"

"They're in no hurry," she said. "As long as they know where Lok Sun is, he can't harm anybody."

"And what about whoever hired him to murder Oksana Sutin?"

"Slauson is certain it's the governor, and he knows, win or lose the election, Omphrey isn't going anywhere."

"Let me guess," I said. "Slauson is waiting, hoping Omphrey wins reelection before the FBI takes him down. Not only will it be a bigger story, but the lieutenant governor will take Omphrey's seat and keep the party of law enforcement in office."

"This *isn't* political, Kevin."

I smirked. "Don't be naïve. Everything is political."

CHAPTER 49

"Call your first witness, Mr. Corvelli."

"The defense calls Mindy Iokepa."

Turi Ahina suddenly grabbed my left arm and pulled me back into my seat. "What the fuck you doin', Mistah C?"

I pried his thick fingers from my suit jacket. "Saving your ass."

Jake distracted Turi as I rose and stepped over to the podium. Meanwhile, Flan escorted Mindy Iokepa through the double doors in the rear of the courtroom, up the aisle, and helped her onto the witness stand.

"Good morning, Miss Iokepa," I said. "Thank you for being here today."

She smiled at me and nodded, then glanced over at Turi and mouthed, *It's okay.*

"May I call you Mindy?" I said.

"Of course you may."

"Mindy, would you please tell us your relation to Turi Ahina?"

After the slightest hesitation she said, "Turi is my daughter's father."

I glanced back at Turi, whose cheeks were rosy, his good eye welling up with tears. This was precisely what I wanted from him today, raw emotion. Of course, that wasn't why I'd never told him I planned on putting Mindy Iokepa on the stand. He would never have allowed me to if I had. He might well have chosen to fire me or, worse, pled guilty. That was how far Turi would have gone to protect the mother of his child, the daughter of a state senator running for reelection.

"And your own father is?" I asked.

"Dave Iokepa. He is the state senator for District Sixteen."

"And your father is up for reelection this November?"

"Objection," Dapper Don said calmly. "Leading."

Narita chuckled. "That is no secret, Mr. Watanabe. I am sure all of us have seen a few yard signs in recent weeks." He turned to the witness. "You may answer the question."

"Yes, my father is up for reelection in November."

I moved to the defense table and picked up an envelope. From the envelope I removed an eight-by-eleven-inch, green page, with the heading "Certificate of Live Birth."

"I would like this document marked as Defendant's Exhibit H," I said.

The clerk marked the page with a removable sticker then handed it back to me, while Jake provided original certified copies to the Court and Donovan Watanabe.

"May I approach the witness, Your Honor?"

"You may."

"Mindy, I'm going to show you a document marked as

Defendant's Exhibit H, and I would like you to tell me if you recognize it."

"I do," she said as soon as I handed it to her.

"What is this document?"

"It's our baby's birth certificate."

"What's your child's name, as it is listed on the birth certificate?"

"Ema Leilani Iokepa."

"A beautiful name," I said, smiling.

Ema Iokepa's birth certificate proved easier to get than Barack Obama's. All I needed was the father's signature on a letter authorizing the release of the certificate to me. I snuck the authorization letter into a bunch of forms I had Turi sign. He never read anything I gave him to sign, not even the Queen for a Day agreement, which could easily have affected the rest of his life. So what the hell was one more? I figured. I made a photocopy of his driver's license. I included the photocopy, along with the signed authorization letter, my own letter of request, and a check for $10, made payable to the state Department of Health. I sent the letter off and waited. If I received a phone call from the Department of Health telling me I had the wrong dad, nothing lost, nothing gained. But I didn't receive such a call. Instead, a few days after I mailed the request, I received a certified copy of Ema Iokepa's birth certificate.

"What name is listed as the mother's name on the birth certificate?" I asked.

"Mine. Mindy Iokepa."

"And what name is listed as the father's name?"

"Turi Ahina."

"Thank you." I took the birth certificate back from the witness and entered it into evidence, then asked, "How old is Ema?"

"She'll be sixteen months on Election Day."

"Is there any court order granting Turi Ahina visitation rights?"

"No, but Turi knows he's welcome to visit with Ema anytime he likes. He's a wonderful father."

Nice touch. "Is there any court order granting you child support from Turi Ahina?"

"No, there is not. But Turi gives me money to help raise Ema every month. I never once had to ask him for a penny."

"How much money does Turi Ahina provide you every month to help raise Ema?"

"Five thousand dollars."

I waited while the number echoed through the courtroom, then said, "How does he pay you this five thousand dollars? By check?"

"Always in cash."

"On the evening of July twenty-third of this year, did you speak with Turi Ahina?"

"I did."

"What was that conversation about?"

"He simply told me he'd drop by my home with the envelope at around eleven o'clock."

"Where do you live?"

Mindy supplied her address on Kolohe Street, and I asked her where that was in relation to the shooting.

"The shooting happened just a few doors down from my house."

"Did Turi ever deliver the envelope that night?"

"He did not."

I switched gears. I was about to elicit testimony that would corroborate the defense theory that Detective Kanoa Bristol fired at Turi first. Of course, now that I had established Mindy's relationship with Turi, this particular testimony would be taken by the jury with a grain of salt. Clearly, as a witness, Mindy Iokepa was biased.

"Did you hear the gunshots fired at approximately eleven o'clock on that evening Turi was supposed to visit you, the night of July twenty-third?"

Mindy started tearing up on the stand. "I did."

"Did you answer when the police arrived and knocked on your door?"

"They never knocked on my door."

"Are you sure?"

"I'm positive."

"Had the police shown up at your door and asked you whether you had heard gunshots, what would you have told them?"

"I would have told them that I had."

"Think carefully, Mindy. How many gunshots did you hear that evening?"

"I heard three gunshots, one right after the other after the other."

I paused to allow her words to sink in. Then I continued, "Do you know a man named Max Guffman?"

"Barely. But he's my neighbor."

I asked her to identify where he lived in relation to her

house. Once she supplied the answer, I asked about the navy
Honda Civic with the Jesus fish and the KEIKI ON BOARD sticker.

"I'd seen the car plenty of times, yes. But never again after
the shooting."

Although we learned that Max Guffman did indeed hail
from Washington State, the Washington State Department of
Licensing informed us that no vehicles were currently registered under his name. Without the number of the license plate
the defense would have to rely on the testimony of Mindy Iokepa and Max Guffman himself, along with the single photograph downloaded from Brian Haak's Facebook account.

"Did one of my investigators, a Mr. Ryan Flanagan, ever
come by your house and ask you about seeing this navy Honda
Civic?"

"Yes."

"What did you tell him?"

"That I'd never seen it before."

"You lied?"

"Yes."

"Why did you lie?"

"Because I was scared. Scared for my baby."

"What about Turi?"

"I knew he didn't want me to say anything or else he
would've told you and you would've come looking for me. He
told me before the shooting that he trusts you with his life."

I tried not to get choked up at the podium. I cleared my
throat and asked, "Is there any other reason you didn't come
forward?"

"My father. I knew that if it came out that Turi was Ema's

father, he'd lose the election because of all the press attention Turi was getting."

"But when I came to you with Ema's birth certificate, you changed your mind. Why?"

She smiled at Turi while wiping a tear from her eye. "You told me I had no choice."

CHAPTER 50

The next day, a Saturday, I called the Honolulu Police Department and reported my Jeep stolen from in front of my office building. Twenty minutes later Detective John Tatupu arrived on South King Street to take my statement. Scott Damiano greeted him downstairs and led him up to my office.

"What the hell is this?" Tatupu said as soon as he stepped into reception.

"Sorry, John," I said. "But I didn't feel like taking a swim to Chinaman's Hat tonight."

Once Scott left, Tatupu and I stepped into the conference room. We sat next to each other, a copy of the Hawaii Penal Code resting on the table between us.

"The answer is no," he said before I asked. "I can't testify. Maybe you can pack up and leave these islands after the trial, but I can't. I have a family to think about."

"You stood up in the face of corruption during the last

federal probe, when Kamakana sued the department. Why won't you stand up now?"

"Things were different then, Counselor. Then if a cop stood up, he risked getting shunned, maybe a broken leg. But now . . ." Tatupu shook his head. "They won't just kill me. They'll kill my family. They'll kill my friends."

I sat back in my chair and regarded him with a look of disdain. I respected John Tatupu, respected him more than any other cop I'd ever met, here or back East. He was one of the few cops I feared facing on the witness stand. During the Gianforte murder trial, I'd treated him with kid gloves for fear that the jury would turn on me if I hammered away at his experience. During the Simms arson trial, I'd counted on his doing the right thing, telling the truth, even if it burned the prosecutor, Luke Maddox. And he had.

"What good is being a good cop if you're afraid to take on the dirty ones?"

Tatupu leaned forward till he was inches from my face. "Don't you try to guilt me, Corvelli. Remember, I *know* you. I *know* what you are. You think this is a fucking game."

A fierce anger immediately swelled within me. The anger had been building, an anger fueled by dirty cops, by political corruption, by self-righteous sons of bitches who looked down on me because of what I did for a living.

"A *game?*" I said, rising from my seat. I ripped open my collared shirt, buttons arching across the room, a few skittering onto the table, making a sound like loose change. I pointed to the upper-right section of my abdomen. "Does this scar look like something I got playing a fucking *game,* Detective?"

Tatupu stared up at me silently.

My chest heaved. "Nikki Kapua's locked away in a mainland prison. Erin Simms is *dead*. That's my life. That's what comes with the business I've chosen. I could have walked away from the law after Brandon Glenn. After Nikki. After Erin. But I didn't. Because there's too many fucking injustices in this world. Because people like you, John, make too many fucking mistakes."

I turned away from him. "Don't make another one," I practically begged. "Don't let an innocent man spend the rest of his life in prison for killing a cop who should've never been on the streets to begin with." I kept my back to him, unable to face him.

"If I had the power to stop this, I would," Tatupu said calmly. "But I don't. The jury will never believe one man's word against an entire department's. I did my job, Corvelli. I went to the feds. I told them the NIU was accepting protection money from Masonet. I told them there were cops acting as couriers between here and Mexico. I told them everyone from the chief on down was getting his dick sucked in exchange for looking the other way when they could have made a bust. I told them that money and drugs and guns went missing from the evidence locker every month. I told them the NIU acted more like a hit squad than a unit of the police department, taking out witnesses and competing gang members as if they were the goddamn Sicilian Mafia. I told them *everything*."

I finally turned to face him.

Tatupu jumped out of his seat. "So I'm sorry, Corvelli, if what I've done isn't enough for you or your client. Because it's enough to clear my conscience."

"What about the dirty cop the feds told you might cooperate? Do you have any idea who he is?"

Tatupu shook his head. "I told you, Counselor, I don't even know if he really exists. The feds knew I couldn't keep talking unless they found someone to back me up. For all I know, this dirty cop was no more than a figment of their imagination."

We stared at each other in silence. Here was an opportunity for a cop and a defense attorney to team up on the side of right, to seek the truth through a cloud of corruption. And John Tatupu was content to allow that opportunity to pass us by. But I wasn't.

I had made plenty of mistakes in my ten years as a criminal attorney. Back in New York, I'd put my career before my clients. I'd determined retainers based solely on how much my clients could pay. I'd needlessly adjourned cases in order to collect additional fees. I'd advised clients to plead guilty in cases I knew I could win. I'd taken shortcuts, manipulated witnesses, pointed my finger at innocent people solely to hear the words *not guilty*. There is a fine line between being a criminal lawyer and being a criminal. Sometimes it was easy to decide the next course of action, to determine what was wrong from what was right. Other times, such as now, it was nearly impossible.

Detective John Tatupu finally turned from me and opened the conference room door.

"Be ready," I said calmly to his back. "Because I'm going to call you to testify on Monday."

"Don't," he said, looking back at me from the doorframe. "You'll be making a big strategic mistake, Corvelli. One you might not be able to come back from with this jury."

I lifted the Hawaii Penal Code off the table and held it up in front of him.

"The only mistake," I said, holding the heavy book, "would be you not telling the jury the truth on Monday."

I opened the hollowed-out code book and allowed him a glance at the running microcassette recorder inside.

"Because, Detective, I have every goddamn word you just said on tape."

Tatupu took a step toward me, eyes blazing, fingers curling into fists. "So help me, Counselor, if any harm comes to my family, you are going to wish you never even heard of these islands."

CHAPTER 51

I ate four Percocet, then entered the jail, signed in, and asked to see Turi Ahina. During the wait, the pills kicked in, but I didn't feel quite as good as I would have liked. That's how it is with pills. It gets so that the anticipation is more exhilarating than the payoff.

Once Turi and I were safely sealed away from the world, I said, "Lying to me about Mindy Iokepa was a no-no."

Turi shrugged his colossal shoulders. "You know why I did it, Mistah C."

I stared at him. "Makes me wonder though."

"Wonder 'bout what?"

"What else you're lying to me about, Turi."

Turi shook his head, shifted in his seat. He remained quiet for longer than I would have liked. "That's it, Mistah C. I was just trying to protect Mindy and my *keiki*."

In the last twenty-four hours my mind had been working overtime, running through scenarios in which I could truly fuck things up. The possible state prosecution for the murder of Alika Kapua still bothered me. But worse was the thought of harm coming to John Tatupu or a member of his family. After what I had done, that was something I knew I could never come back from, even though my first duty was to my client. Even though Tatupu had no right at all to withhold information that could potentially free an innocent man.

"I am about to put another man's life on the line to save yours, Turi. So I need to know the truth."

"I told you all the truth awready, eh?" he shouted at me. "What you think, Mistah C?"

For a few moments the room fell quiet. I eyed Turi the way I might eye a prospective juror during jury selection. I wanted to read his mind, to know exactly what he was thinking. Whether he was telling me the truth or manipulating me, feeding me lies.

I decided to come right out with it. "I think that maybe Doris Ledford really only heard two shots. I think that maybe there was no third bullet, and no navy Honda Civic with a bullet hole in it."

Turi didn't flinch. His good eye remained locked on my face.

"I think maybe Masonet really did order a hit, only it wasn't on you, it was on Kanoa Bristol. In that case, of course, Kanoa Bristol wouldn't have been the assassin; it would have been the other way around."

Turi still didn't flinch even as I accused him of being a cold-blooded killer.

"And I think maybe that five thousand dollars you had wasn't for Mindy, it was yours. Your payment for assassinating

Kanoa Bristol, a dirty cop who had decided to come clean and corroborate another cop's story."

Turi said nothing, just stared at me with that one good eye, the other still hiding behind a bandage.

"Tell me, Turi, is it just a coincidence that Mindy Iokepa and Karen and Brian Haak are Facebook friends? Or is that how Mindy found this random Honda Civic standing behind Karen's mother and Max Guffman?"

Turi backed his chair away a few feet, the metal legs screeching.

"Tell me, Turi, did you contact Tam after we left his bar in Chinatown? Did you tell him that this whole jet thing was a scam devised by the feds?" I punched the table and said through gritted teeth, "Tell me the *truth*, goddamnit!"

Turi said in a low voice, "The truth is, you paranoid, Mistah C. And I know why, eh? I can see it in your eyes. I seen it at the trial. Before that even. You high, brah. You *always* high. What you on, eh? Oxy? Vicodin? Percocet?"

I suddenly felt smaller than the room we were sitting in. My heart raced, my jaw exercised on its own. "You lied to me about Mindy," I said again, almost in defense of myself.

"Yeah, brah. But not 'bout nothing else, yeah? The rest, it's the demons in your mind tellin' you these things 'bout me. Everything you just said, I don't have the smarts for all that. Maybe some crazy motherfucker like Masonet, eh? But not me. Me, I'm a thug, Mistah C. You, you the one with the mind that works like that. You, Mistah C, you could be a thousand times the criminal I ever was. 'Cause you a million times smarter. And a million times meaner."

———

I spent that entire night sitting up on my mattress in the living room, unable to sleep. I had just accused a man who'd saved my life of an elaborate plot against me. And I'd accused Mindy Iokepa, a helpless single mother caught in a hellish situation, of being in on it.

The sliding-glass door to my lanai remained open, and trade winds blew in from the sea. I was dressed in nothing but boxers, yet I was still sweating. Sweating and trembling and trying to keep my teeth from chattering.

I thought about the governor and whether he could have hired Lok Sun to murder Oksana Sutin. Did Omphrey know she was pregnant? Did he know she was a spy? Either was reason enough for him to off her.

Or was it whoever hired Oksana Sutin to spy on him in the first place? Could it have been his opponent John Biel or someone who worked for his campaign?

Could it have been Pamela Omphrey? After all, she'd admitted at the fundraiser to knowing about the affair.

It wasn't my job to determine a client's guilt or innocence. I wasn't supposed to care. I asked for the truth from my clients only so that I could devise the best strategy to get them acquitted, guilty or not. My objective was supposed to remain the same in every case. Defend my client to the best of my ability. What was I doing, sitting up in the middle of the night, trying to discern truth from fiction?

Not long after I flipped my lights on that morning, I received a call from Jake. "Turn on the television, son."

I stared at the spot in the living room where a television had once been. "Don't have one, Jake."

"Then go to the Internet."

"Why?"

"Because they just pulled a woman's body out of Lake Wilson in Wahiawa this morning. They haven't identified her yet, but the description sounds a hell of a lot like Iryna Kupchenko."

"A lake?"

My head felt dizzy with exhaustion, and the sharp pains rising in my gut did nothing to jerk my mind into motion. If the body was indeed Iryna Kupchenko's, then I was directly responsible for her death. I came close to crying right there on the phone, almost screamed at the top of my lungs. I nearly broke down and begged Jake to take my place in court, to handle Tatupu's direct examination.

But in the end, all I said aloud was "I didn't even know Oahu had any lakes."

CHAPTER 52

Judge Narita gazed out over the gallery and said firmly, "Is there anyone protecting and serving our island today?"

He was referring to the dark blue uniforms overflowing the courtroom. More silent witnesses than I could count, none of them cheering on our side, the side of right.

"This is not Aloha Stadium," Narita continued. "If you would like to support your fallen comrade, you may do so with a select group of representatives, no more than six, I'd say. Having a gallery full of law enforcement may not be grounds for reversal on appeal, but I do believe it hinders the defendant's chance of receiving a fair trial. So before I call the jury in, I would ask that all but six uniformed police officers leave. You have three minutes to decide amongst yourselves which six that will be. If there are more than six officers remaining after those three minutes, I will clear the courtroom. Your three minutes begin now."

Narita rapped the gavel, and behind us, chaos ensued.

I took the unexpected free time to turn to my client. I

leaned toward him and said, "I apologize for my behavior yesterday. Sometimes I take the role of devil's advocate a bit too seriously."

Turi nodded. "No worries, Mistah C." With his good eye, he glanced back toward the gallery, at the dozens of cops, any one of whom would gladly have put a bullet into his skull. "I just ask you one favor, yeah?"

"Anything."

"If I get convicted and go to prison, brah, I need you to take care of Mindy and my *keiki*, eh? Specially if something happen to me on the inside."

I bowed my head. "You can count on it, Turi. But I have a much different outcome in mind."

Fifteen minutes later the jury was seated, and I had called the next defense witness. Detective John Tatupu sat in the witness stand just as he had in my last two homicide trials, only this time he was *my* witness, a witness for the defense.

"Good morning, Detective."

"Counselor."

I didn't waste any time. I walked the detective through his long, winding career with the Honolulu Police Department, slowing only to focus on his years in Homicide and his abrupt transfer earlier this year to Auto Theft.

Then together, cop and defense attorney, we entered the abyss.

Tatupu testified at length to what he had witnessed over the past several years within the department. He had discovered drugs and money recovered from raids missing from the evidence locker. Observed officers within several divisions, including the Narcotics Intelligence Unit, receive envelopes filled with cash from businesspeople and known drug dealers. Overheard plans for off-duty officers to carry contraband to the islands from Mexico and the US mainland. He had seen officers offer prostitutes, drug dealers, even perpetrators of domestic violence, leniency in exchange for sexual favors.

Tatupu testified that he had taken his complaints first to Internal Affairs then to Chief of Police Patrick McClusky but received no satisfaction. He'd been warned by more than one officer to mind his business or risk losing his badge, or worse.

I repeatedly glanced in the direction of the prosecution table. Throughout my direct examination of John Tatupu, Dapper Don had plenty of opportunities to rise and object, on the grounds of hearsay in particular. But instead of rising and offering objections, Dapper Don sat riveted, listening to Tatupu as he set the entire Honolulu Police Department on fire.

"Let's turn specifically to the Narcotics Intelligence Unit," I said. "Did you know Detective Kanoa Bristol personally?"

"I did."

"Did you ever witness Detective Bristol engage in any of the illicit behaviors you mentioned earlier?"

"I did. In May of 2007, I witnessed Detective Bristol accept an envelope filled with what looked like large bills from a known ice dealer in Makaha."

"How did you happen to be in Makaha during that time?"

"I was investigating a fatal stabbing at the apartment complex in which this known drug dealer lived."

"Did you confront Detective Bristol following this transaction?"

"I did not."

"Why not?"

"Because by this time I had already witnessed similar events take place and I had brought these issues to both Internal Affairs and Chief McClusky, and I was essentially told by each to mind my own business and stick to investigating homicides. And I had already been physically threatened by a member of the Narcotics Intelligence Unit."

"You were threatened by whom specifically?"

"Detective Ray Irvine."

Tatupu went on to say that he witnessed Detective Bristol accept cash again in March and December of 2008, July of 2009, and February and November of 2010. In July of 2011, Tatupu witnessed Bristol receiving oral sex from a known prostitute in a parked motor vehicle on Monsarrat Avenue across from the zoo.

When Tatupu said this, Bristol's wife, Dana, stood up, cursed at the witness, and exited the courtroom.

During Tatupu's testimony, I watched the twelve jurors and three alternates. They seemed jaded, and I feared the gravity of what the detective was testifying to wasn't getting through. We had started the trial with raw violence, and now they were hearing about envelopes and blow jobs and Internal Affairs investigations that never happened. I needed to turn the dial, return them to the world of gunshots and bullet holes and dead bodies.

"In your capacity as a detective in the Homicide division," I said, "did you ever investigate the murder of anyone associated with a gang known to compete with the syndicate known as the Masonet Organization?"

"All the time."

Never ask a question you don't already know the answer to, Kevin.

"During any such investigation did you ever suspect members of the Honolulu Police Department, including the officers of the Narcotics Intelligence Unit, to be involved?"

Tatupu took a deep breath, then repeated, "All the time."

At that moment I revered John Tatupu even more for staying on the job all these years. I couldn't begin to imagine how difficult it must have been for him investigating homicides on this island. I instantly forgave him his mistakes in the Gianforte investigation and fully understood his reluctance to testify here at the trial of Turi Ahina. John Tatupu was an extraordinary man, but a man just the same. A man once charged with the impossible task of solving the most heinous of crimes on an island gripped by corruption.

How, I wondered, do you begin to solve murders, how do you begin to control violence, when all the usual suspects wear guns and badges and dark blue uniforms, and every witness you discover is determined to remain deathly silent?

CHAPTER 53

"If they come after me, Corvelli, I come after you."

John Tatupu spoke these words in my ear once he was finally released from the witness stand late in the afternoon.

Once the courtroom cleared out, Jake and I gathered our things, walked down the hallway, and stepped into the empty Lawyers Room.

"Tatupu was right," Jake said immediately. "His testimony alone isn't going to prove enough. At the end of the day the jury might want to pat Turi on the back for shooting Bristol, but they're not going to acquit him of Bristol's murder."

I turned on my cell phone and punched in Audra's number, but the call went straight to voicemail.

"I fucked up," I said, running my hand through my hair, which was damp with sweat. "I should have went with a straight defense. Explained away the five grand in Turi's pocket with Mindy Iokepa, hammered away on the fact that there was no gunshot residue on Turi's hands or clothes, carved up the eyewitness, and brought in a dietitian to explain to the jury how many obese men live on Oahu." I rested my elbows on the folding table and dropped my head in my hands. "I'm a terrible fucking lawyer."

"You're an excellent lawyer who employed a terrible fucking strategy by forgetting that trials aren't about getting to the truth."

Jake was right. Somehow in the months since Erin's suicide I'd grown a conscience with respect to my moves in the courtroom, and it was going to kill my client. What the hell had I been thinking?

"All we have left," I said, "is Max Guffman and our own ballistics expert, who can't really say much of anything at this point unless it's framed in a hypothetical."

"What about putting Turi on the stand?"

"I can't. If I put him on the stand, we have to talk about the gun, and that opens the door to the gun's history and the bullets found in Alika Kapua."

Jake was flipping through his yellow legal pad. "Let's not forget who this trial is really about." He tapped a page where he'd written one name in large letters across the center. "The man who either ordered Kanoa Bristol to execute Turi Ahina or at the very least was the reason behind Bristol's murder attempt."

MASONET

Strangely enough, just seeing the name helped me retain focus. "You're right, Jake. It's all about Masonet. I have to start at the beginning. After the raid on the Tiki Room but before the shooting."

"Where does that put you?"

I hesitated, a rotten feeling filling my gut. "Chinatown," I muttered.

I stared at the page with the single name and thought about my next step: returning to the bar where the feds' plan to capture Masonet went awry. I had to confront the giant, Lian, and Tam himself. Find out who Tam relayed Turi's message to. I had to trace that message all the way up to Masonet himself.

And if Masonet hadn't yet left the island . . .

Maybe he could be captured before Turi's case was given to the jury.

I stared at Jake's page, envisioning myself back in Chinatown with Scott and his Walther.

M A S O N E T .

The letters began to move on the page.

T E N O S A M

10

O

S A M

"Son of a bitch."

Jake looked up from the folding table. "What is it?"

"A number, a letter, and a name."

I jotted them down and slid the legal pad across the table back to Jake, cursing myself for not seeing it sooner.

"So?" he said.

"So that's the code if you want to score a high-priced harlot in Honolulu."

"You mean . . ."

"Yeah. Orlando Masonet is behind the Eastern European sex trade here in the islands."

It made perfect sense. The night of the shooting in Pearl

City, Audra told me the feds suspected that, in addition to the manufacture and sale of ice, Masonet controlled the four G's in the islands: girls, gambling, guns, and ganja.

"What does that mean for Turi?" Jake said.

I thought about it. "Maybe nothing. But what it means for me is that I don't have to go back to a deadly dive bar in Chinatown to try to track down Masonet. What I have to do is head on down to Waikiki and pay a long overdue visit to Gavin Dengler."

CHAPTER 54

Scott Damiano stepped out of the towering Aloha International Hotel on Saratoga Road, walked across the street, and hopped into the passenger seat of my Jeep.

"No problem," he said.

"No problem?" Gavin Dengler lived in the penthouse suite, and to get there you needed a special key for the elevator. That, in my mind, constituted a problem.

But apparently not in Scott's. "Ever hear of Gene 'Piss Pie' Spinelli?"

"The wiseguy who owned a bakery on Long Island?"

"Yeah, him. Know why they called him Piss Pie?"

"I can hazard a guess."

"Right," Scott said. "Anyway, you know how he died?"

"Fell down an elevator shaft in Queens."

"Not so. That's what it said in the papers. See, the fucking feds were trying to get us to talk about it, so they fed that bullshit to the *Post*, hoping one of us would say, 'Whoa, that's not how he died!' on a tapped phone."

A moment of silence as we watched a pair of bikinis cross the street.

"So anyway," Scott said, "Piss Pie didn't fall down no elevator shaft. The whole fucking elevator car went down, twelve floors over the course of a few seconds."

"How do you know?"

Scott shrugged as though I were being obtuse. " 'Cause my brother, Chris, and I rigged the fucking thing."

"Your point?"

"My point is, Chris and I didn't learn how to rig an elevator overnight. We went to elevator school."

"Elevator school?"

"Well, not elevator school, but we took on an apprenticeship, all right? With this company that installed and repaired Alto elevators."

"And the elevator across the street . . . ?"

"It's an Alto."

"So we don't need a key?"

"We don't need a key. I just need a few minutes alone with the elevator."

Scott got his few minutes alone with the elevator when a fire alarm went off across the street. Nothing pulls people away from whatever they're doing like the possibility of witnessing death firsthand. Or at least serious injury. But the alarm's going off was my doing, so in a strange, warped way I felt like a bit of a tease.

Twelve minutes later we were cruising up forty-two floors to the penthouse suite.

"Nice elevator," I said.

"Alto does good work," Scott agreed.

"No music, I like that."

"I disconnected it when I rigged it to work without the key."

"Really. Think you can do that at my office building?"

"No problem."

When we reached floor thirty-nine, Scott started sniffing the air.

"What's wrong?" I said.

"I don't know, maybe it's nothing."

The elevator doors opened right onto the suite, a massive space appointed with the most luxurious of everything, from furniture to appliances to tapestry.

But what Scott sniffed from the elevator wasn't nothing. It was far from nothing. I covered my nose and mouth with my tie to try to help block out the stench. But it wasn't working.

The body on the floor was a bloated green-black, with blood vessels and blisters rising out of its rotting flesh. Most of the dead man's blond hair had retreated to the hardwood, and his nails had vacated the tips of his puffed-up fingers.

"This guy has to have been dead a week," I said, still holding my tie over my nose.

"Don't be so sure. We're in the tropics. Heat speeds up the process of decay."

"Sounds about right."

"Of course it's right," Scott said, lowering himself to his

haunches in front of the body. "That's why back East, when-ever you can, you wait until winter to do somebody."

I stood behind him and watched over his shoulder as he examined the corpse.

"Humidity or not," I said, "I still say this guy's been gone five or six days."

"You never know," Scott said, shaking his head. "Could be due to sepsis."

"Sepsis?"

"A blood infection that accelerates the decay process. Can easily make a day-old body look like a week-old corpse. Only way to really tell is to open him up and examine the internal organs."

"Well, we're going leave that to Charlie Tong."

"Who's that?"

"The new ME." I stared into Gavin Dengler's protruding eyes. "You think he was poisoned?"

"Not unless you mean lead poisoning." Scott pointed to a hole on the right side of Dengler's head, just over the ear. "Execution-style. Point-blank from behind. This fucker was on his knees with a gun pointed to his head and he knew it was coming."

I glanced around the room as I removed a set of latex gloves from my suit jacket. I slapped them on and tossed a pair to Scott. "Let's take a look around because I don't think Gavin Dengler's going to be doing much talking."

"What are we looking for?"

I began in the living area, checking shelves and opening drawers. "A photograph of Orlando Masonet with his name

---

under it would be nice. Maybe his address and telephone number on the back."

After inspecting the main area, I moved from bedroom to bedroom, while Scott checked out the kitchen.

"This fucker eats a lot of steaks," Scott called out.

"Not anymore," I mumbled.

I met him back in the living room ten minutes later.

"Nothing," I said. "Not a laptop, address book, day planner . . ."

"I could have told you that. This was a professional. Professionals don't leave any of that shit behind."

"Check his pockets for a cell phone."

Meanwhile I checked the caller ID and speed-dial buttons on his landline. Nothing.

"No cell," Scott said.

"Let's go. We'll call it in from a paypho—"

The landline suddenly rang so loudly I felt it in my chest. When I finally recovered from my initial reaction, I glanced at the caller ID. "Restricted."

"Answer it."

I hesitated. Something about answering a dead man's phone didn't sit well with me. Still wearing my gloves, I lifted the receiver and didn't say anything.

"Mr. Corvelli," an accented female voice said hurriedly.

My stomach sank like an ice cube in wine as soon as I heard my name.

"I need your help. I saw you enter the hotel and I knew you were there to visit Dengler."

I steadied my voice as best I could. "You've been watching the place?"

"Yes. Ever since the murder. Days ago I came to visit Dengler, to bring him money, when I saw someone else punch in the penthouse floor in the elevator. Whoever he was, he had a key. So I punched a different floor and didn't try to return until later. When I did, Dengler was dead."

My mind raced with excitement at the thought of a material witness. "So you saw the killer."

"Yes, Mr. Corvelli." She paused. "But worse, I think the killer saw *me*."

"Where are you now?"

"Just outside the hotel, hiding between some hanging surfboards on the beach."

"Stay there. We'll come and collect you. What's your name?"

"It's me, Mr. Corvelli. Iryna Kupchenko. Oksana Sutin's friend."

CHAPTER 55

Seated in the passenger seat of my Jeep, in the glow of the tiki torches lining Kalakaua Avenue, Iryna Kupchenko appeared ragged, her long blond hair now unkempt and unclean, her tight black skirt and blouse disheveled, her makeup smeared, mascara running from both eyes down her cheeks. The smell of cigarette smoke mercifully masked her body odor.

"We thought you were dead," I told her.

"I moved from Diamond Head to Kahala, but I have not been home in three days," she said. "Not since I saw Dengler's body."

"There was a woman's body . . . ," I said gently.

"In Lake Wilson, yes. She was my friend. Her name was Hannah."

"Who killed her?"

Iryna placed her face against the passenger-side window and wept. "One of the drivers. They are killing everybody they think will talk."

Scott had chosen to walk back to his apartment on Tusitala. Now we were headed back to my villa in Ko Olina because Iryna refused to stay alone in a hotel.

"I'm sorry about your friend," I said as I turned up Paki Avenue. "But we might be close to bringing all this death to an end. You saw Dengler's killer. And Dengler's killer may well have been Orlando Masonet." At the end of Paki Avenue, I made a left onto Ala Wai Boulevard, speeding alongside the canal. "Tell me what he looked like."

"He was tall. Dressed very well. But I did everything I could to avoid looking at his face."

My chest heaved with disappointment. "Tell me you caught a glimpse at least, Iryna."

"I glanced back as I left the elevator, just to be sure he wasn't following me. I saw him just quickly before the doors closed. He had a hard, handsome face."

"How old was he?"

"It was difficult to tell. Young forties, I would have to guess. Not heavy but very well fed."

Our half-hour drive on H1 West was silent as I contemplated my next move. I needed a sketch artist but I couldn't exactly bring Iryna to police headquarters. The only cop I knew I could trust was John Tatupu—and he'd threatened my life just a few hours ago.

As I pulled into my driveway, it finally struck me. I leapt out of the Jeep, helped Iryna out, then took her inside through the front door. Skies greeted us immediately. He didn't like strangers but he did indeed adore beautiful women. Even when they looked and smelled as though they hadn't bathed in days.

"Something to drink?" I said as Iryna stared in wonder at the mattress on my living room floor. "Beer, scotch, soda, Red Bull, bottled water?"

"Do you have red wine?"

"No," I told her emphatically. "I no longer keep red wine in the house."

"Then water will be fine."

I double-checked the cap before I handed her an ice-cold bottle of FIJI. Then I pulled my cell from my pocket and dialed Audra's number. As it rang, I stepped into the bedroom and closed the door behind me.

"I need a favor," I said when she picked up.

"If it has to do with Slauson, the answer is no. He kicked me out of FBI headquarters this morning after accusing me of sleeping with the enemy. He said he should have me fired and prosecuted for treason."

"I may not need him. What I do need is access to a forensic artist. FBI, if at all possible."

The FBI did good work. Without that notorious sketch of the Unabomber, which will be forever ingrained into America's collective memory, the Bureau might never have captured Ted Kaczynski.

"What's this for?"

"I have Iryna Kupchenko here in my villa. She may have seen Orlando Masonet."

"You have a call girl at your place? Isn't one charge of prostitution enough for one year?"

"You would think, but no. I'm going for the record."

"I'll call Mike Jansen. He's the one who's been after Masonet from the beginning anyway."

"Special Agent Jansen of the DEA? It was his stupid fucking plan that got us into this mess to begin with."

"Look, he's the only one I can go to, Kevin. Take it or leave it."

"I'll take it."

After she showered, Iryna passed out naked in the center of my bed. I threw a sheet over her, then sat outside on my lanai and waited for Audra to call back. My thoughts carried me back to July and SoSo's sentencing, Boyd's warning that a Waialua meth lab had been raided, Turi's frantic plea from the FDC, the late-night call from Jason Yi, and the gruesome sight of Oksana Sutin's corpse at the Diamond Head crime scene. Had that all really happened in a single day and night? Could I have somehow avoided it all by marching back down the courthouse steps before the sentencing, returning home, shutting my phone off, and going to sleep?

At some point in the night, as the trade winds blew through my hair and the geckos chirped, I drifted off into a dreamless sleep in the wicker chair. I woke to the bell of my cell phone just as the sun began to rise over the Pacific.

"Eight a.m.," Audra said. "At the DEA's Honolulu District Office."

"No go," I said groggily. "Have Jansen send the sketch artist here. Last thing we need is to have someone spot Iryna visiting with the DEA."

"Jansen can arrange for protection."

"I've experienced Jansen's protection firsthand. Iryna came to me; I'll protect her."

"I'll call him back," Audra said, annoyed. "If you don't hear from me, Jansen and the sketch artist will be at your home at eight." She disconnected.

Without closing the clamshell I dialed Jake's number.

He picked up on the sixth ring. "Getting revenge for me calling you so early yesterday morning, son?"

"Yes, but I also need to ask a favor. I need you to cover for me in court this morning. Call our ballistics expert to the stand. Keep him up there until Narita breaks for lunch, then cut him loose. I'll be there this afternoon to toss Guffman around the courtroom."

Jake didn't ask any questions. "You got it."

I ended the call and dialed Flan. Casey picked up.

"Sorry, Casey," I said. "I didn't mean to wake you."

"Oh, no probs, Kev. Actually, I just got home. Don't tell Dad."

I heard a door creak open, I heard Flan snoring, then I heard Casey yell, "It's for you!" just before the door slammed closed again.

Flan picked up the phone.

I said, "I need you to head to Pearl City this morning, Flan. Make sure Max Guffman makes it to court today. If he gives you any trouble, tell him if he doesn't testify, I'll put his lady friend, Meredith Yancy, on the stand. And her daughter, Karen Haak. And I'll subject them all to charges of perjury. And if none of them show, the whole family, baby Kyle included, will be thrown in jail for contempt."

"Can a baby be held in contempt?" Flan asked, mid-yawn.

"Hey, if I could convince a judge to allow a four-year-old to testify in a murder trial like I did in the Erin Simms case, I figure I can pull off just about anything."

"Let's hope for Turi's sake you're right."

CHAPTER 56

"You are bringing the *police* here?" Iryna said, dressed again in her tight black skirt and blouse, which I'd thrown in the washer and dryer and shrunk overnight.

"Not the police," I explained. "A sketch artist. And an agent with the DEA."

"What is DEA?"

"Drug Enforcement Administration."

"Oh my God," she shouted, running across my living room in bare feet. She grabbed her purse, opened it, stuffed her hand inside, and came out with four vials of white powder. "Quick, you hide these for me!"

"No one is going to go through your purse, Iryna."

"*I have no documents,*" she yelled at me. "They will send me back to Odessa!"

I put up my hands, palms out. "No one's going to Odessa."

"Do you know how fucking cold it is there?" Iryna reached into her purse again.

I walked toward her to try to calm her. "Listen, as soon as the sketch is finished, I'll send my receptionist to Ala Moana Center to buy you some new clothes. Her name is Hoshi and—"

Before I could finish the sentence, Iryna's arm was extended, and I was rewarded with a faceful of pepper spray.

I experienced immediate agony. My eyes shut instantly, and when I tried to open them, it was as though I were attempting to gaze directly into the sun. The pain was burning and intense and I didn't dare try to open my eyes again. Meanwhile, my nose ran, I coughed and coughed, and I could barely breathe. I sank to the floor and rubbed at my eyes with my hands, only spreading the chemicals.

As for Iryna, I shouted her name over and over, though it was no use. I heard her shoes clop toward the stairs, then down them, then I heard the front door open and close with a slam.

I felt around the floor for my phone, then felt the bed. Blind and sick, I pushed myself to my feet, moved across the room, and ran my hands across the surface of the kitchen counter, knocking over empty beer bottles, a small black-silver globe, and a number of file folders from the Turi Ahina trial.

I went to the sink and tried flushing my eyes with water, to no effect. Blinking vigorously helped, but not much.

I dropped to the floor again and pushed myself along the cool tiles until I could prop myself up against the refrigerator.

My cell phone finally sounded from the left pocket of my shorts. I ripped the phone out, opened it, and held it to my ear.

"Who's this?" I shouted, coughing violently.

"It's Scott. What the fuck happened to you?"

"I just got pepper-sprayed. What do I do?"

"Nothing to do but wait it out. At least thirty to forty-five minutes. Longer, depending on how much of that shit you were hit with."

"Great," I muttered between hacks.

"Who pepper-sprayed you? The hooker?"

"Yeah."

"Christ. What kind of kinky shit are you into, Kevin?"

"Just get over here. We need to find her. I've got a sketch artist showing up here at eight, along with a DEA agent expecting his first glimpse of Orlando Masonet."

I ended the call. Tried opening my eyes. Too soon. I needed to get out of the kitchen, so I crawled back into the living room. Used the coffee table to push myself to my feet. Still coughing, still unable to breathe.

Blindly I moved toward the bedroom, made a left into the bathroom. I opened the medicine cabinet and knocked dozens of pill bottles down until I thought I had the right one. I sat on the bathroom floor inches from the toilet and popped the top on the bottle. I stuck my fingers inside. They were the Percocet all right. I needed to get them in me and fast to ease the unbearable pain, to hopefully dull my sensitivity to light—a truly intolerable sensation in a well-lit villa in Hawaii.

I lined four pills up on the floor and started to crush them beneath my can of Gillette shaving cream. It took five minutes, maybe ten, but I soon had a nice fine powder on the tiled bathroom floor. But all the work had caused me to sweat. So I took off my T-shirt and shorts and threw them out into the bedroom, after removing a pen from my pocket. I broke the pen and used it as a straw, placing one end into my left nostril and holding the other end to the pile of powdered Percocet. When I snorted, my nose and eyes and throat burned even worse and I howled in pain.

"Jesus fucking Christ," I suddenly heard a voice say.

I swung around, startled. Tried opening my eyes again. The image was fuzzy, but I could just make him out. Special Agent Michael Jansen of the DEA.

"I have a valid prescription," I said.

CHAPTER 57

Special Agent Jansen dug into my closet, ripped a shirt off the rack, picked a pair of jeans out of my hamper, and threw them at me in the bathroom. "Put these on, and hurry. I don't know what the hell this woman looks like. I need you to help me find her."

"I can't *see* anything," I told him as I slipped into my shirt. "I can't help you find Iryna if I'm blind."

"I sent the sketch artist down to the ABC Store to pick up some baby shampoo. That'll remove the spray and you should have your vision back within ten minutes."

Jansen helped me off the floor once I'd dressed, then guided me into the living room. "Why the hell did she run anyway?"

"She's not documented."

"Did you tell her I don't give a rat's shit about her immigration status? That I just want to find this killer Masonet?"

"She's ignorant. And scared."

Once the sketch artist returned, she rubbed the Johnson's

baby shampoo gently into my eyes over the kitchen sink. I'd all but stopped coughing and my breathing was beginning to return to normal. Five minutes after the shampooing, I could open my eyes into narrow slits.

I walked through the bedroom and glanced into the bathroom mirror; the entire top half of my face was blotchy and red.

"Come on," Jansen said. "We're not going out to pick up women, just to find the one."

Three hours later and not a sign of Iryna Kupchenko. Scott Damiano was staking out the Meridian, while Jansen and I stood in the main lobby of the Kupulupulu Beach Resort, our eyes peeled. I removed my phone from my pocket and dialed Jake's cell.

Jake picked up on the first ring. "Where the hell are you?"

"Ko Olina. Long story. Look, I'm going to need you to put Guffman on the stand this afternoon."

"He could be our last witness. Son, you can't pull this shit in the middle of a murder trial. Narita is *not* happy. He just called us into chambers and asked me where you were. The *jury* is not happy. They watched you the entire trial, and they're looking at me like I'm the fucking understudy. And *Turi*, that young man is not happy at all. He's scared shitless. He thinks you ran out on him."

"Jake, we're close to finding Masonet. We've had a setback. But you assure Turi that what I'm doing is absolutely vital to his defense. Promise him I'll be there to deliver closing arguments."

The moment I hung up, a soaking-wet Scott Damiano materialized with a soaking-wet Iryna Kupchenko on his arm.

"She went for a swim," Scott said. "Only she can't swim.

She tried to doggy-paddle her way to a yacht that had just left the marina. Good thing I spotted her when I did or we'd be fishing her body out of the drink."

I stepped over to Iryna, took her hand gently in mine. "It's all right. I talked to the DEA agent. He has no intention of having you deported. But we need you to come back to my house to give the sketch artist a description of the man you saw in the elevator of Gavin Dengler's building."

Iryna refused to look at me. "I don't believe you. All men are liars."

I placed my arm around her shoulders and guided her toward the main lobby. "Maybe. But this time, all we're trying to get at is the truth."

CHAPTER 58

An hour later we were back in my villa, Jansen and I standing around the kitchen, arms folded, biting our nails, while Iryna and the sketch artist worked together in my bedroom.

"So, what's with the painkillers?" he said.

"Got stabbed in the abdomen last year."

"Wanna tell me about it?"

I shook my head, motioned to the paperback on the counter. "Read the book."

Jansen picked Sherry Beagan's book up off the counter and started flipping through it, settled on the photographs in the middle. "She's beautiful," he said, pointing to a picture of Erin Simms in her wedding dress.

"Was."

Jansen turned the pages again and again until he reached the final photograph—the picture of me in a soaked-through suit, sunglasses covering my eyes, a Panama Jack hat atop my head, standing, covered from head to toe in blood, on the beach abutting the lagoon outside the Kupulupulu Beach Resort.

"I'm sorry," he said.

I nodded. "Thanks."

"So, with the pills, what are you doing, doctor-shopping?"

I gave him a look as though I might kill him right there in my kitchen. "What?"

"You know, going from doctor to doctor to get multiple prescriptions."

"Are you on the job, Jansen?"

"Always."

I took the book out of his hands and tossed it back onto the counter. "Buy your own copy."

"You think what I do is a joke, don't you, Counselor?"

"Not always. When you take down a Mexican cartel trafficking black tar heroin, I'm all for it. When you raid a meth lab that might blow up at any second, you have my utmost respect. But when you take down a farmer with a marijuana field on the Big Island and try to put him away for life, I think you're wasting taxpayer money and being naïve and an all-around son of a bitch."

We remained silent after that. Waiting for Iryna Kupchenko and the sketch artist to exit my bedroom with a usable depiction of our one common enemy, the man known as Orlando Masonet.

"It's not going well," the sketch artist announced a half hour later. She set several stray sheets from her sketch pad onto the kitchen counter and spread them out. "She's confused. And her command of the English language isn't helping."

"Shit," Jansen said, pounding his fist down on the counter. Everything on the counter shook, all the piles of papers and folders I'd accumulated the past few months that weren't directly being used in the trial. A few items fluttered to the hardwood floor.

I swallowed hard, suddenly thirsty and desperate for a few pills. My cell phone buzzed and I picked it up without looking at the caller ID.

"Trial is adjourned for the day," Jake said. "I put Guffman on the stand, and he didn't budge, not even an inch, not even when I entered the Facebook photo into evidence. He insists he's never once seen that car."

"You didn't get anything from him?" I said, suddenly angry at myself for wasting the day here in Ko Olina and not being in the courtroom to question Guffman myself.

"I got Guffman to admit that someone else may have parked in front of his house if they knew he wasn't home. That's it."

As I was telling Jake what had transpired on this side of the island, Iryna Kupchenko stepped out of my bedroom, crying.

"I've got to go," I told Jake. "I've got to get to work on my closing argument."

"All right, son. I think maybe you need to visit Turi, too. Prepare him for the likely verdict and inform him about the appeals process."

I dropped the phone onto the floor and buried my face in my hands. My eyes still felt raw from the pepper spray. My stomach ached, a combination of nerves and withdrawal. I was one closing statement away from losing this trial. Which meant that the man who once saved my life would be going away for the rest of his, thanks to my shortcomings. And on the inside, Turi's life expectancy wouldn't be long at all. Knowing what he knew, there was no way Masonet could allow him to live. Turi Ahina would be murdered at Halawa just as Brandon Glenn was murdered at Rikers Island.

"This, it is him," I suddenly heard Iryna say from behind me.

Jansen stepped around the kitchen counter as I turned and saw Iryna leaning over some papers that had fallen to the floor.

In her hands was a brightly colored brochure. "This, it is him. I swear it."

Jansen took the brochure out of her hands and studied the photograph she'd been pointing at. "Who is this guy?"

I looked over Jansen's shoulder, my heart pounding hard in my chest. The brochure was Audra's—media material for the towering new condominium building being constructed in Kakaako.

Water Landings—your private oasis in the center of it all.

"That's a property developer," I said to Jansen. "The most prolific in all of the Hawaiian Islands." I grabbed the brochure from him and stared at the rich, familiar bloated face. "His name is Thomas S. Duran."

"Duran?"

"The governor calls him Tommy," I said.

CHAPTER 59

"Ladies and gentlemen of the jury," I said at the start of my closing, "first off, I want to apologize for my absence from the courtroom yesterday. Although I am prohibited by evidentiary rules from explaining what transpired yesterday, I can assure you it had nothing to do with me not wanting to be here, and it had everything to do with ultimately achieving justice for my client, the defendant, Turi Ahina."

I waited for Dapper Don to object, but the prosecutor sat silent, his lips pursed, his eyes set on the table in front of him. He appeared pensive, untypically unsure of himself, unsure of his case.

"Turi Ahina," I continued, "is the *victim* in this case. He is the *victim* of a crime, namely the attempt on his life by Detective Kanoa Bristol of the Narcotics Intelligence Unit of the Honolulu PD. He is the *victim* of a cover-up, specifically the attempt by Detective Ray Irvine to circumvent justice by tampering with and removing evidence from the crime scene and manipulating witnesses to deceive you during the course of this trial. Finally, Turi Ahina is a *victim* of this system, a system that allows an innocent man to be prosecuted and convicted in the media before the first witness ever takes the stand. A system that fails to take into account that some police and prosecutors are corrupt and will do anything in their power to obtain a conviction, especially when it means saving their own asses."

"Language, Counselor," Narita said in a bored tone from the bench.

I paused. I had considered putting Iryna Kupchenko on the stand. But who on the jury would believe an undocumented prostitute called at the eleventh hour? And so what if the jury did believe her? What could she say except that she'd witnessed a billionaire land developer named Thomas S. Duran pay a visit to her pimp just before he was murdered? How could we possibly connect all the dots?

"Ladies and gentleman," I said, "you heard during this trial from Mindy Iokepa, daughter of a state senator and mother to Turi Ahina's child. She testified as to why Turi was on that dark street in Pearl City at that time of night, and why he was carrying five thousand dollars in cash. The five thousand dollars—what Mr. Watanabe tried to convince you was *drug money*—was actually funds to help Mindy Iokepa raise and support her and Turi's year-old daughter, Ema.

"So what do we make of the prosecution's assertion that Detective Bristol came upon Turi Ahina in the middle of a drug transaction? What do we make of Mr. Watanabe's assurance that Detective Bristol was merely trying to apprehend Turi Ahina when shots suddenly rang out? I'll tell you what we make of it. We make *everything* of it. Because that alone constitutes reasonable doubt."

And this was true. Once we introduced some credible evidence of the existence of justification, the prosecution became burdened with proving beyond a reasonable doubt facts that negated the defense. In this, I felt, Dapper Don had failed miserably. But there was no telling what a jury would do in the face of such legal and factual complexities.

"Let's examine seventy-two-year-old Doris Ledford," I said. "Mrs. Ledford testified that she heard two shots, not three, which would bolster the prosecution's claim that Detective Bristol never fired his weapon. Frankly, I believe Doris Ledford. Not that she actually heard two shots rather than three, but that she *thinks* she did. After all, Mrs. Ledford testified that she had never, in her seventy-plus years of life, heard gunshots before that night. She thought she was hearing firecrackers. She called Emergency Services thinking that she was reporting some fat kid playing with fireworks. It wasn't until she saw Detective Bristol lying on the ground that Mrs. Ledford realized she'd heard gunfire for the first time in her long life. And before she could come to her own conclusion as to how many shots she heard, she was informed by Detective Ray Irvine that she only heard two.

"Mrs. Ledford didn't intend to deceive us, but Detective Ray Irvine undeniably fed her the facts necessary to cover up Detective Kanoa Bristol's crime. And *why* did Detective Ray Irvine go to such lengths—removing and tampering with evidence at the crime scene, and manipulating witnesses—to cover up his fellow officer's murder attempt? Because Detective Ray Irvine himself had, and continues to have, plenty at stake."

I watched the jurors, and they told me nothing, not with their eyes or any other part of their bodies. They simply watched me, and I had to be content in the belief that they were at least listening, that they hadn't already made up their minds.

What if I could have showed them Orlando Masonet? What then? Jansen didn't have enough evidence to haul Tommy Duran in. And even if he had, Duran would have lawyered up the minute he stepped into the station. If I had called him to testify, he would have lied, and with his reputation I would've been laughed out of the courtroom. At best, Tommy Duran would've taken the Fifth. I would just be standing here begging the jury to make an inference.

"What does Detective Irvine have at stake? You heard during this trial from Detective John Tatupu. He testified at length to the corruption he witnessed within the Honolulu Police Department, particularly the Narcotics Intelligence Unit. Detective Tatupu discovered drugs and money missing from the evidence locker. He observed officers, including Detective Bristol himself, receive envelopes filled with cash from known drug dealers. He overheard plans for off-duty officers to carry contraband to the islands from Mexico and the mainland. He saw officers trade leniency for sexual favors. Detective Tatupu watched the disease of corruption spread throughout his beloved department like a cancer, and he risked everything to take the stand and tell you about it. To tell you that the Honolulu Police Department is run not by Chief Edward Attea or Honolulu's mayor, but by a cold-blooded killer known widely as Orlando Masonet."

I stepped across the courtroom and swallowed some ice water, allowing the jurors' eyes to follow me to the defense table and a sympathetic-looking Turi Ahina.

"When Judge Narita instructs you on the law, he will define for you once again the legal term *choice of evils*. He will explain the *reasonable person standard* and inform you that the critical factor in determining whether Turi Ahina's actions were justified is his state of mind, or his belief with respect to the facts and circumstances. By selecting each of you as jurors, Mr. Watanabe and I, and of course Judge Narita, made the determination that you were twelve reasonable people. Thus, applying the reasonable person standard in this case should be reasonably easy. All you will have to do is ask yourself this: What would *I* do if I were staring into the barrel of a loaded gun on a dark street in Pearl City? If I were armed, would I fire back? Would I fire first in order to save my own life? Would I fire to remain on this earth with the ones I love? If I fired at my attacker's chest only to find the bullet bounce off his Kevlar vest like some homicidal Superman, would I fire again? And if so, would I aim higher? Maybe at the throat, maybe at the head? Would I kill to keep from being killed? Under the law, if you are a reasonable person, the answer is yes."

I swept my hand across the jury rail as I looked each of the twelve jurors in the eyes. "You were cautioned by Mr. Watanabe at the beginning of this trial to expect smoke and mirrors from me. He referred to me as an illusionist, implied that I'd wave my wand and whisper hocus-pocus and make evidence disappear, just as Detective Ray Irvine did at the Pearl City crime scene. But I have something better than smoke and mirrors, something far more powerful than magic. Ladies and gentlemen of the jury, I have the truth on my side. And whether you choose to believe the truth or Detective Irvine's lies will mean the difference between justice and a terrible, irreversible injustice. A vote of guilty is a vote to continue the status quo, to permit the stench of corruption to continue to permeate every inch of our lives in these islands until every man, woman, and child has been exposed to the disease. I therefore ask that when you retire into the jury room to deliberate, you do so with the intention of righting a series of terrible wrongs. And I ask that when you return to this courtroom to deliver your verdict, you send a loud and powerful message to those who would destroy this city—and deliver a verdict of not guilty on all counts."

CHAPTER 60

Judge Narita read the jury instructions late Friday, meaning the jury wouldn't begin deliberations until Monday. Which meant I had the entire weekend to think about all the things I'd done wrong during the trial. The third bullet bothered me most. Technically, it wasn't necessary to the choice-of-evils defense. Legally it didn't matter whether Kanoa Bristol fired first or fired at all, so long as Turi reasonably felt his life was in imminent danger. But to the jury I knew it *did* matter, and it could mean the difference between a conviction and an acquittal.

Problem was, so little evidence supported my claim. I based the defense on Turi's word, and to me, Turi's version of the events made perfect sense. Especially the details he provided. A navy Honda Civic. A Jesus fish. A sticker in the rear window that read KEIKI ON BOARD. But the jury never got to hear Turi say anything about this, or anything at all for that matter. That would've been too risky. Indeed, it could have proved suicidal.

And the ghost bullet allowed me to introduce new depths of police corruption. To villainize the lead detective in the Bristol investigation. By confronting him with accusations of tampering with and removing evidence from the Pearl City crime scene, I put Detective Ray Irvine on the defensive from the beginning. I hoped what the jury would remember most about his appearance at trial was not his investigation, but my cross-examination.

I had never known a lawyer who didn't second-guess himself between his closing statement and the verdict. If one existed, he was either indifferent or plain stupid.

"With the trial over and less than three weeks until the election, it's time to focus on all things Omphrey," I said.

Jake, sitting across from me at the conference table, nodded. "We think now that it was Thomas Duran who hired Oksana Sutin to have an affair with the governor, right?"

"If Iryna Kupchenko is correct in her identification, yes. Then I think it's safe to assume that Thomas Duran *is* Orlando Masonet."

I had sat down with Jansen this morning and together we'd gone through the DEA's file on Masonet. Jansen was keeping everything close to the vest until he had something more concrete than an undocumented prostitute's identification of a man on a brochure. Aside from the sketch artist, no one in the Drug Enforcement Administration even knew Jansen suspected Thomas Duran of being Orlando Masonet.

With everything we knew, Masonet had gotten filthy rich—billionaire rich—long before Thomas Duran the land developer arrived on the scene. Ironically, we knew less about Tommy Duran than we did Orlando Masonet. But following some research we decided that Orlando Masonet had laundered his money through hundreds of false businesses spread throughout the Caribbean and Northern and Eastern Europe.

"So, presumably," Jake said, "Tommy Duran hired Oksana Sutin—who was one of his girls to begin with—to spy on Wade Omphrey and press him for information about some pertinent land-use decisions, including one in Kakaako and several up North Shore."

"The Waimea Valley project was going to be the most lucrative and therefore the most important," I said. "In addition to the millions Duran would have made on that project, a decision falling in his favor would have inevitably opened the floodgates to developing the North Shore."

"But Omphrey was the big-business candidate," Jake said. "Why the hell kill Oksana Sutin and try to bring the governor down?"

"Multiple reasons, I suspect. One, Oksana Sutin was pregnant with Omphrey's child. She may have told Duran 'no more.' And Duran couldn't risk her spilling what she'd been doing to the governor or anyone else. Two, I have a feeling Omphrey was going to stand up to Duran on the Waimea Valley project, not because of any sudden crisis of conscience, but because his wife, Pamela, felt strongly enough about preventing further North Shore development to pack up and leave him. If she left him and news of his affair broke, he'd finish out his term as governor, but he'd have to kiss goodbye any chance at running for Senate or being chosen to serve in a cabinet position."

"So, have you told Omphrey any of this?"

"Not yet," I said. "The FBI is watching Lok Sun. Jansen is searching for Tommy Duran. And our job for the moment is to sit and wait for Turi's jury."

CHAPTER 61

That night I knew I'd sleep like the dead. When I arrived home, I fed Skies, then myself, then performed what had become a ritual since Audra Karras nearly died on my living room floor. I went downstairs and checked the lock and the deadbolt on the front door, then on the door that led into the garage. Upstairs I closed and locked all the windows except the ones in the living room on either side of my mattress. I wasn't giving up the trade breezes no matter how many people wanted me dead. Though I did lock the sliding-glass door leading to the lanai. After all, I didn't want to make killing me *too* easy.

It felt good to get out of my suit, and the hot shower felt even better. In the shower I thought of all the things I'd have to do once the verdict was finally read. I owed Josh Leffler a phone call. If he was game, I'd go online and purchase two tickets to the NFL Pro Bowl, which was being held in February at Aloha Stadium. Maybe I'd order three tickets, and we'd bring Audra along.

I would need to see Audra long before then, of course. Despite my initially being an ass, she had helped me every chance she could. Neither of us was the same person we were sixteen years ago. I thought I'd like to get to know the Audra Karras of today, learn about her experiences in college and law school, her stint as an AUSA in the Southern District of New York, her marriage to Marty Levy and her divorce. Maybe, if I could keep myself from pushing her away, I'd even like to date her, just to see where it took us. Maybe, I thought.

Back in the living room, I killed the lights and lay down on my mattress, covering myself with only a sheet. Grey Skies curled up next to me as I explored my feelings for Audra Karras. Soon enough my eyes closed on their own and I fell into a warm unconsciousness.

I may have made it to the first stage of sleep before my cell phone started ringing on the kitchen counter. I rolled off the mattress and dug through the clutter to find my cell.

The caller ID read RESTRICTED.

"Speak."

"Mr. Corvelli, it is Iryna," she said in a small voice.

My first thought was, *You can save your thanks for the morning.* "What is it, Iryna?"

"They have me."

"Who has you? The DEA? They're protecting you, Iryna. You're free to leave anytime you want, but don't. Wait until this is over, and I'll help you out, help you find a place. Maybe we can even work on doing something about your immigration status. I've been toying with an idea."

Actually, it was Flan's idea. He was ready to remarry, especially if it was to a Ukrainian bride with legs as long as a foot-ball field.

"I have already left," Iryna said, crying. "I went looking for one of my friends. Mr. Corvelli, I made a terrible mistake. Now they have me."

"*Who* has you?" I said again, suddenly struck with a wave of anxiety.

"These men, I do not know their names. They want *you* to come to collect me."

"Me?"

"Yes, they insist that it be you."

"Can they hear me right now?" My voice was suddenly soft and trembling.

"No, just me."

"Tell me where you are and I'll call Special Agent Jansen."

She sobbed. "No police, they said. If the police come, they will kill me before the police ever get through the door. They said you must come alone."

I walked across the living room, opened the sliding-glass door and stepped out onto the lanai. If I went downstairs and walked out my door tonight, it would be like walking straight toward the barrel of a loaded gun and hoping it misfired.

"Please, Mr. Corvelli," she said, crying. "I need you to come for me."

I stared deep into the night. It had been my choice to dig for the truth that had placed Iryna in danger. Right or wrong, I had to live with my decisions. But if there was a chance of saving her, however slim, I had to try.

Didn't I?

Without ending the connection I held the phone away from my ear and stared at it in the darkness, the seconds of the call ticking away like a time bomb.

You can't let her die.

I'd seen enough death the past four years to last me a lifetime. But I was scared.

"Please," she cried. "You must help us."

I held the phone against my ear again. "Us?"

"There is another woman here, too."

"Another woman?"

"They have her gagged and she may be unconscious."

"Who is she?"

"I do not know," Iryna said, weeping. "They tell me she is a lawyer."

CHAPTER 62

"They have Audra," I said into my cell.

Scott was groggy but he gathered himself quickly. "Are you sure?"

"I'm parked in front of her house in Ewa now. She's not here."

I told him about Iryna's call.

"Where do they want you to go?" he said.

I drew a deep breath. "Chinatown."

"Come pick me up, Kev."

"I have to go alone."

"Bullshit. Go in there alone and they're going to kill you *and* Iryna *and* Audra. We go in there together and maybe some of us come out alive and some of them go out dead. It's your only fucking choice, Kev."

"Be downstairs in twenty minutes," I said. "And bring an extra gun."

"This is a thirty-eight Special," Scott said. "You ever fire a gun?"

"No, but I had a gun fired *at* me once."

"A little different, but let's not split hairs. Okay, this is how it works."

In my Jeep, parked in front of Scott's apartment building in Waikiki, he showed me how to fire the weapon. "This is a double action, which means you don't have to cock the hammer. Squeezing the trigger will do it for you." He released the cylinder using the thumb piece and loaded the revolver with bullets. "You got five rounds."

"Only five?"

"How many men you plan on killing tonight? Just use the front sight and take good aim."

I held the gun in my hand. It somehow felt too heavy and too light at the same time. "You don't have Kevlar vests, do you?"

"Back East, yeah. Here, no. I didn't realize I'd be getting shot at in Hawaii. Milt Cashman left that part out when he handed me the plane ticket."

I started the Jeep.

It was a short drive between Waikiki and Chinatown even though they were two entirely different worlds. I parked again in the business district. A fast getaway wasn't going to be possible anyway. These criminals weren't stupid; they'd disable my Jeep if I was dumb enough to drive directly into Chinatown.

Scott and I walked. I felt no safer with the .38 Special in my jacket pocket. The streets were no brighter, the denizens lurking in the shadows looked no more friendly and no less tough. And when we reached the spot, Tam's bar felt no more inviting.

This time we didn't have to knock. As soon as we stepped into the nook, the giant opened the door and trained his piece on Scott.

"You were told to come alone," the giant said to me.

"Yeah, well those are the breaks," I said.

With his piece still leveled at Scott, the giant grabbed my collar and dragged me inside. Scott followed. The door slammed shut behind us.

I turned and saw Lian standing in front of the door, holding a knife.

Then Tam said, "Who is this, Corvelli?"

"If you knew who I was," Scott said, "you and the fucking elephant man here and the Chinese whore would all be running out the back door."

Tam laughed. "Is that so?"

Across the room, Tam pulled a .357 out from behind the maroon seat cushions and aimed it at Scott's head.

I glanced at the bar. The bartender stood behind it holding a shotgun.

I had five bullets. There were four of them, each armed to the teeth.

"Frisk them," Tam said.

As the giant patted me down, Scott turned and grabbed Lian by her straight, jet-black hair. She screamed as he twisted her arm and took the knife away from her. In one swift move Scott positioned Lian in front of him, holding the knife to her throat.

Scott said, "Let's just say every man in this bar is armed and leave it at that, okay?"

The giant looked back at Tam, who nodded. The giant threw me down hard on the floor, my head bouncing off the cement. But at least I still had the gun.

Slowly I got to my feet. "Where are the women?" I said.

Tam leaned toward the back door and shouted something in Vietnamese. A few moments later the door opened and a single thug hauled in Audra and Iryna. Both women were blindfolded. Both appeared drugged. Both had been beaten. Badly.

I seethed but kept my hand out of my jacket pocket, knowing I'd be burned down before I could even draw. When all this was over, if I made it out of this shithole alive, I planned on spending some time at the Waikiki firing range. As much as I hated guns, just too much garbage littered these mean streets.

Tam turned to the bartender. "Telephone."

The bartender reached under the bar and placed a large, black business phone onto the bar.

"Call him," Tam said.

Holding the shotgun with one hand, the bartender dialed ten digits then punched the button for speakerphone. The ringing resonated through the bar. One ring. Two rings. Three rings. Four. Then someone picked up.

"Is he there?" a male voice said through the speaker.

"The lawyer is here," Tam said. "And he brought a friend."

"Kill the friend."

Tam swallowed hard, the first emotion other than rage I'd seen from him. "The friend is holding a knife to Lian's throat."

"Then kill her, too."

Lian screamed out.

"Wait!" I stepped in front of Scott and Lian.

Tam had had his .357 aimed at them. Now he had it aimed at me. "The lawyer is blocking my shot," Tam said to the phone.

The man on the speaker sighed. "Mr. Corvelli, do you know how much of a fucking pain in the ass you are? The only reason I don't tell Tam to blow a hole right through you to get to Lian and your friend is that I want to hear you die a slow and painful death."

The voice was unmistakable. It was Tommy Duran's.

It was Orlando Masonet's.

"If that's all you want," I said, "then let Scott and the women go. I can die slowly and painfully without their help."

"No. I think we'll do things my way from now on." Duran paused for twenty seconds, then said, "Tam."

With his left hand, Tam immediately pulled out a .44, held it to the left side of Iryna Kupchenko's head, and fired. I instinctively shut my eyes tight and waited for the ground to shake as Iryna's head exploded into a cloud of blood, brains, scalp, and skull.

I opened my eyes expecting to see her body drop to the floor.

But Iryna just stood there, blindfolded and trembling, until the thug shoved her aside.

Duran said, "Given the part of the world she's from, I thought it only fitting that with Iryna we play a round or two of Russian roulette. Of course, AUSA Audra Karras has Greek blood, so she doesn't receive the same courtesy."

The thug dragged Audra closer to Tam, stood her in the exact spot where Iryna had stood a few moments ago.

Duran said, "Unless you want to watch Audra Karras die, Corvelli, you'll answer my questions quickly and concisely. If you do, I'll have Tam let her go. Are you ready?"

I couldn't speak.

Duran said, "Tam."

Tam put the .357 to the left side of Audra's head.

I shouted, *"No."*

"See?" Duran said. "That's what I mean, Corvelli. I asked you if you were ready and you didn't answer at all. That's precisely the kind of thing that's going to get Ms. Karras killed. So, are you ready?"

"I'm ready," I said, my voice cracking like ice.

"Good. Let's start with Governor Omphrey. What does he know? And if you say one fucking word about the attorney-client privilege, then Ms. Karras loses a breast. Now go."

"Omphrey doesn't know anything about you. He knows Oksana was a spy but he doesn't know whose. He knows she was pregnant. He knows she was poisoned by Lok Sun but he doesn't know who hired Lok Sun either."

"Good. Now, I know you hadn't told Ms. Karras because Tam here tortured her for hours and she didn't talk." Duran spoke about torture and death so casually, he was unquestionably a sociopath. "So, Corvelli, besides your friend needlessly holding the knife to Lian's throat, who else did you condemn to death? Your partner Jake maybe?"

"There was no point in me telling anybody," I said. "I couldn't trust anyone. The more people I told the better your chance of escape."

Duran said, "So, ostensibly, so long as I gave Jansen the

slip, I could leave Honolulu without so much as a second look. Is that what you're telling me, Counselor?"

"I can only speak to what I know. And I know that I didn't tell anybody about Iryna's identification."

"Are you satisfied, Tam?" Duran said.

"I think we should shoot him in the kneecap, see if he tells the same story."

"We'll get to that," Duran said. "But first, let's hold up our end of the bargain. Tam, you're satisfied that Ms. Karras cannot identify you or any of your friends? That she can't identify your bar?"

"She's been blindfolded the entire time, and she has had so many drugs pumped into her, I am a little surprised she is even alive."

"Good. Let her go."

Tam hesitated. "Not until the American releases Lian. He still has a knife to her throat."

"Kevin," Duran said, "explain to your friend that he has to let Lian go or else Ms. Karras is going to get shot in the head."

I turned to him. "Scott," I said quietly.

Scott handed the knife to Lian, who bolted in a straight line toward her protector Tam.

To me, Scott said, "Shoot the giant," as he pulled his Walther from his pants.

Without a thought I reached into my jacket, grabbed the revolver by the grip, finger across the trigger, extended my arm full length in the direction of the giant, saw his head through the front sight, and squeezed once, squeezed twice.

The first shot struck the giant's left eye, the second caught him in the ear as he was already falling.

Scott fired two rounds into the bartender before the bartender could raise the shotgun to his shoulder. Then Scott turned on the thug and fired a bullet just over Audra's shoulder, jacking the thug's head back as though he'd just heard someone calling him from the sky.

Iryna ripped off her blindfold, grabbed Audra, and pulled her to the floor, out of the line of fire.

Tam turned the .357 on me, but before he could get off a shot, Lian planted her knife through the bottom of his chin and stabbed upward until blood poured from his mouth.

"What the *fuck's* going on?" Duran shouted.

Scott casually stepped over to the phone.

"Why don't you come down here and find out, cocksucker?"

I rushed across the room to Audra's side, removed her blindfold, and looked into her blackened eyes. She was beaten and drugged, and for a moment I wished Tam were still alive so I could kill him myself.

The line went dead and that awful dead-line noise filled the bar.

"See?" Scott said to me, punching the button to silence the room. "Every motherfucker in the room is dead, and you still have three bullets left."

CHAPTER 63

I had been about to dial 911 when I thought better of it. Instead I called Special Agent Neil Slauson, and he and his team arrived within ten minutes. Down the street another FBI SWAT team took down Lok Sun, aka the Pharmacist, and four of his men at the abandoned brothel they'd been watching since Audra informed Slauson of Lok Sun's whereabouts.

I told Slauson nearly everything that had transpired inside Tam's bar after telling Scott to keep his mouth shut. My only real concern was the guns. I didn't know where they came from and I didn't want to know. Luckily, after telling him about Scott's being on parole in New York, neither did Neil Slauson.

Hours later, as the sun rose over Chinatown, Slauson informed me that Thomas S. Duran, aka Orlando Masonet, had been captured.

"He wasn't even on the island when you were talking to him," Slauson said. "He had indeed given Jansen the slip and was already in his jet heading west. Of course, no flight plan was filed, but it appears he was headed to Hong Kong."

"How did you catch him?" I said.

"Immediately after you called me, I contacted the FAA. Turns out, a commercial airline pilot had just received a warning via his collision-avoidance system. Air traffic control requested that the pilot of the unidentified aircraft squawk IDENT, but the pilot failed to respond. When I got off the phone with the FAA, I contacted a friend who is a lieutenant colonel at Hickam Air Force Base. Hickam scrambled two fighter jets to escort the unidentified aircraft back to Oahu. Said craft held none other than Thomas Duran, his wife, Holly, and a Chinese crew."

I swallowed hard as I considered the implications of Orlando Masonet's remaining at large. If not for Slauson's quick thinking, Audra, Scott, Iryna—none of us would ever feel safe again.

I took a deep breath. "You have enough to convict Lok Sun?"

Slauson frowned. "Nothing found at the abandoned brothel implicates Lok Sun in Oksana Sutin's murder, or the attempted murder of AUSA Karras."

"But you have Zhi Zhu," I said. "You have Zhi Zhu's testimony."

Slauson shook his head. "Zhi Zhu was found dead just over an hour ago. The ME suggests suicide, but we won't know for sure until the autopsy."

My head sank into my chest. "Now that I've rested my case in Turi Ahina's trial," I said softly, "can you at least tell me whether you're going after the dirty cops in the Honolulu Police Department?"

"There's an open investigation," Slauson said cryptically.

I looked him in the eyes. "You could have testified."

Slauson shook his head again. "You wouldn't have wanted that, Counselor."

"You weren't investigating Kanoa Bristol?"

"Oh, we were investigating Kanoa Bristol. In fact, at the time of the shooting, the agent you met in my office, Wendy Chan, had been undercover, posing as a single mom with kids at the school Bristol's own children were attending."

"And?"

"And that's all I can tell you, Counselor."

A few minutes later, ducking through the crowd of agents, I pulled Scott aside. "So tell me, Scott, how did you know Lian was going to turn on that son of a bitch?"

"She's my massage therapist."

"You mean she jerked you off a few times."

"Whatever." He lowered his head and spoke in a low, conspiratorial tone. "Look, I'm all right with the hand-job part, but the massage itself makes me kind of uncomfortable. So, Lian and I got to talking. Around my seventh or eighth visit—"

"Seventh or eighth? Jesus, Scott, how many times have you been there?"

He shrugged. "Four or five times a week since I got here. Anyway, Lian told me all about this son of a bitch who owned a bar down the street, how he likes to smack her around and shit. So I offered to take care of him. She said no, she wouldn't let me go near him. So I didn't, though I thought about it a lot." Scott glanced over his shoulder to make sure no agents were within earshot. "So last night, soon as I saw her, I grabbed her. And I said in her ear, 'Is that the guy?' She nodded. Soon as she did, I knew we were getting out of there alive. So when the time came, I handed her the knife and said, 'Run straight at the motherfucker like you're running for help and then bury the blade in his throat.'"

I reached around and felt the bulge at the base of my neck. No more professional massages for me. Masseuses were just too dangerous these days.

Up the street I spotted Flan's jalopy pull over to the curb. Jake exited the passenger side and hurried along the sidewalk. Twice he was grabbed by an agent, twice he pushed the agent aside.

"Kevin!" he shouted. "Kevin!"

Jake's face was pale as paste, his eyes bloodshot. When he reached me, he grabbed me by my arms as if to make sure I wasn't a hallucination. "The local news stations are reporting that you're dead."

I thought about it, then shook my head. "I'm not, Jake."

"Yeah, well . . ."

"Everyone's fine. The FBI has Lok Sun in custody. Tommy Duran, too."

Together, Jake and I stared down at the pavement. In a few hours the blacktop would burn hot as a stove.

Finally, Jake turned his face toward the sky, the fresh light making him look older than ever before. "Where do we go from here, son?"

I shrugged. "Back to the office, wait on Turi's jury, I guess."

He stared at me. "That's not what I meant."

I shrugged again. "Nothing changes, Jake."

He nodded slowly, without looking at me, his gaze again fixed on the street. "That's what frightens me most."

I turned my head, watched as the giant, covered by a large white sheet, was finally rolled out on a gurney. I didn't know the giant's name. I didn't want to know it.

Three bodies, one after another after another, were rolled out after the giant's. All anonymous under their white sheets.

Jake looked away from the bodies, away from me. "You spend your entire life trying to do some fucking good, all the while everyone around you is fighting it. There's no way out, Kevin. We're all captives of society. And there aren't enough well-intentioned people to change a fucking thing, you know that? Not nearly enough."

I thought about Turi's trial, about what a not-guilty verdict could mean for Detective Ray Irvine and the rest of the Honolulu PD.

"We can effect some change," I said absently. "One thing at a time, one place at a time."

"And where do we start, son?" Jake smirked. "Here?"

I looked at the street signs and windows, all adorned with mysterious symbols, and slowly shook my head. "Maybe. Maybe in Hawaii. Maybe in Honolulu. Maybe we already have right here in Chinatown, Jake."

CHAPTER 64

I stepped into the courtroom carrying nothing but a single yellow legal pad and William F. Boyd's Montblanc pen.

The jury had been out four full days. Was that good for the defense? Bad for the defense? As Milt Cashman once told me, "Nobody really knows, and anyone who says they do is a fucking schmuck."

I took my place at the defense table and opened my legal pad to the first clean page. Most defense lawyers I knew jotted down three letters before any verdict was read: G and NG. I usually jotted down two: W and L.

But not today. Because this wasn't just a game. This wasn't win or lose with no extra points for owning the truth. The truth mattered. Only when it came out was justice ever truly done.

Dapper Don rose from his chair at the prosecution table and walked across the aisle, offering his hand. "I find it is seldom possible to shake hands after a verdict is read, so I thought perhaps we could shake hands now."

I took Dapper Don's outstretched hand and shook it without saying a word.

Five minutes later the defendant was led in. It struck me that this would probably be the last time Turi and I would be in a courtroom together. We'd stood beside each other so many times before. More than I'd ever stood beside any other client in my career.

We hugged after he was uncuffed.

"We goin' home today, brah?" he said with a smile.

"I know I am."

For a moment I thought he was about to burst into tears, but then his face contorted and broke into laughter—a big, bad belly laugh I hadn't heard since the raid on the Tiki Room.

"No be so sure," he said, still chuckling. "Judge find you in contempt again, you might be movin' into my cell, eh?"

Maybe, I thought. *Either for that or for shooting Tam's giant in the face.*

When I glanced back at the crowd in the gallery, I had to do a double take. Scott Damiano was seated alone in the back row.

"Excuse me, Turi," I said, walking toward the rear of the courtroom.

"Hey, Magnum," Scott said.

"So what the hell are you doing here?"

He grinned at me for a long while, then motioned with his chin to the empty jury box. "I just love to hear the words *not guilty.*"

I smiled back at him. "Yeah, me, too."

"That and *on the house.*"

I nodded. "You know, Scott, you and I may have a hell of a lot more in common than I originally thought."

Fifteen minutes later I was seated at the defense table with Turi again.

"All rise."

The grand entrance of Judge Hideki Narita was announced, then His Honor blew in.

"You may be seated," the judge said. "I understand the jury has reached a verdict. Let's bring them in."

While the court officer went back to retrieve the jury, Judge Narita provided the ubiquitous warning to the gallery. No excessive outward displays of emotion or I'll clear the courtroom. That sort of thing. I tried to count in my head how many times I'd heard those words uttered in court. Too many for a lawyer my age, I thought.

Once the jury was seated, Judge Narita asked the foreman if they had indeed reached a verdict.

"We have," the foreman said.

As the form passed from the foreman to the judge, then back to the foreman, I turned and said to Turi, "No matter what happens next . . ."

"I know, Mistah C," he said seriously. "I know you got my back."

I nodded just as Narita said, "Will the defendant please rise."

I helped a wobbly Turi to his feet.

At this point, time doesn't freeze as a lawyer fresh out of law school might expect it would. Merely a few seconds passed between the time Turi and I rose to our feet and Judge Narita read aloud from his copy of the verdict form, "As to count one named in the indictment, murder in the first degree, how do you find?"

The foreman cleared his throat and said, "As to count one named in the indictment, murder in the first degree, we, the jury, find the defendant, Turi Ahina, not guilty."

"Not even guilty on the charge of illegal possession of a firearm," I said to Flan over the phone as I walked through the courthouse lobby with Scott.

Turi, of course, wouldn't immediately be released. It would take a few hours for paperwork and to gather his things.

"No worries, won't take too long," Turi had said to me. "With you as my lawyer, I figure I no can lose, so last night I packed my things and got ready to go."

I closed my phone, then paused in the courthouse lobby, knowing I would be overwhelmed by reporters the moment I stepped outside. I gathered myself and started walking through the lobby toward the courthouse exit again.

As the doors opened before me, I was immediately struck with a mad sunlight. I shielded my eyes with my right hand as I stepped up to the microphones with Scott Damiano at my side.

With a broad smile I said, "I'm even going to let you take my picture today. No hat, no sunglasses. Just one hundred percent pure, unadulterated Kevin Corvelli this morning, folks."

Those reporters who knew me—all of them, I suspected—laughed.

I'm back, I thought as I adjusted the group of microphones. *This is how it was when it all began, me in front of the lights and cameras, me speaking into dozens of microphones right on the courthouse steps.* I glanced down and noticed the shadow gathering around me.

"Today," I said to the reporters, "justice was done. One of my heroes, the American lawyer Clarence Darrow, once said, 'There is no such thing as justice—in or out of court.' Today, twelve men and women proved him wrong. There is justice both *in* court for Turi Ahina, and *out* of court for the rest of us. Because today, those twelve men and women didn't just make a statement about the *innocence* of Turi Ahina; they made a statement as to the *guilt* of the Narcotics Intelligence Unit of the Honolulu Police Depar—"

From the crowd I heard someone shout, *"Nico Tagliarini says to keep it in the family."*

The sound of a single gunshot filled the light Hawaiian air, and without thought I stepped in front of Scott.

As I moved, I suddenly felt as though I'd been punched in the chest. I gazed down at my gray suit jacket as it turned a liquid black, and next I dropped to my knees. Then fell to the side, rolling down one, maybe two, concrete courthouse steps before coming to a stop and hearing a scream.

"He's been shot in the chest!"

Another three, four, maybe five shots fired in the distance. Quickly drowned out by an odd humming in my ear. I opened my eyes, not realizing I had closed them, and saw that the humming was emanating from Scott Damiano's lips.

"You're going to be all right, buddy," he said, reaching into his pocket.

"Someone call an ambulance!"

"There's too much blood! He's not gonna make it!"

"Make sure you're getting this on film, goddamnit!"

Scott ripped my tie off, then tore my white, button-down shirt open to get to the wound. I heard the buttons rattle down the courthouse steps and thought of my meeting with John Tatupu not long ago in my conference room.

I tried to lift my head but Scott held it down. "Don't look at it. Just look at me. Stay focused on my face."

I did as he said, stared up at Scott's head. The look on his face was intense and not once did it shift into anything other than determination.

In the distance, sirens.

My vision blurred. I could barely see Scott produce the vial. Before my eyes he twisted the cap and poured a generous helping of white powder into his hand. I felt a gurgling in the back of my throat that frightened me more than anything else had ever frightened me in my entire life.

"This may burn a bit," Scott hummed. "Stay with me, Kevin. Don't you go into fucking shock."

The sirens grew closer.

I thought, *Thirty-five years wasn't enough. Where are the cheerleaders? Bring on the halftime show. We still have another two quarters to play.*

My chest burned and suddenly heaved up.

"Relax, Kev," Scott said. "This will help absorb the excess bleeding just like it did for Nico Tagliarini and the Vietcong."

I stared at him through wet eyes, a white fog washing over me. "What are your two favorite words again, Scott?"

He smiled, leaned over, and kissed me on the forehead. "Not fucking guilty."

"That's three words, you bastard," I rasped, blood spilling over my lips.

Then I passed out, unsure whether I'd ever wake up again.

NOWEMAPA

(NOVEMBER)

CHAPTER 65

Lying in a bed at the Queen's Medical Center, I opened my eyes to find Audra standing over me, a fifth of Glenlivet resting in her delicate hands.

"For when you get better," she said.

I parted my lips to ask her to move in with me, but I couldn't speak. *A lawyer without his voice is . . . almost human*, I thought.

Hours earlier I'd had a chat with Jake through Hoshi via instant messaging. They were at the office and kindly let me know that the pink message slips were piling up.

By the end of our chat, we'd decided to have the law firm of Harper & Corvelli go on indefinite hiatus so that I could fully recover, both from the gunshot and my addiction to narcotic painkillers. We'd refer out our current cases and close the office, though we'd continue to pay the rent at South King Street for as long as we could, hopefully with the help of a sublease.

Audra set the bottle down on the nearby tray table and sat

on the edge of the bed, taking my left hand, IV and all, into both of hers. She still appeared frail, but she'd clearly gained back a few of the pounds she'd lost since she was poisoned. The torture she'd endured at Tam's bar was another story altogether. She refused to talk about it, and I didn't push. Whatever came of our relationship, we'd always have scars, both physical and emotional, to remind us of our inauspicious start.

Truth is, I wasn't sure if I should be more surprised by the number of people who died during these past four months, or by the number of people who survived.

Wade Omphrey survived. Though not on Election Day. The governor had been six points ahead on the first of November. Then someone anonymously sent Rolando Dias of the *Herald* a copy of the DVD depicting the governor in Oksana Sutin's apartment.

"Did you send it?" Flan had asked me when the story first broke. He was standing next to me as I lay flat on my hospital bed.

"How could I have sent it?" I rasped. "I've been here the entire time."

"But Scott hasn't."

"If I had Scott send it, I could be disbarred. I received that video in connection with my representation of the governor."

"Okay, so you didn't send it," Flan said, nodding. "But whoever did send it turned out to be a kingmaker. And I think they did the right thing. I think Hawaii's gonna be a better place with Wade Omphrey gone."

John Biel seemed sincere enough. He promised during his campaign to fight for better education for Hawaii's *keiki*, a more genuine equality for all races and ethnicities and orientations, and for the legalization of marijuana. And if he didn't follow through, I vowed I would stand high up on the court-house steps one day and call him on it. Because I'm best when I'm behind a microphone. Hell, while standing behind a bevy of microphones, I may even be immortal.

Maybe they should lower the drip on my morphine.

Miles Flanagan survived Election Day, too. So Flan would get to hear his father rant about Flan's ex-wife, Victoria, for one hour, six days a week, for as long as it took Miles to die. Miles assured Flan he wasn't going anywhere anytime soon.

Iryna wasn't going anywhere either. Not if Flan had any-thing to do with it.

Of course, plenty were dead, too: Oksana Sutin and Iryna's friend Hannah, two beautiful young women who had merely tried to make better lives for themselves by putting their trust in dangerous men; Gavin Dengler; Tam and friends. In one way or another, they were all victims of Orlando Masonet. Or Thomas Sean Duran, or whatever the hell you wanted to call him.

Whoever he was, the scourge known as Orlando Masonet was now behind bars on enough charges to fill a phone-book. Lok Sun, too, was being held at the Federal Detention Center, as Special Agent Slauson and AUSA William F. Boyd meticulously built their case.

Tragically, after learning he was under investigation, De-tective Ray Irvine took his own life with a single shot to the side of the head from his own service revolver. He left behind an ex-wife and a twelve-year-old son on the Big Island.

The man who'd tried to shoot Scott and hit me was dead, too. Shot and killed by Detective John Tatupu in the ensuing chaos in front of the courthouse. His name was Frankie "the Flash" Bianchi, so called because he was so fucking fast. But apparently not fast enough.

I'd always known John Tatupu was all right.

Even if he didn't feel the same way about me.

"I'm being released today," I told Scott over the phone.

"I'll be there to pick you up and take you back to Ko Olina."

"Not so fast. We've got one more job to do."

CHAPTER 66

"It was originally Jansen's idea," I said to Turi in the darkness. "So I can't take all the credit. If you remember, this was how he and Boyd planned on taking down Masonet."

We stood on the runway of a small, rarely used airfield in front of a jet owned by the rap star M.C. WMD. While I was still at the Queen's Medical Center, I'd called in a favor from Milt Cashman. When Milt heard the plan, he said, "Kev, you're fucking crazier than I am. I like that in a lawyer. Give me ten minutes to call Mr. Fucking M.C. WMD and you've got yourself a jet."

"We all cool inside," WMD called from the plane. "Whenever y'all motherfuckers are ready, let's jetty."

"Hey, WMD," I said over the roar of the idling engines, "you ever been shot?"

"Nah, man," he said, revealing a mouthful of gold teeth.

"You ever been stabbed?"

WMD removed his sunglasses. "Nope."

"Ever been arrested?"

"Nah, but there was this one time, man, I came real close. Hey, whatchu getting at?"

"And you call yourself a gangster," I said, smiling.

WMD shook his head while smiling back at me. "Not Guilty Milty told me alls about you, Corvelli. A lawyer out there doing gangsta shit. But lemme tell you something, Counselor. Doing gangsta shit don't make you a gangsta."

"No? What does?"

He pulled out a wad of green the size of his head and said, "M-O-N-E-Y, money."

I thanked him again for the favor, then turned back to Turi.

"How 'bout you, brah?" Turi said. "You gonna be awright?"

"Oh, yeah."

Mindy, with Ema held tightly in her arms, said, "We could never thank you enough, Kevin."

"It's the other way around," I said. "Now go get on that plane before M.C. WMD changes that platinum heart of his."

When Turi and I were alone, we shared a brief hug. No more bear hugs, not for me. My chest was all stapled up and couldn't take it.

"Mistah C, before I leave, I wanna clear the air, yeah?"

A cold dread suddenly crawled up my spine. What Slauson had begun to tell me outside Tam's bar had been tugging at me ever since the verdict.

In that moment, I was sure Turi was going to tell me that the five large the cops had found on him was cash he'd picked up before entering Pearl City. That it was advance payment from Masonet for the hit on Kanoa Bristol.

My lips parted but I couldn't speak. I wanted to hit rewind, to say goodbye and put Turi on the plane without ever having to hear him say he wanted to clear the air.

But it was too late.

Was Bristol the dirty cop who'd decided to come clean and back Tatupu's allegations? Had I risked a good man's life to save that of an assassin?

I thought about Dana Bristol and her two children. About Ray Irvine and his ex-wife and son. I thought about the hole in my own chest.

If I'd been deceived, it was by my own strategy. I had put the words in Turi's mouth. *I* was the one who'd suggested to *him* that Bristol was going to put a hit on him that fateful night in Pearl City.

I stared over Turi's shoulder at the plane. I had the power to stop this right now with a single phone call. Turi could still do twenty-five to life on the federal drug and racketeering charges if he remained in Hawaii. Why should I put my ass on the line for someone who lied to me? For someone who killed in cold blood.

Sometimes life just grabs you by the throat, I thought. *Grabs you by the throat and chokes you and leaves you for dead on the floor.*

I searched Turi's wide, watering eyes and decided. I wouldn't turn back now. Whether he'd lied to me or told the truth, Turi Ahina had once saved my life. And when it came right down to it, all I'd really done during the trial was my job. I'd fulfilled my duty. I'd won an acquittal. That was all I was ever supposed to do.

"I was scared," Turi said finally. "I didn't wanna tell you

during the trial 'cause I didn't wanna seem soft. But now I wanna clear the air. I was scared, Mistah C."

I immediately felt my chest deflate and realized I'd been holding my breath. "That all?" I said above the sound of the engines.

Turi cleared his face of tears and managed one of the legendary smiles I would forever remember him for. "That's all, Mistah C."

I nodded. "For a moment there I was scared, too."

"Well, I guess this is it, Mistah C," Turi said as he backed into the darkness. "So say goodnight to the bad guy. Unless you wanna come, too. I'm sure WMD's got an extra seat."

It was tempting, of course. Running always is. But if I'd come to any realization at all during my mend in that Honolulu hospital bed, it was that I was through running. Hawaii was, and would always be, my home.

When I shook my head, the big guy acknowledged me with a grin, turned, and started his way up the ladder into the airplane, shrinking from my sight.

"Aloha," I said softly.

When he finally disappeared into the jet, I knew I would never see my friend Turi Ahina again.

AUTHOR'S NOTE

Last Lawyer Standing is a work of fiction that depicts a very different Hawaii from the one I know and love. When I began work on this novel, I didn't know who would be serving as Hawaii's governor when this book was released. Needless to say, the governor depicted in *Last Lawyer Standing* is a figment of my imagination and not based, in whole or in part, on any actual Hawaii governor, past or present.

Likewise, the Honolulu Police Department depicted in this novel is not the same department that protects and serves my island home. The mention of the Kenneth Kamakana case against the City and the County of Honolulu is mentioned solely to add authenticity to the story.

Honolulu's Chinatown is a lively place that boasts one of the greatest cultural experiences in the Hawaiian Islands. It is in no way, shape, or form the dark and frightening place depicted in *Last Lawyer Standing*.

In crafting this novel, I attempted to remain as true as possible to the laws and geography of the state of Hawaii. But I did bend both when I felt that it better suited the story. As a lawyer and a novelist I've learned that on occasion the truth must take a backseat to getting a point across.